# NERDS & BABIES

## A SEASONED ROMCOM COLLECTION

MELLANIE SZERETO

amatoria press

Nerds & Babies: A Seasoned Romcom Collection
Copyright © 2025 Mellanie Szereto
Published by Amatoria Press
Cover art by Amatoria Press

ISBN-13: 978-1-942522-58-4

BOOKS BY MELLANIE SZERETO

Cowboys of Science series ~

No More Mr. Gneiss Guy

Taken for Granite (coming soon)

Creekside series ~

Sexy Claus

Roll With It

Already Gone (coming soon)

Love on the Menu series ~

Love Served Hot

Red Hot Pepper

Hot Tamale Nights (coming soon)

Love on the Menu...Extra Hot standalones ~

Just Desserts

Iced Latté

A Little Appetizer

The Main Dish

Dressing on the Side

Flavor of the Day

Love on the Menu…Steamed trilogy ~

Egging Her On

Sweetening Her Up

Reeling Her In

Love on the Menu: Steamed Boxed Set

Marry Me series ~

Mom I'd Love to Marry

Dad I'd Love to Marry

Nerd Love series ~

Comma Kaze

Comma Sutra (coming soon)

Nerds & Babies series ~

The Nerd Next Door

The Nerd Upstairs

The Nerd Downstairs

Nerds & Babies Boxed Set

Romancing the Phone series ~

Call Me…Maybe

Smooth Operator

Hang-Ups (coming soon)

Telephone Lines (2025)

Dialed Up (2026)

Mixed Messages (2026)

The Homegrown Café Book Club series ~

Makin' Bacon

The Farmer Takes a Husband

The Butcher and the Baker

When Harry Met Wally

And Baby Makes 2½

The Homegrown Café Book Club Boxed Set

The Jerk Series ~

Jerk in the Box

Playing in the Raine: A Toy Story

Bound by Voodoo: Legends

Bewitching Desires series ~

Two if by Sea

Two Knights of Passion

Two Fated for One

Two Pirates to Treasure

Two Times the Trouble

Two Roped and Ready

Two from the Triangle

Beyond Bewitching

# THE NERD NEXT DOOR

## NERDS & BABIES #1

# CHAPTER ONE

CARSON HINES SLOWED TO CHECK THE HOUSE NUMBERS ON THE mailboxes, not trusting the accuracy of his phone's GPS for the final leg of his nearly three-thousand-mile drive. It had already tried to take him on a much longer route than he'd deemed necessary, missing a turn off the main road and forcing him to backtrack through a maze of side streets to correct the course the app had obviously screwed up. Analyzing DNA required less concentration than driving a fifteen-foot U-Haul with his car trailing behind in this sleepy little college town.

After a quick glance at the map on his phone, he followed the hairpin curve toward his temporary residence. The gray bungalow with pale-green shutters from the pictures appeared through the trees a few hundred yards away.

*Finally.*

As the road straightened, his patience—and the pavement—came to an abrupt halt. A metal guardrail painted reflective yellow blocked the green space beyond the unannounced cul-de-sac. Tall stalks of dark purple buds and thick bunches of white flowers with feathery leaves lay between him and the house that was his destination.

He shut off the engine and climbed out to search for a path through the swath of nature blocking his way. The least he could do was be on time to pick up the keys from his landlord in the house next door.

Buzzing caught his attention first, and then movement among the chest-high blooms revealed hundreds of honey bees and bumblebees bouncing from flower to flower. An assortment of colorful butterflies also flitted in and out of the strip of what was most likely native plants, suggesting someone had purposely cultivated this obstruction for polli-nators. A worn trail led into the thick mass near the left side of the dead end, but it was too narrow for his size-thirteen feet.

*Made by wild critters, no doubt.*

Nixing that plan, he tapped in a text message to his new neighbor. *"Good morning, Ms. Trimble. I'm running behind schedule. I should be there to pick up the keys in about five or ten minutes."*

His cell buzzed in his hand within seconds.

*"Trouble finding the house, Dr. Hines? Use your GPS. See you soon."*

He lifted his gaze to the dwelling next to his rental as he huffed out a sigh. A shadow in the window under her porch roof assured him the old woman had a clear view of him and the moving van. He hadn't fooled Zinnia Trimble for a second.

"Busted." Instead of responding to her message or waving, he returned to the truck and followed the advice she'd given him in her email last week. That was acknowledgment enough of an error on his part. Besides, this cul-de-sac and the one on the other side shouldn't have the same road name if they weren't connected.

The GPS took him back along several familiar-looking streets to the main thoroughfare. Seven minutes later, he parked along the curb on the opposite side of the weed patch, making sure he didn't block Ms. Trimble's driveway.

A last fortifying gulp of coffee from his insulated mug prepared him to meet the person who'd called him out on his rare mistake. He pocketed his phone, exited the truck again, and crossed the grass to his new neighbor's walkway. Thankfully, she wasn't waiting for him on the porch with a pitcher of lemonade and a mouthful of grandmotherly advice.

Giggles drew his attention to the sidewalk behind him, but the baby in the three-wheeled contraption held his thoughts for all of half a second. A gorgeous blonde with her hair piled on top of her head and a heart-stopping smile halted him in his tracks, reminding him that man couldn't live on genetics research alone.

*Another neighbor?*

*Is she single?*

Lively dark eyes shone through the lenses of lime-green glasses. They matched the tank top hugging her incredible breasts. "Dr. Hines, you made it."

*God, I hope she's single.*

"Ma-ma-ma-ma!" The kid—a girl maybe, since she had a bow at the base of her dark-brown ponytail fountain—whacked a ring of brightly colored plastic keys on the padded crossbar in front of her. Blue eyes stared up at him from a chubby-cheeked face, and all four central incisors appeared when she grinned at him. "Ma-ma-ma-ma!"

He finally managed a nod. "Yes, I made it. Did Ms. Trimble tell you I was moving in today?"

Instead of confirming that she'd been told about his pending arrival, the bombshell narrowed her pretty eyes and scrunched up her sexy mouth. "I'm Zinnia Trimble. You were expecting someone else?"

Telling her a name like hers conjured the image of a much older woman seemed like a really bad idea. "No, I just thought you'd be home when I got here."

"I am home." She swerved around him, engaged the stroller's wheel locks, and bent to retrieve the baby from the seat, giving him an amazing view of long legs and a perfect backside in skintight bike shorts. "The road doesn't go all the way through anymore. I know exactly how long it takes to drive from the other side of the pollination planting, so Daisy and I went for a walk. And, for the record, I told you to follow the GPS directions in the email I sent. You know, the one with the receipt for your security deposit and first month's rent."

*Fine, you told me so. And you could've warned me about the road.*

The plastic keys flew over her shoulder at his face, and he nabbed them right before they would've made contact with his nose. "Yes, you did. Do you need help?"

She swung around, her arms extended like she was about to hand off the baby to him instead of directing him to carry the three-wheeler up the porch steps.

He jerked back and tripped over the sidewalk, windmilling his arms to keep from landing in her flowerbed.

High-pitched squeals bubbled out of the kid, showing off a hint of a cleft chin like the dimple he hid beneath his beard. Was she laughing at him?

"You should see your face. She's past the frequent spitting-up stage, but she likes to gnaw on anything and everything that'll fit in her mouth, in case you're wondering. That includes fingers, ears, and toes." Zinnia's tempting lips spread into a wide smile. Before he could respond, she perched the baby on her hip, bounced the stroller up the stairs on the rear wheels with her free hand, and unlocked the front door. She obviously had the babysitting gig down pat. "Would you like to come in? I'll need a minute to get the keys to the bungalow."

Against his better judgment, he followed her inside.

"HAVE A SEAT. I'LL BE RIGHT BACK." WAVING HER NEW TENANT toward the couch, Zinnia continued through the living room and into her home office. The extra income from the rental would add a nice chunk of change to Daisy's college savings, but being ogled by a man too full of himself to listen to simple instructions was more than an annoyance.

*There's a reason I'm single and planning to stay that way until the right man comes along.*

She guided her daughter's quick little fingers away from the wireless keyboard as she reached to open the desk drawer. "You can play on one of those when you're a bit more gentle with breakable things. How about we have a yummy snack instead? Do you want some banana?"

"Bana, bana, bana." Daisy smacked her palms together.

"Yes, banana. They're yummy, aren't they?" With the keys to her rental tucked inside her fist, she hurried back to her guest, who'd chosen to peruse the framed photo collages on the wall above the couch instead of sitting.

*Surprise, surprise. The man can't follow directions to save his life.*

Dangling the keyring from her index finger, she held out her hand. "Your set of keys. Do you have any questions?"

His thumb brushed her fingers, probably on purpose, but she suppressed her reaction to the contact to avoid feeding what was probably a monstrous ego.

He stared at her with narrowed eyes and a crooked frown. "The baby. She's yours? She doesn't look anything like you or any of the other people in the pictures. Her facial structure and coloring are completely different."

Every hair on the back of her neck rose, along with her impatience. She aimed a glare at him, but his gaze now seemed focused on the photo her mom had taken when the nurse placed newborn Daisy in her arms eight months ago. "Yes, she's mine. No, she isn't adopted, not that it's important *or* any of your business. Being a geneticist, you should know dominant genes aren't always passed on directly from parent to child. Before you ask, her biological father isn't in the picture, literally or figuratively. Again, not that it's any of your business. And she has my ears."

He shot a cocky smirk over his shoulder, his blue eyes smoldering like he expected her to swoon in his presence. "Is anyone else?"

"Is anyone else what?" The empty-headed look she'd mastered at twelve fell into place with no effort. If he wanted to know her relationship status, he could damn well ask the question without all the outrageous flirting and leering.

His grin widened, as if she hadn't blown him off with the clichéd dumb-blonde act. "Are you—"

The doorbell chimed, saving her from his asinine come-on.

She turned her back to him and walked away—an enormously

satisfying action, even if she hadn't initiated it. A peek through the glass erased her irritation.

Shifting Daisy higher on her hip, she swung open the door for her guest. "Hi, Mom."

"Gam-gam!" Her daughter leaned forward into her grandmother's outstretched arms.

Sharing a slobbery lip-to-lip kiss with her only grandchild, Zinnia's mom grinned. "How's my favorite baby girl in the whole world? I saw your stroller on the porch. Did you go for a walk this morning?"

"Dr. Needleman?" Carson's voice stuck a pin in the joy of seeing the connection between her mom and her daughter.

Her mother adjusted her hold on Daisy as she looked toward the obnoxious man in the living room. "Dr. Hines, I'm glad to see you've arrived. Three students will be here in a few minutes to help you unload the moving truck. I see you've met Zinnia and Daisy. Oh, and please call me Iris."

A grimace appeared and disappeared almost too fast to see, but he'd obviously noticed their flower names and judged the tradition too peculiar for words. "Iris, good to finally meet you in person. Yes, I've met your daughter and granddaughter. Thank you for making arrangements for some hired help. I'm looking forward to our meeting and the campus tour on Monday."

"You're welcome. I think someone's ready for her mid-morning snack." She lowered her squirming armful to the floor and laughed when Daisy rolled toward the kitchen at a turtle's pace. "One of these days she's going to discover crawling is faster. Speaking of food, Carson, did you get the invitation to Sunday's cookout and picnic? I'm sure you'll appreciate a break from unpacking by then."

"Of course. I wouldn't miss it." His charm-the-pants-off-the-ladies expression made another appearance.

Not bothering to hide an eye roll, Zinnia followed her daughter. "Mom, would you mind showing Dr. Hines out? My girl is on a mission that requires supervision. Tell Dad I'm bringing dessert tonight."

Footsteps, muffled conversation, and then the thunk of the front door closing brought relief.

*One day of living next door to a cad down. Only four more months to go.*

# CHAPTER TWO

DESPITE HIS BUFF PHYSIQUE, SUPERIOR INTELLECT, AND PRACTICED facial expressions to show a woman she had his full attention, Carson had failed to bamboozle his target for the first time in nearly two decades. That trick had saved him from looking like the nerd he was in most social situations.

Zinnia Trimble had been unimpressed by him, or at least indifferent.

His face had quite possibly betrayed his muscled body and his formidable mind. Only a moment of visible shaky confidence could have caused her interest to evaporate, as it had so often before he went from a scrawny twelve-year-old to the coolest guy in high school after a growth spurt practically overnight.

Since Friday morning, he'd been too busy moving into the bungalow next to hers and unpacking his belongings to make a concerted effort to cross paths with her again. Of course, every time he'd gone outside—checking his mailbox or taking out trash—to accidentally meet up with her, she'd vanished into her house or wheeled off in the opposite direction with her baby.

The other half of the kid's DNA still stirred his curiosity. He himself had as many obvious physical traits in common with the subject than its own mother, if not more.

*Hair color, eye color, cleft chin.*

Carson frowned into the mirror and skimmed the trimmer through his beard, careful not to thin the right side more than the left. A comb-through revealed no gray hairs yet, but the hint of distinguished silver would make itself known soon, based on the history of male aging in his family.

*What's the deal with the baby's father?*

He brushed the trimmings into the wastebasket and washed his hands.

*One-night stand? Dumped when she discovered she was pregnant? Divorced?*

Zinnia's lack of receptiveness might have something to do with how that relationship had ended. Unfortunately, her past experience could potentially taint his attempts to form a neighborly friendship with her.

*Yes, the problem is definitely on her end.*

Another possibility sprang to mind, but he didn't want to consider that she might be a young widow. Wouldn't she have pictures of her late husband hanging on the wall if that was the case?

Her kid was the star in most of the photos, although a few included Zinnia, her mom, and a man about the same age as Dr. Needleman.

The woman was too damn complicated to be a four-month girl-friend he could practice his rusty dating skills with.

Opting to leave his button-down shirt untucked from his shorts, he slipped his feet into his favorite pair of boat shoes and pocketed his wallet and keys. As he headed out the door, he slid his sunglasses into place.

The humid wall of midwestern August heat that hit him at the bottom of the porch steps tempted him to drive, but Iris had informed him the walk to her house wasn't a long one. Not taking any chances this trip, he tapped a few times to bring up directions on his phone.

*Less than a mile and no major street crossings.*

Content with his decision to leave his car in the detached garage, he set off down the sidewalk, doing his damnedest to ignore the house next door. The chances of Zinnia being invited to what sounded like a work-related function seemed slim to none, which was probably for the best. Flirting required too much thought for his science-focused brain.

Fifteen minutes later, his phone told him he'd arrived, and voices and the mouthwatering scent of grilled meat led him to the backyard of a brick ranch. It reminded him of home—the house in Pittsburgh his parents had lived in since before he was born. He made a mental note to plan a visit for next month, given that it was less than two hundred miles away.

Iris emerged from a group gathered near the deck, holding a baby sporting a blue bow in her dark hair. "Carson, I'm so glad you could make it. Come meet the students and faculty you'll be working with."

*She's here.*

He buried the strong urge to search the crowd for Zinnia and walked to his host with his hand extended. "Good to be here. Thanks for the invitation."

As Iris reached to shake his hand, the baby lunged toward him. "Goodness, Daisy, where are you going?"

He caught his attacker around her middle faster than he'd reacted to her toy flying at his face two days ago.

Iris raised her eyebrows and released the baby's legs. "She usually only likes to be held by people she knows well when Zin isn't right there. I wonder if she remembers you from move-in day."

Dangling from his grasp, Daisy squealed and kicked her blue-socked feet. "Bana ma-ma gam-gam."

A flash of orange and blue swooped in and rescued him from the chattering handful. The mass of hair on top of Zinnia's head bobbled as she lifted the baby to her hip. "Pop-Pop is getting your banana. Let's go find the high chair and a bib."

Tiny fingers flapped open and closed as the baby twisted toward him. "Bah-bah. Bah-bah. Bah-bah."

His hand rose of its own accord to wave at her, but his eyes were glued to the swaying backside of his shorts- and tank-top-clad landlord.

*Complicated is what I do best.*

❧

READY TO MAKE A RUN FOR HOME WHILE HER TENANT WAS ENGROSSED in a conversation about genetics and hereditary diseases, Zinnia hugged her dad. "Thanks for the leftovers. They should get me through some of this week's deadlines."

"Any time, Zin. Give me a holler if you need a babysitter." He winked and leaned down to kiss her daughter on the forehead. "I miss you already, sweet girl. Have a good nap."

Blinking up at him, Daisy patted his cheek. "Pop-pop."

"Yep. Pop-pop loves you." The adoration in his eyes reminded Zinnia why she'd chosen to have a child on her own instead of holding out for a man who'd likely gotten lost and fallen off a cliff on his way to finding her. Her father stepped back from the stroller and grinned. "She'll be zonked out before you make it half a block."

"That's the plan." Zinnia unlocked the wheels and prepared for a bit of rough terrain before the long stretch of sidewalks. "See you soon. Love you."

"You bet, kiddo."

The stroller bumped along the grassy yard with a bit of effort, but she soon hit a measured stride on the driveway. Her mind wandered as she walked, ideas forming for a project she planned to start tomorrow morning. Three-quarters of the way home, she slowed her pace to add a few notes to her phone. As she sped up again, steady footsteps registered in her head. Ready for a curt "passing on the left," she moved into the driveway on her right.

"You didn't say you were leaving. We could've walked home together." A boat shoe attached to a hairy leg popped into her peripheral vision.

*Can't you take a hint?*

"Excellent food. Interesting people. Your parents know how to put on a good party." Carson's muscley calves flexed with each step. Unfortunately, his mouth did too. "It looks like your baby fell asleep."

"Mm-hm." Maybe the noncommittal response would make him go away. She kept her gaze on the view in front of her, wishing she could teleport to her living room and avoid the great Dr. Hines the majority of guests had worshipped at the get-together.

"You spent a couple years in Silicon Valley as a programmer. You're also a teacher. Or you used to be until you started a graphic design business last year so you could be at home with your daughter. Your mom mentioned it." He dodged a dog-walker by merging in behind her and then moving back into his previous position. "With undergrad degrees in art, computer science, and math, plus master's degrees in programming and education. Impressive."

She snorted a laugh and increased her pace as her house came into view. "You were expecting a PhD in cheerleading and an MRS? Sorry to disappoint you, but I'm not what you would probably consider the typical blonde."

He matched her speed without much adjustment to his stride. "I have no idea what an MRS is, but hair color has no direct correlation to IQ, according to Zagorsky. As a geneticist, I concur, although I haven't conducted my own study. It seems like a waste of time and resources. Too many factors influence intelligence to commend or blame a single gene. Are you seriously, casually, or otherwise engaged in a relationship or non-relationship?"

His abrupt change of topic stalled her mind, mouth, and feet at her driveway.

He stopped beside her. "I was interrupted when I tried to ask you on Friday."

She made a hard left turn, hoping to escape his line of questioning.

When she locked the stroller wheels to unbuckle Daisy, he marched toward her. "I'll move your three-wheeler to the porch while you carry the baby. She went to sleep faster than I would've thought. Don't babies cry a lot when they're tired?"

"You ask a lot of questions." She lifted her daughter to her shoulder and climbed the porch stairs. "Babies are all different, just like everyone else. Daisy is a happy baby for the most part. And, no, I'm not dating anyone or otherwise engaging in a relationship or non-relationship. When I have time off from running my business and being a parent, I sleep, clean house, and do laundry."

THE NERD NEXT DOOR

"I could help with some of those things." He wasn't even winded from hoisting the stroller into the air with one hand to follow her.

A sarcastic chuckle leaked out as she unlocked the door. "You mean like sleeping with me?"

His neck flushed noticeably pink against his white cotton shirt. "Okay, I'll be the first to admit I'd sleep with you in a heartbeat, but you're smart and beautiful and challenging. I'm sure we'd have cerebral discussions before, during, and after sex."

"Ha! If I can carry on an intelligent conversation during or after sex, it's a pretty good indication you're doing something wrong."

He set the stroller out of the way and joined her at the door. "That's true. However, I enjoy talking to you, partly because you don't suck up to me because of who I am and what I can do for your research record."

"Then why did you agree to be a visiting scholar?" Unsettled by his honesty, she shot him a frown as she entered the living room. "It doesn't make sense, especially when you seemed to be in your element at the picnic. Make yourself comfortable while I put Daisy in her crib."

The slight creak of the couch almost drowned out a noisy exhale as she hurried down the hall to the nursery. Was his superior attitude and women-should-fall-at-my-feet swagger all a façade to cover up frustration with his professional life?

Daisy's sigh as Zinnia laid her on the mattress, on the other hand, was a sound of happiness, contentment, and utter relaxation. A smile curved her daughter's mouth and stayed there.

"I love you, Daisy Mae. Sweet dreams." Her heart full to bursting, Zinnia returned to the living room. She was surprised to find Carson sitting with his elbows braced on his knees and his furry jaw resting on his palms. "Want something to drink? Water, iced tea, coffee?"

"No, thanks." He straightened and looked her in the eye. "I haven't told anybody this yet. I'm thinking about leaving my current position. After ten years of strictly research, I want to teach."

His stern expression convinced her he might actually be serious. "You're doing the visiting professor thing to see if the grass is greener at a small teaching-focused university?"

"I suppose so. I haven't taught since I was a TA over ten years ago." Some of the soberness in his face eased, but he seemed much more intense than during their other interactions. "Presenting at conferences to people with similar educational and professional backgrounds to what I have isn't the same. I'd like to observe faculty in a classroom setting and give some guest lectures to students so I can make an educated decision and relearn how to communicate the knowledge I've accumulated during my research."

She offered him a supportive smile, almost liking this other side of him. "Hmm. Maybe your ego isn't quite as humongous as it seems to be."

His eyes lit up like a clear sky on a sunny day. "Of course not, but another part of me is."

"Just when I thought you might be a decent human being, you had to go and ruin it." She shook her head and dropped onto the opposite end of the couch from him.

He leaned toward her with one of those familiar smirks playing on his lips. "Shame on you, Ms. Trimble. Such a dirty mind. I was talking about my brain."

"Sure you were." A flutter in her belly warned her not to let her imagination go in the direction he'd suggested, but the dirty mind he'd mentioned had already gone there.

# CHAPTER THREE

CARSON CLOSED HIS BARREN REFRIGERATOR AND WENT IN SEARCH OF his phone. Eight hours of interacting with people had shorted out at least a dozen synapses, leaving nothing for a trip to the grocery store. Only delivery would keep him from starving.

He tromped back to the bedroom, where he'd dumped his wallet, keys, and computer bag to change clothes. His sport coat, pants, and shirt still lay across the desk chair, but the charger on the nightstand didn't have a phone attached to it.

"Pockets." He patted his workout shorts first and then his pants pockets when his cell wasn't there. "Empty. Where did I put it?"

Retracing his movements, he returned to the living room. The limited number of surfaces—coffee table, futon, end table—were bare.

"Think, think, think."

*Toured campus, met with every faculty member and grad student who's remotely interested in genetics, ate lunch with Dr. Needleman and her fellow administrators, checked out my office space, and had a preliminary discussion with my research collaborators in the newly expanded lab.*

Not once during his time on campus had he gotten a call, text, or email notification. He'd had no reason to take it out of his pocket.

*My jacket pock—*

A trio of raps on his front door scattered his thoughts. The silhouette through the textured glass didn't look human, but he answered the summons anyway.

His pulse sped up as a blonde ponytail came into view. "Zinnia. Hi."

She turned toward him with a box almost as long as she was tall leaning against her shoulder and a breath-stealing smile on her face. "This was delivered for you earlier. It was halfway in the street, and I didn't think you'd appreciate having someone run over it before you got home."

His fingertips grazed the side of her breast as he tried to grip the package. *Dick move, dude, even if it was an accident.* "Sorry. Thanks."

As soon as he had the box in his possession, she gestured toward her feet. A pair of sandals showed off sexy red toenails. "Oh, and I found a cell phone in the flowerpot here by the door. Did you set yours down while you were finding your keys? Or maybe drop it?"

"Thanks. It's mine, and I have no idea how it got there. Today was…long." He shoved the door open wider with his foot and stood the lamp he'd ordered against the wall. "I've spent the last ten minutes looking for it so somebody can bring me food. No time or energy to find the grocery store yet."

Her snicker matched the amusement she couldn't hide behind her red-framed glasses. "I know you're not asking for an invitation, but I was just starting supper when I noticed you were home. Salmon, rice, roasted veggies. If you help, I'll share."

Not about to turn down an easy meal, he fished his phone from the overflowing pot of brightly colored flowers. "Give me thirty seconds to grab my keys. Next time is my treat."

A soft coo came out of nowhere, and she skittered down the steps. "Daisy's awake. Come on over when you're ready. I'll leave the door unlocked."

His exhaustion lifted with the realization that she didn't want a piece of him. He was accustomed to being in demand and the people around him tugging him in multiple directions. As much as he loved being recognized for his research, he hated the fakeness it attracted.

Zinnia was real. She'd offered him a simple meal they would prepare together and share, for no other reason than kindness and generosity. Her beauty went far deeper than her physical appearance.

When she paused on her porch and glanced toward him, something inside him switched on—energizing him, bringing him to life in a way he didn't expect. His initial reaction to her had been filled with the immaturity and selfishness his public persona had found necessary to put on display. She made him want to trust that she saw *him*, not his accomplishments.

Finally snapping out of his ruminations, he retrieved his keys, plugged in his phone, and headed next door.

Zinnia's voice, mixed with nonsensical chatter from her daughter, greeted him as he entered her house. Then they appeared in the hallway, their identical cheery moods outweighing the dissimilarities of their hair, eyes, and facial structures. They were alike in the most important way.

The baby flung her whole body toward him, like she had at yesterday's cookout, and strung together at least two full sentences of gibberish. Her mother barely caught her before she took a nosedive to the floor. The yellow bow atop her head met with a different fate.

He picked up the hair decoration, studying its construction and weighing the possibility of returning it to its proper location. He gave up and placed the bow in the tiny outstretched hand. "You lost something."

Daisy giggled and dropped it at his feet. Another indecipherable statement followed.

"She's training you." Zinnia grinned at him, sending his heart into a lovesick rhythm once again. "Pavlovian conditioning is something children figure out very early. Drop a toy. Someone picks it up. The reward is a smile, a laugh, or another positive reinforcement."

He raised an eyebrow at the baby. "Are you learning how to manipulate my behavior?"

"Ma-ma-ma." She tangled the fingers of one hand in Zinnia's pony-tail and reached for him again with the other hand. "Ba-ba."

"I'll take that as a yes."

ZINNIA ALMOST GAVE IN TO THE TEMPTATION TO HAND OFF DAISY TO their supper guest before he knew what was happening. Instead, she shook her head at him and led him to the kitchen. "Are you uncomfort-able around all babies? I just changed her diaper, so the chances of a mishap are pretty slim."

"I wouldn't say uncomfortable. Just no experience." He stopped at the sink and turned on the water. After a squirt of soap, he scrubbed his hands like he was about to perform surgery. Then he pulled the chef's knife from the block near the cutting board and lined up the blade on a carrot. "Anything need chopped besides the broccoli, cauliflower, and carrots?"

"That's it." Determined to ignore the flexing muscles his sleeveless shirt brought to her attention, she buckled Daisy into the high chair and squeezed the squeaky part of the toy suctioned to the tray. "No nieces or nephews? Friends with kids?"

"I'm an only child and I don't socialize much. A few colleagues are married with kids, but I don't think I've ever met their families. I work in the lab sixty or more hours a week. I go home to work out, sleep, and eat. Twice a year I visit my parents for three or four days. The only times I deviate from that schedule is when I attend conferences or travel somewhere to give a talk." He pivoted toward the stove, forcing her gaze from his remarkable glutes to his equally impressive biceps. "I prefer the lab. Vegetables go on the baking sheets, right?"

"Yes. I already sprayed them with olive oil, and the oven should be done preheating." She frowned at her wayward thoughts and stalked to the pantry. She'd made her business and motherhood the big priorities when the pregnancy test had displayed a plus sign. Any man who wanted to be part of her life had to accept that she and Daisy were a package deal. She wasn't holding her breath for that longshot. Her lungs would've shriveled up decades ago, waiting for someone to want more than a roll in the hay from a curvy blonde, let alone one with a fatherless baby.

*Ugh.*

Grabbing the supplies for the pilaf, she returned to the counter on the opposite side of the sink from him. The saucepan banged the granite a bit harder than she intended, but her disappointment needed an outlet. "I'll start the rice as soon as you put the veggies in the oven. The salmon is seasoned and ready to go."

"Okay." His curt answer sparked a twinge of guilt over the tone her suddenly frustrated mood had allowed.

He stepped aside every time she came near him while they finished cooking and sat in silence across from her while they ate, clearly expecting her to bite off his head for no reason. His food was gone in less than fifteen minutes.

He drained his water glass as he pushed away from the table. "Do you want the dishes in the dishwasher? Or should I wash them by hand?"

"In the dishwasher is fine." Contemplating how to ask him to stay a little longer as he cleaned up after himself, she fed Daisy a bite of applesauce. The vast majority of it ended up back on the spoon, a sure sign supper was done. "Carson, I'd like to talk to you about something. Can you stick around for a bit? Or we can talk another time if you need to go."

"I said or did something to offend you, didn't I?" He glanced up from adding his silverware to the utensil basket. "I apologize if I did. I'm used to putting on a show for my...*admirers*, so I don't get much practice being me."

"Actually, I'm the one who should apologize. I—" Not wanting to delve into her issues without his full attention, she used the least messy part of the bib to wipe the goo from her daughter's mouth and chin. "You know what, let's wait until we put the leftovers away and clean up. I have more to say than I'm sorry. And I *am* sorry."

The shadow that had dimmed his eyes faded. "I was planning to lift and go for a run, but I can stay for a half hour or so. Don't want to exercise too soon after a meal. Where do I find the plastic bowls? I can take care of the food while you wipe down the eater-in-training."

Glad for his help, she directed his search for containers and focused on Daisy's mess.

He sat on the couch a few minutes later and rested his ankle on his opposite knee, looking relaxed again. "I don't understand. What do you have to apologize for?"

She settled in the chair not much more than an arm's length away —one of *his* arms anyway. "I was thinking about things that put me in a grouchy mood and I took it out on you. Would you be uncomfortable if Daisy nurses while we talk? I'll use one of her blankets to keep from flashing you."

His cheeks flushed slightly pink, but he shrugged. "If you don't mind, it's fine with me. I'm not sure I'd be brave enough to breastfeed a baby with teeth. She doesn't bite, does she?"

"Not yet, but I have a nipple shield in case she does." With the flower-print piece of flannel from the arm of the chair draped across her shoulder and chest, she unfastened the cup of her bra and cuddled Daisy to her breast. "All set."

"Already?" He lowered his foot to the floor and moved the other one to his knee, mirroring his previous position. "I guess you've had lots of practice since she was born."

"Mm-hm." *Here goes.* "Do you like me?"

His dark eyebrows dipped low over his light eyes, and wariness seemed to tighten his jaw. "Is that a trick question?"

"No." She huffed out a noisy sigh. "I'm having a hard time reading your intentions. At first, you had this swagger-y macho thing going on, like you expected me to swoon like a groupie or something. Then you ignored me until I left the picnic before you. Now... Now you're giving off I-want-to-date-you vibes. I'm confused, and dating hasn't been on my to-do list since...I found out I was pregnant. So, do you like me?"

# CHAPTER FOUR

*DO YOU LIKE ME?*

Zinnia's question had been direct and to the point. Their follow-up discussion had given him hope, despite the cringe-y middle school memories it had inspired. Most importantly, Carson didn't regret the honest answers he'd given her four nights ago.

Yes, he liked her. Wildly infatuated might be a better description, but telling her the extent of his feelings probably wouldn't have made a good impression. Dweebiness wasn't a good look on anyone, especially not a thirty-eight-year-old guy who hid a nerd under his compensatory muscles and public persona.

Yes, he understood and accepted that her parental duties took precedence over everything. Last-minute cancellations or changes in plans might happen, but the same could occur with his or her job.

Yes, he wanted to date her—and do other things he wouldn't rush her into, considering she already had a baby she likely hadn't planned for. His impending search for a position with a balance of teaching and researching had seemed to convince her he wasn't going to disappear at the end of the fall semester or expect her to conduct a long-distance relationship indefinitely.

*And last but not least...*

Yes, he was fully aware of Daisy's impact on any relationship that might develop, including the possibility of immediate fatherhood.

Did the final admission scare the living daylights out of him?

*Absolutely.*

As much as Zinnia's daughter seemed to like him, he didn't have the first clue how to be a good dad, even though the one he'd grown up with had been a decent role model. Focusing on his career had all but taken over his life, with no thoughts of starting his own family.

*I can do this.*

*She's worth the effort.*

He laughed out loud at the gross understatement. No other woman had filled his mind day and night or coaxed his focus away from work.

The timer buzzed on his phone, alerting him to his Friday night guests' arrival in five minutes. After a careful check of the place settings, he made a quick sweep of the living room and bathroom to be sure both were presentable, even though he'd done it twice already.

Did women obsess about having a clean house and making an edible meal for men?

As he moved the freshly washed bath towel—in case she needed a cover-up while she nursed the baby—from the left side of his new chair to the right, movement through the window sent his pulse thumping faster than his target heart rate during a hard workout. Although he'd texted with Zinnia several times since Monday, neither of them had been able to carve out more than a minute or two here and there to talk. Between her project deadlines and making sure his lab space was organized for next week, they hadn't seen each other at all.

*She's here.*

He hurried to the front door, wishing he could greet her with a kiss. A whisper of his lips against hers would do. It might not cure his first-date jitters, but he wouldn't have to spend another second wondering about the experience.

"Ba-ba-ba-ba." A high-pitched squeal carried from his driveway, but the wail at the tail end assured him someone was in a terrible mood today.

The dark circles half-hidden by her purple-framed glasses when

Zinnia climbed the porch stairs with a still-crying Daisy announced she wasn't her usual self, either. "I thought a change of scenery might improve her disposition, but she's been fussy for most of the week. She doesn't have a fever, but maybe she's teething. Do you mind if we try again tomor—"

"Ba-ba-ba-ba-ba-ba." Excitement lit up Daisy's tear-stained face as she reached for him with both of her tiny arms. Her squatty legs wiggled and her socked feet kicked back and forth against the Super-Mom t-shirt clinging to her mother's gorgeous curves. "Ba-ba-ba-ba."

Swallowing his uncertainty in favor of scoring points with Zinnia, he lifted the baby to his torso and secured her with a palm across her back and his forearm beneath her padded bottom. "Is this right? I don't want to drop her."

"Ba-ba." Her grouchiness seemingly forgotten, Daisy patted his beard and giggled. "Ba-ba."

Zinnia nodded. The tiredness lingered in her eyes, but she looked happy again. "Perfect. I guess she missed you."

A fuzzy feeling spread through his chest. "Did *you* miss me? I missed you this week."

Going with his instincts, he pressed his lips to her forehead. The softness of her skin tempted him to move to her mouth. He surrendered to a gentle first kiss, exactly like the one he'd wished for.

Her soundless exhale tickled his neck. "Evidently not as much as Daisy since my middle name wasn't cranky-pants all week. That means yes, in case you're wondering."

Pretty sure she now owned his heart, he grinned. "Come on in before the neighbors start complaining. We're having enchiladas, corn on the cob, and fruit."

"I'm not going to complain. You're a life saver." She led the way inside, the sway of her hips distracting him from the baby fingers grasping his sideburns. "It smells *so* good. I've been living on leftovers, bagged salad, and peanut butter crackers for days."

The stove timer started singing as soon as they entered the kitchen, but the sound Daisy made when he tried to hand her off to her mom wasn't harmony by any stretch of the imagination. "Maybe you should take the enchiladas and the corn out of the oven. Potholders are in the drawer to the left of the stove."

"Are you sure you don't mind holding her? She'll stop fussing eventually."

He hooked his foot around the chair leg and dragged it away from the table so he could sit. "But I may not have any facial hair left by the time we detach her from me. Besides, you deserve a break from momming. How did work go this week? It couldn't have been easy with a crying baby. Were you able to finish the jobs that were due by today?"

"Yes. All three authors loved their cover mockups, and I sent the last set of marketing graphics at two o'clock this morning. I even got a jump on one of next week's big projects after we took a catnap this morning." Transferring the casserole dish to the stovetop, she surprised him with an orgasmic moan. "Oh, wow. This looks amazing."

He willed away his body's immediate reaction to the sound, but it didn't fully cooperate. "So you'll let me cook for you all weekend?"

ZINNIA PLATED THE ENCHILADAS AND CORN, FILLED THEIR GLASSES, and retrieved the fruit salad from the refrigerator to hide the fact that she was dumbfounded.

The man sitting a few feet away, who'd offered to feed her for the next forty-eight hours and held her daughter like he didn't mind at all, was quiet until she turned to face him. "We both have to eat, and you deserve some payback since it's my fault Daisy's been out of sorts. I also think we should spend more time together to prevent that from happening again."

Taking the blame for her daughter's grouchiness made up for his self-satisfied smirk, but she wasn't about to dive into a serious relation-ship without dipping her toes in first to test the waters. "Remember when I mentioned taking our time getting to know each other?"

"How can we get to know each other if we don't spend more time together? It's been four days since I saw you. That's too long, especially when you live about fifty feet from me." He reached past the bowl of guacamole and produced a small banana. "And I'm not above using bribery to convince you."

Daisy squealed and grabbed for the perfectly ripened prize. "Bana!"

He laughed as he held tight to his gift. "That's right. Ba-ba got banas and some jars of strained peaches for you to prove to your mama I'll be a good boyfriend. Man-friend? No, that sounds creepy. Partner? Yeah, I like that."

Blinking away the tingling feeling in her nose and eyes, Zinnia transferred their plates to the table and sat across from this thoughtful, persistent, patient man she could suddenly picture as a husband and father. "You're not playing fair. Hand me the banana. I'll peel it and cut it into pieces small enough for you to feed her. FYI, your food's probably going to get cold before you're done."

"Won't be the first time I've eaten cold food." His mouth lost its playful curve, and he set the banana in the middle of the table. Then he carefully shifted Daisy so his thigh served as a high chair seat, an arm still cinched around her. "I'm not playing, Zinnia—fair or otherwise. No games. Ever. I promise."

The seriousness in his direct gaze and no-nonsense tone told her to take his declaration at face value, in spite of her past relationships telling her to tread carefully. Her heart had led her astray before, but her gut never steered her wrong. "Okay. Go ahead and take a few bites while you have the chance. Feeding Daisy is pretty much a full-time job until she decides she's done eating."

He tugged the dish towel free of the oven handle and tucked it in the neckline of her daughter's romper. "Did you hear that, Daisy? Your mom thinks I'm partner material. Don't let me screw up, okay?"

She drummed her hands on the table. "Ba-ba. Ma-ma."

"Ba-ba and ma-ma. Sounds right to me." His cocky grin made another appearance. It was, however, tempered by the look of pure happiness in his eyes and the genuine bond between him and her child.

When Zinnia pulled the extra place setting closer to work on prepping Daisy's entrée, he picked up his fork. As she laid the peel next to her plate, the utensil in his grasp slipped in above it with a chunk of honeydew melon stuck on its tines.

"Here. Have a bite." Something sweet yet intense glowed in the look he gave her. "All the teasing and flirting aside, I'm really glad you decided to stay for supper."

"Me too." She parted her lips, treasuring the intimate moment. Why couldn't she have met him sooner?

*No regrets. I have Daisy because of the timing.*

*I wouldn't change any of it.*

The illusion of family continued while they ate and through the mess Carson's inexperience created and his one-handed help with cleanup. Not until Zinnia settled into his chair in the living room did her daughter release him from dad duty.

*If the last hour is anything to go by, he'd be a great father.*

As he lowered Daisy to her arms, he sighed. "Holding her wasn't as hard as I thought it would be. Thanks for letting me help."

*And a wonderful partner.*

She grasped his shirt, urging him close enough for a quick kiss when he would've straightened. "Thanks for helping."

"You're welcome." He unfolded the towel resting on the chair near her head and draped it over her shoulder. "So you have some privacy while Daisy nurses. I'm going to put on a clean shirt. Be back in a minute."

# CHAPTER FIVE

"HAVE A GOOD WEEKEND, DR. HINES. CARSON." INEZ, ENTHUSIASTIC grad student number three, waved as she headed out of the lab, her hero worship having thankfully waned somewhat to excessive respect over the last week.

"You too. See you Monday." He returned the gesture and shut down the desktop computer.

The clicking of shoes announcing her presence, Dr. Needleman entered his work area looking surprisingly cheerful for the end of the first week of the semester. "Do you have a minute, Carson?"

He slung the strap of his laptop bag on his shoulder and met her halfway across the room. "Can we talk while we head to the parking lot? I have—"

"Plans with Zinnia and Daisy at five. I know." Her broad smile seemed to indicate her approval. "I'll walk you to your car."

He pulled the door closed behind them and double-checked the lock. "We're grilling at her house and then taking Daisy for a stroller ride."

"She said you've been having supper together every night. My granddaughter apparently adores you. Ba-ba, she calls you, according to my daughter." The elevator opened as they arrived, and she pressed the first-floor button when they were both inside. "I'm glad to see Zin hasn't given up on love."

Curiosity wouldn't let him keep his mouth shut. "She told you she loves me?"

Her laughter echoed in the small space. "Good gracious, no, but I'd venture to say *you* love *her*, based on your hopeful expression. Don't worry. Your secret's safe with me. And my husband, of course. For now, anyway."

Heat flooded his neck and face, even though they hadn't stepped out into the late-August humidity yet. "It wasn't part of my original plan, but feelings happened. I don't think she's ready to hear it."

"You're probably right. I'm sure she will be soon, so be patient with her." The elevator door slid open and she led the way down the main hallway. "That isn't what I wanted to speak to you about, though."

He pushed out of the exit and held the door for her, getting the distinct feeling it was something every bit as big as falling in love. "Did another proposal receive funding?"

"Not that I'm aware of." Her pace along the sidewalk allowed him full strides, suggesting she never moved in slow motion. "Your counterpart in the visiting scholar exchange called me yesterday. We had quite an interesting discussion. She intends to stay in California after the agreement ends and plans to email her resignation letter to the department chair next week, effective the last day of December. Obviously, that leaves us with her classes on the books but no one to teach them during the spring semester. While we can't officially offer you her position just yet, I'd like to gauge your interest."

His leg muscles froze, stalling him next to the building where her office was located. This opportunity seemed like a sign. It meant he wouldn't have to leave Zinnia, even temporarily, when his current gig was done. He didn't need to think about the decision or weigh the pros and cons. "Yes, I'm interested."

She backtracked a few steps and stopped beside him. "I thought as much, but I couldn't presume to know your intentions. As I'm sure you know, we'll have to follow certain procedures that may take several weeks to a few months."

He nodded, familiar with the slow processes and miles of red tape required to do anything at a university. "I'm guessing you want me to keep this to myself for now."

"I would appreciate it. I'll keep you updated as much as I can." Her all-business manner shifted to a pleased one as she set off in the opposite direction. "Go enjoy your time with my girls."

Walking home would've burned off the excess energy coursing through his body, but driving got him there faster. He jogged up the front steps and hurried inside to dump his bag on the desk in his bedroom. His phone buzzed against his palm as he emptied his pockets.

Zinnia's name appeared on the screen. *"The grill is preheating. Daisy says to hurry up! :D"*

A grin tickled his cheeks. *"Changing clothes. Be there in five minutes. LOL"*

Three minutes later, he stood on her porch with his fist poised to knock. The door swung wide before he made contact, and his two favorite people greeted him with kisses. One was wet and sloppy on his cheek. The other was sweet and sexy on his lips. Both greetings filled him with so much emotion he wanted to stow them in his memory forever.

"Ba-ba!" Daisy rubbed her fingers along his beard and giggled.

"My whiskers feel funny, don't they?" He hoisted her against him with his left arm and wrapped his right arm around Zinnia's waist. "Hi there. How was your day?"

"Good, but it just got better." Wisps of blonde silk had escaped her messy bun, but the look suited her and made him wish he'd been the reason for her disheveled hair.

"Mine too." Unable to resist, he kissed her for a heartbeat longer than she'd done to him. "Am I on cooking or entertainment duty this time?"

"What do you think? She's been talking about you all day. I didn't expect her to become so attached to our next-door neighbor." Zinnia's teasing tone didn't match the seriousness in her eyes. Was she feeling a connection with him too?

Telling her about his discussion with Iris would be too easy if he didn't find a distraction. "You say that like it's a bad thing. We have similar interests, right, Daisy? Eating, laughing, spending time with your mom. Speaking of time, your swing should be in the shade by now. After that, we can read a book or two and watch your mama flaunt her grilling skills."

"Ma-ma. Ba-ba. Ma-ma. Ba-ba." His partner-in-crime clapped her hands and bounced on his forearm.

"Yep. Ma-ma and Ba-ba and Daisy. Perfect together, like breakfast, lunch, and supper." Linking his fingers with Zinnia's, he walked with her toward the kitchen.

She shook her head, but the hint of a dimple below her cheekbone gave away her amusement. "Always thinking about food. You two are something else. Go play while I decompress."

Concern hit faster than he'd fallen for her. "Wasn't your dad supposed to babysit this morning?"

"His fuel pump bit the dust on the way home from the hardware store, and he spent an hour waiting for roadside assistance and another three hours for the repair to be done." She released his hand as they approached the fridge. "I'll get the chicken and garlic bread. Would you mind carrying the potatoes and zucchini? They're in the container by the stove."

"Got 'em. It sounds like your day got derailed." A slight adjustment to his hold on the baby let him carry the vegetables and slide open the door to the patio. "Did you finish the marketing package for your new client? Daisy and I can keep each other occupied if you need to work after supper."

The answer was obvious when she set down her load on the picnic table and sighed. "I'm about halfway done. You have a deal if it includes diaper changes."

❧

DIAPER CHANGES HADN'T BEEN A DEAL-BREAKER. IN FACT, ZINNIA HAD meant it as a joke, but Carson had agreed to her terms—and followed through—without a complaint or argument.

She attached the last file to her email and sent the completed graphics a few minutes after ten. An invoice sent and her project spreadsheet updated, she shut down her computer and turned off the lights in her office. The lamp in the living room still glowed down the hall, but she checked Daisy's room first, on the off chance Carson had put Daisy in her crib.

Finding it empty, Zinnia walked to the front of the house. Her aging ovaries nearly exploded at the sight of him stretched out on the couch, her daughter cradled against his chest and their eyes closed. A tiny hand rested on his beard and his much larger one cupped the headful of hair that looked so much like his. This was what she'd imagined before her biological clock had forced her into action. She'd wanted happily-ever-after with her true love and their child. Having a baby had been within her control, but finding love hadn't.

*Is what I'm feeling real? Or is it wishful thinking?*

Honesty demanded she admit that she'd been falling in love with him over the last two weeks. He was kind, generous, and not the egotistical jerk his first impression implied, and having Daisy's stamp of approval wasn't something she could take lightly. Her daughter treated him like she'd known him every day of her short life, like she'd chosen him to be her father.

*One day I'll have to tell her how she came to be.*

*And him. He deserves to know too.*

Zinnia stepped closer, taking in every detail of the scene so she could recreate it in a sketch. The soft lighting muted their features, but no one would mistake the special relationship—the connection—between them.

He suddenly blinked up at her, sleep still heavy in his eyes. "Hi. Her bedtime story worked on both of us. Did you get done?"

Her heart fell a little farther. How long had she searched for someone who showed more than superficial interest in her? "Yes. Thank you for babysitting."

Shifting Daisy to the crook of his elbow, he sat up. "Do you want me to put her to bed?"

His husky voice woke the part of her she'd let slumber the last two years—since she'd made the decision to make part of her wish come true on her own. This was her chance to have it all.

She nodded and led him down the hall. Each step bolstered her courage, giving her the boldness to seize the opportunity she'd been handed.

He paused at the crib, first pressing a kiss to the top of her daughter's head and then waiting for Zinnia to do the same. "On her back, right? I've been reading up on babies."

She nodded again, too touched by his willingness to take care of Daisy to speak.

In the nightlight's dim illumination, his fingertips lingered for a few seconds on a dark curl at her daughter's temple. "What about her socks? Won't her feet get too warm this time of year with them on?"

"She likes wearing them, even in summer. Not a battle worth fighting."

"Okay." He covered her with the sheet. "Good night, little flower."

Daisy's almost silent sigh was punctuated by a contented smile.

*Are they trying to turn me into a blubbering mess?*

Zinnia sniffled and swiped at the tear trickling down her cheek as they left the nursery. If she hadn't been in love with Carson before, those simple words and actions would've clinched it.

"Why are you crying?" He slipped his arm around her shoulders and gave her a sideways hug when they entered the living room. "You're not feeling guilty about needing to work tonight, are you? I was happy to do it and Daisy knows you're an amazing mom."

"No, that's not it at all. They're happy tears, because the moment you shared with her in there was so beautiful." She turned to face him, confident in the question she was about to ask. "Will you stay?"

"Sure. Did you want to watch a movie? Or we can talk if you—"

"Stay. As in, the night." The way his now-alert eyes searched hers told her she'd gained his complete attention. *All in.* "A sleepover with me. In my bed. With no clothes and lots of kissing and touching."

He swallowed loud enough for her to hear and then inhaled and exhaled on a shaky breath. "Are you sure? I love… Um, I care about you a lot, but I don't want you to feel rushed into something you might regret later."

Relief and a comforting dose of humor mixed with the desire simmering in her lower belly. "I love… Um, I care about you a lot too. I don't feel rushed, and I think we'll both regret it if you leave. I know I will."

He leaned his forehead against hers. "I really want this to last. What if it's too soon? I don't want to ruin what we have because my no-IQ head gets cocky. Ugh. That sounded much less stupid in my intelligent head."

A chuckle escaped, and she held his face in her palms, loving the soft bristliness of his beard. "I'm ready for the next step, but we can leave our clothes on if you're not. Spending time alone together is the important part. No parenting or other responsibilities to think about. Just us, because we have deep feelings for each other."

"Yes, deep feelings." He tipped his mouth down to hers, kissing her with such sweetness she had no doubts about how he felt. "I love you, Zinnia, and I want to stay."

The "but" she half expected didn't make an appearance. Instead, he held her closer and ran his tongue along the seam of her lips, presumably asking permission for a more intimate connection.

*It's a step in the right direction.*

She parted her lips and melted against him with the first glide of his tongue along hers. The gentle stroke lit up every cell in her body and sparked a consuming fire—the kind she'd begun to suspect didn't exist, at least not for her. Another slow sweep followed, still patient and sure. The world faded away, leaving only the two of them and the thorough exploration of what had been building between them every day.

The loss as he eased back for a breath gave way to awareness. She took advantage of the break while she could. "I love you too, Carson. I want to show you how much."

He scooped her into his arms and carried her to her bedroom. The light of the moon filtered through the blinds, casting a slight glow over the bedspread and enough of the floor to keep from having to turn on a lamp.

Stopping beside the bed, he lowered her to her feet and simply stared at her for several seconds. Then he worked the top button of her sleeveless blouse free before moving on to the next. Each one allowed him access to more skin, but he didn't dive in like a sex-starved man. The reverent way he undressed her amplified the feelings she'd admitted, made her wonder if he was trying to savor their first time together as much as she was.

Impatience finally got the best of her, and she tugged his muscle shirt over his head and tackled his shorts. Less than a minute later, he stood facing her, naked and quite obviously ready for the main event.

His erection bobbed up and down at her, and he hissed a breath when she closed her fist around his hard length. His low groan caressed her nerve endings a second before she landed flat on her back with his face between her thighs.

A leisurely lick through her folds sent tingles zinging to her fingers and toes and everywhere in between. She arched into him and clutched at the covers, loving the coarseness of his whiskers against her tender skin and his insistent tongue lapping at her clit. His thumb brushed over her nipple as a tidal wave of sensation rushed through her muscles and over her skin. Every inch of her came alive, forcing a cry from her throat. The peak tapered off for only a few seconds before his caresses carried her up and over again.

She melted into the bed, more relaxed than she'd felt in years.

He kissed her inner thigh as he moved away, but her eyelids refused to let her watch him for the moment. After the telltale crinkle of a condom package, he shifted her toward the middle of the bed and positioned himself at her entrance. Then he glided inside her, stretching and filling her.

A long second passed with their bodies connected, his poised over hers, though he lay still. She opened her eyes and met his euphoric gaze in the not-quite-darkness.

He finally rocked forward and back in a slow and steady rhythm that promised even more pleasure. His mouth covered hers again, their tongues imitating the synchronized movement of their hips.

She wrapped her legs around him and hooked her ankles at his lower back, desperate to be closer to him. Her pleasure soared as he sank deeper. "There, Carson. Yes. More."

The friction changed with his next thrust. He swelled inside her, and his rougher, more erratic in-and-out motion pushed her to new heights. Then everything but their union dropped away, leaving her freefalling safely into his embrace.

He growled against her neck and stiffened as she rose and fell again. His panting breaths feathered across her cheek while she trembled through aftershock after aftershock. Then he was lying on top of her, the wonderful weight of him keeping her from floating away.

A few minutes later, he levered up on his elbows and combed his calloused fingertips through the wisps of hair tickling her cheek. "Someday soon I'm going to ask you to marry me, Zinnia Trimble."

# CHAPTER SIX

⦁

HE'D MADE THE VERY DECLARATION EVERY GUY KNEW NOT TO MAKE in bed.

Technically speaking, he hadn't actually done it, but he also didn't regret telling the woman he loved he planned to do it soon.

Carson rolled over to find Zinnia and enjoy a few more minutes of cuddling before he ran next door for a quick shower and change of clothes. Then they would spend the day together.

The spot she'd occupied much of the night was empty.

"Ma-ma! Ba-ba! Ma-ma! Ba-ba!" Daisy's exuberant wake-up call had likely forced her mother out of bed while he slept like a man who'd discovered heaven the night before.

He shoved away the tangled sheet and grabbed his shorts from the floor. After a quick trip to the bathroom, he padded toward the kitchen —where a little voice chattered his name over and over.

As soon as she spotted him in the doorway, her pink-socked feet started kicking back and forth and she reached for him. "Ba-ba! Ba-ba bana. Ma-ma!"

"Hey there, early bird. Looks like you're having baby cereal and something orange for breakfast. Peaches, maybe? Little girls can't live on banas alone." Not bothering to fight his grin, he crossed to her high chair and kissed the top of her head. Continuing to Zinnia at the counter, he gathered her in a hug from behind and nuzzled her ear. "G'morning. Do you want me to feed Daisy so you can hop in the shower?"

"That's one of the sweetest things anyone's ever offered to do for me. I'm definitely taking you up on it." She turned her head and planted a kiss on his lips. "I'm glad you stayed last night."

"Me too." He held her in place for another longer taste. "Mm. I could get used to waking up every morning to this."

"It isn't always smiles and banas." Her robe slipped apart as she stirred more peaches into the pasty-textured goo, giving him a peek at the physical parts of her he'd explored last night. "You haven't experienced a grouchy-, teething-, or sick-baby day. Or when she wants to be held by someone who isn't there."

Last week's crying fit when they'd arrived for supper at his house gave him a fair idea of what she meant. Still, he could live with a bit of fussiness mixed in with Daisy's usually cheerful mood to have this woman and her child in his life. "We all have bad days once in a while. Being with you makes it better. Should I bother with a bib? I could just hose her down in the sink after she eats."

Zinnia's throaty laughter sparked interest behind his zipper, but she straightened her robe and handed him the kid-sized bowl faster than his body had reacted to her. A quick brush of her delicious mouth on his pec doused him in horniness, only to have to watch her walk toward the living room. "You two stay out of trouble while I take a shower."

"Yes, ma'am." He sat next to her daughter and reined in the desire to follow his lover. If he wanted Zinnia to agree to marry him when he proposed, he had to prove his dedication to being a good father. "Your mama runs a tight ship, doesn't she?"

*A father. I never thought I'd be a dad, not in the raising-a-child sense.*

"Ba-ba. Ba-ba. Ba-ba." Daisy smacked her palm on the tray of the high chair, clearly impatient for her breakfast.

"Okay, give me a second. Let's see if we can put this bib on you."

Working quickly to keep her from wrestling him for control, he whipped the catch-all under her chin and fastened the Velcro tab.

Her mouth opened as he lifted the first bite, making it an easy target. Unfortunately, she also hadn't quite mastered the concept of swallowing all of the miniscule amount of food on her miniature spoon. Half of what he put in came back out, creating a plowable drift above the dimple in her chin.

His training to spot genetic similarities asserted itself for the dozenth time since her mom had tried to hand her off to him the day he'd moved into the rental.

*Dark brown hair. Blue eyes. Cleft chin.*

Of course, noticing that combination had become an old habit over the last twenty years.

Did people who didn't know any different think he was her biological father during their walks? Did he, Zinnia, and Daisy look like a family?

Given that the man who'd contributed to Daisy's DNA wasn't in the picture, adopting her was going to the top of his to-do list once he and Zinnia tied the knot. Until then, he would happily take on the role without legal responsibility or recognition.

Supplies at the ready, Zinnia laid her daughter on the bed in the room she'd slept in during her teen years and unfastened the crotch snaps of the ruffled romper. Carson's declaration on Friday night—that had almost been a marriage proposal—circled her mind again. It had instigated a lot of feelings, but fear wasn't among them. Knowing in her heart they were meant for each other had surprised her the most.

Gam-gam snickered as she offered Daisy a stuffed bunny. "She must've been quite the moving target during her last diaper change."

"Carson said she was bicycling around the block while he was hooking the tabs. I was packing the pie to bring over and could hear them giggling all the way in the kitchen." Zinnia couldn't help smiling at the memory.

"A man who doesn't mind changing diapers? And you're practically glowing. He seems like a keeper." A wink and a smirk accompanied her mother's playful game of peek-a-boo with Daisy. "Your dad and I really like him. Is it serious?"

"Come on, Mom. You can't fool me. You were hoping for serious when you invited both of us to the cookout two weeks ago." The job finished, Zinnia refastened Daisy's romper and picked up the used diaper. "The other night he told me he was going to ask me to marry him soon, and I wanted to say he could do it now. Am I out of my mind?"

"Sometimes you just know, Zin. Haven't you always trusted your instincts? That's why we have this truly wonderful child in our lives." Her mom scooped Daisy off the bed and kissed her cheek. "And you adore Ba-ba too, don't you?"

Even after a long day consisting of a trip to the grocery store, one nap, playtime inside and outside, and Sunday supper at her grandparents' house, Daisy grinned and smacked her palms together. "Ba-ba!"

Zinnia disposed of the diaper and headed to the bathroom in the hall to wash her hands. "What if my instincts are being influenced by hormones? I swear he pickles a bunch of my brain cells every time we kiss. And don't even get me started on Friday night. I invited him to stay, and it was like we'd been a couple for months or years instead of days. Being with him and waking up next to him felt so right, but I can't screw up, not when Daisy could end up hurt too."

"I know she likes most people, but has she ever become this attached to someone she just met like she has with Carson?"

Meeting her mother's gaze in the mirror, Zinnia sighed. "You know the answer to that question. But…what if he reacts badly when I tell him the whole story of Daisy? He's probably already made assumptions, just like most people did when they found out I was pregnant."

Her mom rolled her eyes. "Anyone with an ounce of perception can see he's completely in love with you, and the truth isn't going to change that. The sooner he knows, the better. Besides, *you* can ask *him* to marry you. Can you imagine the look on his face if you proposed?"

"Actually, I can. A little surprised and a lot smug, although I don't think I'd have to worry about him saying yes. Fine, I'll tell him tonight." Her insides finally settling now that she'd talked through the situation and made a decision, Zinnia followed her dad's and Carson's animated voices toward the kitchen. They'd evidently segued from their earlier discussion about the best seasonings for steak to the most effective methods for collecting a non-blood DNA sample from a crime scene.

"Ba-ba." Daisy dove for Carson as soon as he was within reach and immediately rested her head on his shoulder when he pulled her to his chest.

His grin softening to a contented half smile, he rubbed her back. "She'll be asleep before the stroller hits the sidewalk."

Her parents exchanged a look that said everything Zinnia needed to know about their opinion of Carson. They liked and respected him, and they couldn't have picked a better man for her and their granddaughter if they'd tried.

After a round of hugs, kisses, and handshakes at the front door, Carson buckled in a mostly asleep Daisy like he'd been doing it her entire eight-month life. "Do you want me to push the stroller?"

"Sure. Thanks." She hooked her arm through his and fell into step beside him. Knowing her resolve might falter if she put off telling him her story, she took a deep breath. "I've been waiting to see how things went between us before I shared about Daisy, but I think it's time."

Without slowing, he glanced toward her. "You don't owe me an explanation. Babies are made every day. Some have fathers who want the job and some don't. The mothers aren't to blame for that. Being a single mom is no reflection on your morality, at least not as far as I'm concerned. It takes two people and birth control sometimes fails."

His defense of her warmed her heart. "Actually, I chose to have a child by myself. And before you jump to conclusions, I didn't trick anyone into impregnating me."

He paused at the cross street for the count of two and then continued. "I know you didn't. You're not that kind of person. If you got pregnant on purpose, the guy you had sex with knew what the deal was."

"So…" She forced another relaxed breath. "The thing is…I wasn't in a relationship or even dating anyone, but I knew I wanted to be a mom. At forty-two, time wasn't on my side. Although I'm healthy, I was already in the high-risk age group, which meant I needed to research my options carefully."

His attention clearly on crossing again, he was silent until they arrived at their street. "Makes sense."

*Two blocks to go.*

"Besides not wanting to resort to a one-night stand with someone whose medical history I knew nothing about, I wasn't interested in having sex outside of a serious relationship. That left adoption—a process that usually takes years—or conceiving without intercourse." She waited most of the block for him to comment.

"But you said you didn't adopt her." His pace remained even as they neared her house. "I didn't mean to imply there was anything wrong with it when I asked if she was adopted. Curiosity about genealogy is kind of a byproduct of my field. I can be a little oblivious to how my observations about genetics sound sometimes."

"She's biologically my daughter." *Out with it already.* She turned toward him at the end of her driveway. "I chose an anonymous sperm donor by his profile and was artificially inseminated."

# CHAPTER SEVEN

EVERY BIT OF AIR ABANDONED CARSON'S BODY IN AN INSTANT.

*An anonymous sperm donor profile.*

*Artificial insemination. Also known as the turkey baster method.*

Donor insemination had been the topic of numerous conference talks he'd attended in his career, mainly because the industry had grown exponentially over the last decade. It was the top reproductive choice among LGBTQ couples and single women who hadn't found or didn't want a partner. He'd been approached by all sides of the equation—provider, donor, recipient, offspring, and legislators—about representing support for and opposition to more regulation, especially since a single donor could father hundreds of babies.

Of course, he had his own personal reasons for staying informed about the procedure, its consequences, and the changes in anonymity and privacy.

He willed the Broca's area of his frontal cortex to form a response before Zinnia got the wrong idea—that he was opposed to the practice. "I can see why you chose to go with artificial insemination. Sperm donors have to have far more testing than sex partners. Not just for sexually transmitted diseases. Lots of other medical information and health histories. IQ, mental health evaluations, and personality and physical traits are a routine part of the profiles. I'm glad yours was successful."

An amused smirk lifted the corners of her mouth. "Remember how a few minutes ago you said you could be oblivious? You're doing it again. Not that I mind. Most people have no idea what goes into the whole process, so it's nice to be able to talk to someone who's familiar with how it works and why it's an important option. Since genealogy websites have made DNA testing more accessible, Daisy may decide to locate her donor when she's older. Siblings aren't a possibility, though. There are too many horror stories out there about half-siblings dating and marrying each other because they had no way of knowing their biological connection. I asked for profiles with only enough supply for one recipient and narrowed my choices from there."

He nodded to keep from choking on his words. Hope tried to outpace logic, but it receded as all the details requiring alignment to create her baby from a one-time donation he'd made twenty years ago filtered through his thoughts.

He'd lived in a different part of the country then, far from his most recent home in California and not in the same state where she'd grown up and probably lived most of her life.

He hadn't wanted to be notified when his donation was chosen, but it surely had happened in the eighteen years prior to her decision, given the popularity of his particular profile.

Separately and collectively, dark brown hair, blue eyes, and a cleft chin weren't all that unusual among donors, genetically speaking.

His hope came from wishful thinking. Wouldn't Zinnia be more inclined to marry him if Daisy was their daughter in every way?

*Not if she didn't love me.*

Should he tell her he'd been a donor? Yes, but would it cause unnecessary upheaval since the chances that his sperm had been used was miniscule at best, especially when international databases were now in place?

The least he could do before sharing that news was contact the company tomorrow and ask about the status of his deposit. Confirming he couldn't possibly have fathered her child needed to happen first.

Determined to handle it all like a rational human being, he pushed the stroller up the driveway and then along the walkway to the porch. "Avoiding profiles with numerous donations was a wise decision. I've been on a few advisory committees about regulation specifically related to this issue. The demand for sperm has increased exponentially and the pay per donation can provide a decent supplemental income, meaning the chances of crossing paths with a sibling have skyrocketed. Regulation, transparency, and better oversight need to happen."

"I like when you get all intellectual." She gave him a quick kiss on the lips and brushed her fingers over his beard. "It's very sexy."

His pulse sped up with the contact, distracting him from tomorrow's task. "You elevate nerd-sexy to a whole new level. Programmer, teacher, artist, businesswoman. I'll take care of the stroller while you put Daisy to bed. Let's meet on the couch."

"Maybe you should run next door for your work clothes and laptop now, so you don't have to do it in the morning." She peered up at him through her pink-framed glasses as she unbuckled her daughter.

God, he loved her studious look and her gorgeous mind. "Is that an invitation to stay the night again?"

Her husky laugh skittered across her skin. "Unless you want us to sleep over at your house tonight. You're paying me rent for it after all."

He shook his head. "I'll sleep wherever you want, but Daisy will be more comfortable in her crib. And your house feels like a home. Give me about ten minutes to grab my stuff."

"Eight minutes. I've been thinking about making love to you all day. With me on top." With a wink and a seductive wiggle, she lifted Daisy from the three-wheeler and carried her up the steps.

More than willing to accommodate the modified timetable, he collapsed the stroller, stowed it on the porch, and jogged next door to pack for his third overnight stay in a row.

*Shirt, pants, socks, and underwear.*
*Shoes, travel kit, laptop.*
*Condoms.*

Twenty minutes later, she led him from the couch to her bedroom, turning off lights and kissing him every few feet along the way.

&.

*I COULD GET USED TO THIS.*

*I want to get used to this.*

Carson slicked his comb through his wet hair, the dumbfounded expression of his reflection staring back at him in the mirror. He'd made a decision while he showered—probably the most monumental decision of his life.

He was going to ask Zinnia to marry him tonight.

Not once in his thirty-eight years had he ever entertained the idea of proposing to a woman. Sure, he'd dated some, but focusing on his research had taken precedence over having an active social calendar. Despite his reputation as a flirt, he hadn't played anywhere near as hard as his colleagues thought he did.

*Once a nerd, always a nerd.*

Growing ten inches and adding muscles his freshman year of high school hadn't changed his brain at all and not much of his tendency to overcompensate for being insecure. Only years of practice kept that disconcerting flaw under control most of the time.

After a swipe of deodorant in each armpit, he wrapped the towel around his waist and headed to the bedroom to dress for work.

Zinnia still lay on her side with the tangled sheet draped across her from breast to hip, the same position she'd been in when he'd crawled out of bed.

*Trip to the jewelry store at lunchtime.*

As much as he wanted to climb back under the covers with her, he dropped the towel and pulled on the pair of boxer briefs and khakis he'd stowed on top of the dresser. His button-down shirt still hung on a hanger from the top drawer's knob, where he'd hung it to avoid having to iron out the wrinkles this morning.

A soft coo came from the nightstand on Zinnia's side as he pushed the last button through its hole. She blinked once, twice, three times while he crossed to the bed.

He leaned down to press a kiss to her forehead. "Go back to sleep for a little while if you want to. I'll take diaper and breakfast duty."

Her sleepy smile tempted him to go back for a more intimate greeting. "You're the best partner. Love you."

His willpower almost abandoned him, but he finger-combed her hair away from her cheek and straightened. "I'm the lucky one. I love you too."

A contented sigh carried to his ears on his way out the door to Daisy's room.

He hung his damp towel on the wall hook by the shower and continued to his destination. When he opened the door, Zinnia's baby girl sat up and grinned. "Good morning, sunshine. Let's whisper so your mama can sleep in."

Her infectious giggle squeezed into every bit of space in his heart not already occupied by her mother. "Ba-ba."

"Yep, Ba-ba loves you, just like he loves your mommy." He hurried through the diaper change, managing to fasten the tapes straighter than yesterday's disaster. "Are you ready for breakfast?"

"Num-num-num." She patted his beard all the way to the kitchen, repeating the new word she learned over the weekend—the one he'd taught her.

"Num-num in the tum-tum." He laughed with her as he buckled her into the high chair. Hoping to keep her squealing to a minimum, he offered her the smaller of the two teethers Zinnia stored in the freezer. "How about I make some rice cereal and cut up your favorite fruit while you gnaw on this?"

She closed her little fingers around the cold ring and shoved it past her itty-bitty teeth.

"I hope you're this easy to get along with when you're a teenager." With half his attention on prepping her breakfast and half on her, he measured, mixed, and chopped like Zinnia had done the other two mornings they'd spent together. Sharing parenting responsibilities with her would be part of marriage, assuming she accepted his proposal. "We'll just have to convince her we're meant to be a family, won't we?"

A string of indecipherable babbling coincided with the removal of the teether. As he scooped a spoonful of cereal, she tossed the slobber-covered silicone ring onto the table. It bounced and landed in his lap. "Bana!"

"Okay, okay. A bite with banana first." He emptied half the contents of the spoon into the bowl, added a piece of squishy fruit, and tried again.

She opened her mouth wide, her bright blue eyes shining with innocence and trust. The look she aimed at him triggered tightness in his throat and fullness in his chest like he'd never felt before meeting Zinnia and her daughter. His gut told him being with them was the right next step in his life.

They were the family he'd never really thought about having and wanted more than anything.

He stuffed the teether in his shirt pocket to keep it from falling on the floor while Daisy mostly gummed her mouthful. More food stayed inside than came out this time, a vast improvement over his previous attempts at feeding her. "Ready for more?"

Her baby bird imitation made the answer clear. She gobbled bite after bite, getting messier toward the end of her meal. Mashed bananas coated her pudgy hands and cheeks by the time she emptied both bowls.

"Let's clean up before your mom sees how bad I am at feeding you." He wet a clean dishcloth in the sink as he debated the best approach. By the time he turned around to start wiping, she'd spread the sticky goop to the high chair tray and her sock-covered feet. "Hands first. Then remove the tray and wipe the face while I hold your hands out of the way. Fair warning, Daisy Mae. Your socks are dirty, so they're going to have to come off."

She blinked up at him with her sweet baby smile, as if she planned to fully cooperate.

"Prove it, banana girl." He caught her right hand in the washcloth, keeping her at arm's length so he wouldn't have to change clothes before he headed to work. After a thorough between-the-fingers wipe, he repeated the process with her left hand. "So far, so good."

She giggled and reached for the cloth when he refolded it to a clean section.

He kissed her closest hand and snuck his in from underneath to wipe her face. "Gotcha!"

More adorable laughter allowed him a chance to seize what he'd missed the first time on her cheeks.

Satisfied with that part of the job, he slid the tray free and set it on the table. A single tug on each of her socks finished the worst of the task. He dropped them onto the tray. "Look what I found. Cute little Daisy feet."

She chattered away as he lifted a foot toward his beard. Five tiny toes wiggled, revealing webbing between two of them—exactly like his own. Her right foot was a mirror image of her left.

*Bilateral syndactyly.*

*The same as mine.*

The room swayed as he focused on his own bare foot.

*There was always a chance, but...*

*This. Am I her father?*

The question played over and over in his head.

*What do I do now?*

"Carson. Carson, is everything okay?" Zinnia stepped into his wavy peripheral vision. Her toes slowly came into focus—her normal toes.

He nodded and stood. "I just... I realized I'm going to be late for work if I don't get going."

Without waiting for her to reply, he hurried out of the kitchen to find his shoes and socks, wallet and keys, laptop and phone.

# CHAPTER EIGHT

HAD THE FULL AND SOMETIMES-OVERWHELMING IMPACT OF PARENTING whacked Carson over the head?

Zinnia unbuckled Daisy from the high chair and carried her to the living room to nurse, pretty sure he'd suddenly realized what day-to-day life with a baby would be like. Was he having second thoughts about their relationship, proposing, living happily if not perfectly ever after?

A thud and a grunt came from down the hall, and he appeared a minute later, his dark eyebrows dipping low over his eyes and his mouth scrunched in a tight line. His gaze seemed focused on a point somewhere beyond her, like he was in a hurry to escape. He didn't glance her direction until he was halfway out the door, but he still didn't meet her gaze. "I... I'll text you later."

"Okay. I love—"

The front door clunked shut.

Or maybe this side of him came out when he shifted deep into research mode?

*I will not jump to conclusions. This doesn't mean he's already moving on to something easier.*

Instead of stewing in the doubts trying to drown her, she prioritized the items on her to-do list for the day, including a graphics package for a local restaurant. She couldn't afford any melodramatic distractions while her small business grew its clientele and her workload paid the bills.

Knocking cut into her thoughts as she sat Daisy on the rug with a cloth book. "Oh, I bet I know who that is. Want to go play at Pop-pop's house while I work this morning?"

"Pop-pop-pop." Daisy clutched the book in her fist and made a soundless clap.

Leaving her daughter to trail after her if she was so inclined, Zinnia double-checked that she'd righted her shirt on her way across the room. A peek through the glass confirmed her guess, and she welcomed him inside with a hug. "Hi, Dad. Thanks for babysitting. Give me a minute to get her dressed. I'm running a little late this morning."

He scooped the baby off the floor and puckered up for a slobbery kiss. "Did you sleep in for a change, Daisy Mae? Morning, Zin. I can find some clothes for her if you need to start working."

"Actually, I slept in for a bit while Carson fed her breakfast." She followed him down the hall to the nursery. "He left in a hurry after I got up. Do you think he's realizing what's involved in raising a child and getting cold feet?"

"Did you ask him?" He pulled a romper and clean socks from the dresser and stood Daisy in her crib.

She plopped on her bottom, clearly not interested in testing her vertical skills yet.

"No, but he practically ran out the door, saying he was going to be late for work and he'd text me later." Zinnia tugged the ponytail elastic off her wrist and twisted her hair into a messy bun. "I know I'm probably overthinking. It's just that I really want him to be the one. We click. All three of us. And Daisy loves him as much as I do."

With a gentle sweep, he pulled her daughter's pajama top over her head and past her hands. "Does she need a diaper change?"

"Carson took care of it."

"Good for him." The ruffled bottoms came off next. "Yes, you're probably overthinking. I've seen him with the two of you, and I gotta say he's head over heels in love with you or he's an expert liar. Maybe he got a phone call or a text from somebody he's collaborating with. I trust your judgment, and so should you. Give him the benefit of the doubt unless you have evidence that proves otherwise. Snap, snap, snap. Done. I like these summer outfits your mom picked out. Easy on. Easy off."

"You make it sound so simple." She chose a purple bow to match the romper and passed it to him after he gathered Daisy's dark hair into a curly fountain at the top of her head. "Here you go. I'm still amazed she leaves those in."

"She likes being fancy, just like you did when you were little. Let's have those pretty little tootsie-toes, Daisy." He wiggled a sock into place and started on the second one. "Love is only complicated when we make it that way. I knew your mom was it for me on our first date. She needed a little longer, but I didn't mind. It gave me more opportunities to show her how important she was—is—to me. If you really want this and need more time, ask him to wait for you. The right man will be patient."

When he picked up her daughter, she wrapped them both in a hug. "How did you get to be so smart?"

"Sixty-seven years of making mistakes." He draped an arm around her shoulder as they walked out of the room. "We'll take the stroller since I walked here. Do you want me to bring her home around noon? Or would you rather come get her and stay for lunch?"

"My eyes will need a break by then, so I'll come over and you can feed us." She trailed him out the front door with the stroller and bumped it down the steps to the walkway. "Thanks, Dad. I don't know what I'd do without you."

"You're intelligent and resourceful. You'd figure something out." He tossed a grin at her as he strapped in Daisy. "Wave bye-bye to Mommy."

Her daughter folded and unfolded her fingers. "Bah-bah."

Zinnia brushed her lips against her baby's forehead. "Bye-bye. Mommy loves you."

Her mood in a slightly better place than when Carson had left, she waved and headed inside to her office. Her job didn't care about her problems or her love life, let alone a combination of the two.

FLEXING HIS FINGERS AROUND HIS MUG OF COFFEE, CARSON REREAD the twenty-year-old email from the facility he'd visited. It included his donor code, the most personal identifying information recipients received with his profile. Before he could second-guess the decision, he copied and pasted the string of numbers and letters into a new message and requested a status update from the company that was miraculously still operating under the same name and email. Mergers and buyouts had eaten up the smaller clinics years ago. His choice had been one of the first to jump on the expansion bandwagon, becoming a standout in the industry.

He set the cup aside, clicked Send, and pushed his chair away from the desk.

The odds of his sperm having contributed to the creation of Daisy had increased exponentially in the last twelve hours, despite the number of donors in the world. Too many genetic—or coincidental—similarities had come to light to brush off the possibility.

He shoved his fingers through his hair as he rested his elbows on his knees to curb the lingering unsteadiness. Caffeine wasn't helping the nerves already hopped up on adrenaline.

*I need to know if she's mine.*

Not once in the two decades since his donation had an actual child entered his mind. The concept of being a biological father hadn't made him think of anything other than some abstract combination of genetic material.

*She's real.*

*Dark brown hair, blue eyes, cleft chin, bilateral syndactyly of the same toes.*

He couldn't ignore that many coincidences, not with his knowledge of DNA and the incidence of less common parental traits in offspring.

*I need to know.*

Unable to sit any longer, he straightened and pushed up from the chair, sending it rolling backward. Something tugged at his shirt and fell onto the floor next to his shoe.

*The teething ring.*

*That has DNA from Daisy on it.*

He yanked a tissue from the box on his desk and picked up the teether. The textured silicone provided a good surface to trap dried saliva, even if it wasn't an ideal sample.

*I'm an expert at this. I'll make it work.*

*I can find out. Today.*

*I have to know.*

Shaking off the woozy feeling that had been nagging him for the last thirty minutes, he carried his prize into the lab and started prepping her samples for the extraction process, along with three of his own. Nearly an hour passed before Inez arrived, finally saving him from pacing a trench while the new Maxwell 16 isolated the nucleic acid for the next step.

She closed the door behind her, dropped her backpack on the empty counter near the sink, and joined him at the machine. "What's the plan for today?"

*Besides proving I'm a father?*

How could he spin this into a legitimate use of university-owned equipment?

Squeezing the teether in the pocket of his white lab coat, he forced a supply of oxygen to his brain cells. "Training. You're learning how to operate the new equipment. I'm preparing samples from two subjects in the Max. When that's complete, your job is to go through quantification, amplification, and capillary electrophoresis to determine whether or not they have a genetic relationship. I'll walk you through each step so you can make notes if you need to. At the end, you'll write a brief report that explains your findings. That'll be your basic template for future samples."

"Awesome." She rubbed her hands together and grinned. "This is going to be so fun. Are we doing the whole thing today? I did some refresher reading on sequencing, PCR, and genetic profiling over the summer. Doesn't it take ten or twelve hours from start to finish?"

"Usually about ten. Since I started at seven thirty, we should finish about five thirty." Although ten hours seemed like a lifetime to wait for the answer, knowing he had someone double-checking his analysis might ease the pressure about doing it right. Not once in his life had his expertise meant the difference between his having a child or not. If that didn't mess with a guy's mind, nothing could. "We'll be working through lunch, so I'm buying. The food court has a delivery robot, doesn't it? That motorized cooler thing I've seen around campus?"

She laughed. "Yep. They're kind of slow, but if you order online now, it should be here by noon."

"That bad, huh? Maybe I can pay an undergrad to go pick it up." He certainly didn't want to go himself. Iris Needleman was far too skilled at reading people to risk seeing her today.

"Good plan. I'll have a veggie wrap with a pickle and baked chips from the sandwich place. No drink. I brought a water bottle." Raising her pointer finger, she pivoted and returned to her backpack. "Hang on a sec. I need my laptop for notes. Tell me about the samples."

While her back was turned toward him, he peeled off the bandage he'd stuck on his pinkie and pressed the skin to be sure the bleeding had stopped where he'd pricked it. "Blood was collected by sterile means from Test Subject A. This is the best-case scenario. It's reliable. Dried saliva was used for Test Subject B. It's definitely trickier if the item with the dried saliva on it is improperly handled or in some other way contaminated. For our purposes, we'll say the collection method wasn't conventional, but it was done as well as it could be under the circumstances and contamination is minimal. Not necessarily worst-case scenario, assuming extraction is successful."

"I'm guessing you're confident that it will be, otherwise we won't be able to do the training you already said we're doing today." Her wide grin challenged him to argue against her logic.

"Yes, I'm confident we'll have usable DNA. I've worked with less." The normalcy of the conversation didn't relieve the tension in his body, but it enabled him to look at the analysis with scientific intellect instead of a head full of emotion. "We have about fifteen minutes until this step's done, so let's go over what comes next."

His lab partner for the day followed his instructions to the letter as he supervised, observed, and shouldered the growing self-reproach weighing on his conscience for his reactionary response. He'd gone behind Zinnia's back after she'd been honest with him about Daisy's conception. She deserved better from him. How could he face her and admit what he'd done? How could he not?

Inez finally handed him a printed copy of her findings in a sealed envelope at five forty-five, pride showing in her posture and smile. "Done. Lots of wait-time, but the process is...wow. I mean, I really liked the genetics courses I took for my undergrad degree, but applying that knowledge to actual research is like a CSI dream come true. Do you want to know the results?"

Fighting the nausea churning in his stomach, he shook his head and tucked the envelope into his computer bag. "You did everything correctly. I'll take a look at your report later. Good work today."

"Thanks. You're a good teacher." She hefted her backpack, headed out of the lab, and waited while he locked up.

They walked out of the building together and parted ways near where he'd had the discussion with Dr. Needleman last week. Everything in his life seemed like it was up in the air, holding its breath.

Right now, he had to face the music for his panic-induced decision and live with the consequences of screwing up.

# CHAPTER NINE

"Ba-ba! Ba-ba!" Daisy smacked her palm on the high chair tray, tears streaming down her flushed cheeks and the sadness in her appeal a hundred times worse than when she'd gone four days without seeing him.

Zinnia bit her lip to keep from joining her daughter as she rinsed the knife and cutting board she'd used to chop a head of lettuce. No amount of consoling had stopped or even slowed the tears since they'd started at five o'clock, the time Carson had been arriving every day after work. Fifteen minutes late had turned into thirty minutes late, and thirty minutes was about to become an hour. Of course, he hadn't texted her like he'd promised, although "later" could've meant tonight, tomorrow, or days from now.

*Stop being melodramatic.*

*Fine, but this is how the end always starts.*

She put two handfuls of lettuce in each of the pair of salad bowls on the counter to chase away the doubts trying to take root. "He'll be here soon, Daisy. He wouldn't—"

The faint sound of knocking stalled her ability to think. Hope made her legs move.

Unbuckling her daughter from the high chair tested her fine motor skills, but she managed to free her distressed baby from the seat and hurried through the living room. She caught a glimpse of the back of Carson's head through the glass and opened the front door.

He turned toward her, a haggard look announcing he'd had an exhausting day.

"Ba-ba!" Daisy lunged toward him, giving him no choice but to release the large envelope in his hand so he could catch her.

Cradling her against his chest, he closed his eyes for several long seconds. His shuddering breaths set Zinnia's heart racing.

She picked up the item he'd dropped and guided him to the couch. "Something's wrong. What happened?"

"I did something…" His voice cracked over the words, suggesting he was almost as upset as Daisy. He cleared his throat and tried to adjust his hold on her as he sat, but she clung to him. "I did something today that I shouldn't have done. Not without asking you. I panicked and…"

Zinnia set aside the envelope, knelt beside him, and wrapped her arms around them both, anxious to ease his guilt and curious about what he could've done that needed her permission. "It can't be that bad. Tell me what's going on."

"There's something I have to tell you first. I didn't mean to keep it from you, but…" He rested his cheek on the top of her daughter's head, looking more distraught than he had on the porch. "I should've told you last night, but I didn't think…"

What had happened last night?

*It doesn't matter.*

"It's okay." She kissed the smooth skin above his beard, trusting he'd had justifiable reasons for not sharing whatever it was. "You can tell me now."

"You're not going to be so understanding once you know." He met her gaze for a fraction of a second and looked away. "When I was eighteen, I needed money to pay for a couple college application fees. Since I was interested in genetics, I went to a sperm bank. To learn about the process. Make some money if I made it through the screening process. It was the one time. One donation."

Her heart broke a little for him. "And when I told you I was a recipient, it made the possibility that you've fathered a child more real. That's totally understandable. Somewhere out there is a man whose sperm helped me create Daisy. It was a gift I can never repay. If she wants to try to find him someday, I'll help. I have—"

"Zinnia." He pulled away from her and stood, still holding her daughter like she was his lifeline. The comfort they gave each other was tangible, immeasurable. "I think she's... I think I might be her father. Not a one-in-a-million chance. More like, I don't know, one in ten?"

*Carson? Daisy's father?*

She couldn't help but note their obvious similarities, as she had on numerous occasions. "Having the same hair and eye color doesn't prove anything. And you donated twenty years ago. Someone surely chose your profile before I ever considered insemination."

"I've never asked. I have a cleft chin, and we both have bilateral syndactyly. I saw her webbed toes when I took off her socks this morning. They match mine. Most people don't notice, but those of us who have it tend to look for it. She's the same, and all those similarities..." He glanced toward the envelope she'd set on the end table. "I wanted to know. God, I *needed* to know after seeing her toes. But what I did was unethical. I'm sorry, Zinnia. I shouldn't have..."

The low buzzing in her ears drowned out the rest of the words as his meaning dawned on her. He had the technical skills to discover the truth.

*How long does a DNA test take?*

*The envelope. Does he have the results already? Does he know?*

She raised her hand, signaling him to stop talking. Did she dare hope he was Daisy's biological father? Did it even matter?

He hadn't spoken like he knew for sure.

A visual inspection of the seal seemed to indicate only the person who'd placed the report in the envelope could've read the contents.

She stood without touching the package that clearly contained the truth. "Is she ours?"

"I don't know. I don't deserve to know." He rocked back and

forth, even though Daisy had already fallen asleep in his arms, looking like she belonged there. "I gave her a teether while I was making breakfast. She tossed it at me when I started feeding her, and I put it in my pocket without thinking. It had her saliva on it. Her DNA. I could find out without waiting for confirmation that my donation had been chosen. One of the students I'm working with processed our DNA samples and wrote up the report. Only she knows if they're a match, but she doesn't know who the samples came from."

Calmer than she would've expected, Zinnia gestured to the couch. "Come sit down. We'll read it together."

"I did this behind your back." He stood his ground, his tortured expression shattering her heart. "What if she isn't?"

"Look at the way you're holding her and how she settled down so quickly when you came home." The reality she'd built had exploded with his admission, but she regretted none of it. The pieces had fallen into place, as if they finally fit the way they were meant to. She swiped at the tear streaking down her face and willed him to let go of the uncertainty holding him back. "Carson, you're already a wonderful father to her. She *loves* you. *I* love you. Biology doesn't change that."

"But…"

"No buts." Trusting her instincts and her mother's advice, she closed the few feet between them and cupped his face in her palms. "Will you marry me and become Daisy's legal father?"

*Yes.*

Carson wanted to say yes with all his heart and soul.

His conscience, on the other hand, made him hesitate.

Zinnia pressed her lips to his in a kiss that was part whisper, part shout and drove all thought from his head. "I know you love me and I know you want to marry me. You told me you were going to ask me the first time we made love. Have your feelings for me changed?"

If anything, he'd fallen more in love with her since that night. The simplicity of how she viewed their relationship hammered at the complicated mess in his gray matter.

"I'll take the lack of argument as a no." She brushed her fingertips through his beard and then over the fountain-like tuft of hair on top of Daisy's head. "Okay, maybe you should've asked me for permission, but I can forgive that, considering the new evidence you discovered. I can't imagine how you must have felt when you realized you might have a biological connection to her. Or how you feel now. Forgive yourself for that much at least. Please."

He'd violated his donor contract and failed the ethical oath he'd sworn himself to uphold as a geneticist. Some information had to remain confidential in situations like this.

He swallowed, trying to clear the ache from his throat. It wouldn't budge. Another issue chewed deeper than his questionable profession-alism. How could he be so torn between needing the truth and being afraid of it? "I'm not supposed to know."

"I'm not, either, but here we are. We met for a reason, and I wouldn't change it for anything. You've made such an impact on Daisy. A positive one. She misses you when you're not here, in case you didn't notice. I do too." Zinnia smiled and led him back to the couch. "So, I know quite a bit about my donor from his profile. I'm happy to share what I was told if you want to know. If you don't, that's fine too. And we don't have to look at the results if you don't want to. Do what's best for you, Carson, because I want you to be happy."

*Happy.*

What brought him happiness?

Spending every night curled around the love of his life made him happy. Knowing she wanted to marry him and cared more about his feelings than the integrity he'd compromised today made him happy. Sitting here next to her with the baby he strongly suspected was their daughter asleep in his arms made him happy.

Could he live with not knowing if he was Daisy's biological father?

*For now? Maybe. But not indefinitely.*

Zinnia's ever-present messy bun wobbled as she shifted on the cushion. "You need some downtime after such a stressful day. I'm going to finish making supper while you and Daisy rest. Then we'll have a relaxing evening with the three of us. No pressure to make any decisions. Sound good?"

Most of the tension lingering in his muscles finally dissipated. Grateful for her nurturing qualities, he eliminated the space between them and pressed a gentle kiss to her soft lips. "Sounds perfect. I love you."

A slight dimple formed in her cheek when her mouth curved into a radiant smile. "I know, but you're welcome to tell me anytime. I love you too. Close your eyes and relax."

He followed her advice, letting her quiet footsteps and Daisy's whispery breaths lull him toward the bit of peace he could muster with the envelope still laying within reach.

# CHAPTER TEN

*Breathe in for five.*

*Breathe out for five.*

*Close your eyes and relax.*

Zinnia added the pasta to the pot of boiling water, wishing she could follow her own advice.

*It's his decision, and I'm not going to influence him.*

*I know in my heart who he is. Daisy knows. She knew from the moment we met him.*

She set the timer on her phone, stirred the fettuccine, and adjusted the burner. Biology didn't matter, but he'd earned the right to claim the title of father in all ways.

*I will not open the envelope. I will not open the envelope. I will not open the envelope.*

The oven timer buzzed, and her heart tried to jump out of her chest. She jabbed at the touchpad button to shut it off, hoping she hadn't disturbed Carson and Daisy.

*Stir.*

*What if he isn't?*

She'd been practical for his sake, saying all the right things to reassure him, but she had to be realistic. The possibility still existed that another man with many of the same traits had donated the sperm she'd chosen.

Did it matter?

*Stir.*

The man she loved had wanted to be Daisy's father before he'd compared their DNA. Biological connection or not, he'd stepped into the role willingly, and their emotional connection transcended blood ties and genetic markers.

*But he wouldn't have done the testing if he didn't want to know. Honestly, I'd like to know too—because I want him to be, for all our sakes.*

She added the roasted tomatoes to the bowl with olive oil, black pepper, feta, and basil and slowly exhaled as several more seconds passed on the countdown for the pasta. With less than a minute to go, she stirred the pot again and set the table to try to distract herself.

The situation required patience, so patience she would have. A clock wasn't ticking, and confirmation or contradiction wouldn't change their feelings for each other.

Her phone vibrated against the counter from the timer, forcing her to once again concentrate on finishing her task. Steam rose in a cloud as she emptied the pot into the strainer. The fog evaporated quickly— probably a lot faster than her current dilemma would.

*I hate angst and drama.*

She dumped the fettuccine into the bowl, tossed the contents together, and set it on the table. Her stomach growled, in spite of the nerves tangling and knotting in it.

As she placed a basket of warm bread next to it, Carson appeared in the doorway, holding a now-awake Daisy. "Supper smells great. Thanks for taking care of us."

"You're welcome. I know you'd do the same for me." Seeing how much calmer they seemed, Zinnia crossed the room to kiss them both. "I was just about to come get you. Daisy wouldn't eat earlier, so she's probably hungry too."

He slipped his fingers around hers and walked with her to his chair. "I'll feed her. Is it okay if she sits on my lap?"

The uncertainty and hope in his voice wrapped around her heart.

*This man. No wonder I fell in love with him practically overnight.*

"Of course." She grabbed the unused bib from the high chair and fastened it in place. How could she deny either of them more bonding time? "I'll make some fresh cereal for her. You know you're going to be covered in baby food by the time she's done eating, don't you?"

He winced and his eyebrows dipped into a vee. "I'm sorry for leaving you a mess to clean up this morning."

Shaking her head, she focused on gathering what she needed. "No more apologies related to what happened. You experienced extenuating circumstances today, and I'm giving you a free pass because you told me the truth when you came home."

He was quiet while she prepared Daisy's supper, but the weight of his gaze continued when she turned around and placed the dish out of her daughter's reach. "You said I came home. Twice. Do you mean it? Is this our home? Together?"

"Yes. You belong with us and we belong with you." She refused to think about what would happen when his visiting scholar term ended.

"Okay. The answer is yes."

CARSON WRESTLED HIS CONFLICTED FEELINGS INTO SUBMISSION AND forged ahead. "Yes, I'll marry you—on one condition."

Zinnia dropped into the chair adjacent to his, her hopeful stare bolstering his confidence in the decision. "Name it."

That she trusted him so implicitly made the request much easier.

He tightened his hold on Daisy and leaned forward to grasp Zinnia's hand. "The envelope stays sealed until after the wedding. I don't want you thinking I'm marrying you for any reason other than I love you. This has nothing whatsoever to do with anything else. After we're officially married, we'll look at the results."

The possibility that he might not be Daisy's father churned in the pit of his stomach, but he wanted a life with Zinnia, no matter what the report told them. He wanted to be more than a biological father to the baby on his lap.

Her weepy smile and nod eased the ache in his stomach. "If that's what it takes. Even though I know you're more likely *not* to marry me because of your possible link to Daisy. So, here's *my* one condition. We're going to the courthouse for the marriage license and a civil ceremony tomorrow during your lunch hour."

An unexpected burst of relief washed over him, triggering a choked laugh and a tickle in his nose. "Tomorrow. If we could get a license and a judge right this minute, I would, but don't you want a wedding dress and a million flowers?"

She wrapped her arms around him and squeezed. "Nope. I just want you and our happily-ever-after. It doesn't have to be perfect, just forever."

"I'll do my best." He captured her lips for a firm kiss to seal the deal. The contact soothed and aroused him and brought tranquility to his intense emotions.

Daisy patted his beard and giggled, summing up the high he was riding more effectively than any words. "Ma-ma. Ba-ba. Ma-ma. Ba-ba."

Resting his forehead against Zinnia's, he soaked in the rightness zipping through his veins. "Yes, Ma-ma and Ba-ba and baby Daisy. We're a family, starting right now."

The steady hum and buzz of a cell phone interrupted the moment, and Zinnia groaned. "Somebody has terrible timing. I should get that."

"Num-num-num." Daisy twisted toward the table and reached for her supper. "Num-num."

He scooped a spoonful of what looked like a mixture of applesauce and cereal as Zinnia picked up her cell from the counter. "Looks like somebody's hungry. I'll feed her while you answer your phone."

"It's my mom." She tapped the screen and lifted her phone to her ear. "Hi, Mom. Good. Sure. Yes, he's here. Hang on a second and I'll put you on speaker." As she returned to the table, she tapped the screen again. "Okay, you're on speaker."

A stitch of panic pinched his gut as her mom's voice filled the kitchen. What if the job offer had fallen through? Or worse, that she'd somehow discovered his ethically questionable actions today?

"Carson, hello. I tried reaching you on your phone, but it went to voicemail after several tries."

He shook off the dread and fed Daisy another bite. "Hi, Dr. Needleman. Iris."

"I have important news."

"Gam-gam." A spray of slobbery cereal exited Daisy's mouth and landed on his pantleg.

"That's right. How's my sweet Daisy? Gam-gam loves you." At Daisy's happy squeal, Iris chuckled. "What a smart girl. Carson, the department chair received your counterpart's resignation letter this morning and I've negotiated an extension of your visit through the end of the spring semester. That gives us time to go through all the necessary motions of a new hire, assuming you're still interested."

Not caring if he seemed overanxious, he let the confirmation escape before a full second passed. "Yes. Absolutely."

"Excellent. You're such an outstanding addition to the department and the university. We'll talk in more detail over the next several weeks. In the meantime, congratulations. We're very pleased to have you here."

With one less concern weighing him down, he slowly exhaled. "Thank you. It's really good to be here, and I appreciate your support."

"You're welcome. I'd like to celebrate by taking you to lunch tomorrow if you're free. Oh, Zin, before I forget, I ran into Beryl Drechsler, of all people, at a new faculty event today. She said you two lost touch when you left San Jose for Pittsburgh. Goodness, that's been fifteen years ago, hasn't it? Anyway, she was so excited to hear you moved back home to have Daisy. We decided to plan a cookout at your house on Sunday."

*Pittsburgh. She lived in Pittsburgh.*

*Was she already pregnant when she left?*

*Did she undergo insemination there?*

The conversation became little more than background noise to the runaway heartbeat thumping in his ears. Only thoughts of the report's possible outcomes accompanied each spoon-to-mouth motion as Daisy ate bite after bite.

*Breathe. We'll open the envelope tomorrow.*

Zinnia dropped into the chair again. "That sounds great, Mom. So...um, about lunch tomorrow. Carson has plans. Since you invited him, I'm guessing you're available to meet us at the courthouse for a wedding instead."

"Oh my, yes. Of course. What fantastic news, Zin. I'm so happy for you. James! James, come here! You owe me an ice cream date. Zin and Carson are getting married tomorrow!"

Masculine laughter announced his future father-in-law's presence. "I can't say I'm sorry I guessed wrong. Congratulations, you two. This is great news."

"Thanks, Dad. Thanks, Mom. I'll text you the details in the morning."

"Sounds good. Your mom is waving the car keys at me, so it looks like we're heading out to celebrate."

"Enjoy your ice cream date. See you tomorrow." After a round of goodbyes, Zinnia ended the call and leveled a concerned stare across the table. "What's wrong? You went a little pale when my mom was talking about my college roommate. Is she an ex-girlfriend or some-thing awkward like that?"

Carson shook his head, fairly certain neither of them would be able to wait until after their wedding to find out the truth. "I grew up in a suburb of Pittsburgh. It's where I made the sperm donation."

# CHAPTER ELEVEN

ZINNIA BLINKED AT CARSON FOR SEVERAL SECONDS, ALL BUT confirming the scenario that had gone through his head had made a stop in hers too. She finally opened her mouth, as if to speak, and shut it again for a few more moments. "The fertility clinic I used for the insemination is in Pittsburgh. It's been in business for over forty years and it was highly rated when I started looking into that option."

*It has to be the same facility. It's the only one in the tri-state area that's been in business that long.*

His hope soaring to new heights, he tucked Daisy into a football hold as he stood. "Back in a sec."

The wild fluttering in his stomach increased with every step he took toward the answer to his question. He couldn't make Zinnia wait until tomorrow, not when everything pointed to a single conclusion.

*Who am I trying to kid? I need to know now too.*

He snagged the report from the end table and marched back to the kitchen. "Open it while I finish feeding Daisy."

Looking at the envelope, Zinnia scrunched her mouth into a crooked line. "Are you sure? We can't undo this once it's done."

Nodding, he sank into his chair and perched the giggling baby on his thigh. "I'll be disappointed if we're not a match, but it doesn't change how I feel about either of you. We're getting married tomorrow and finding out what we have to do for me to become Daisy's legal dad. Besides, I'm at least ninety-eight percent sure I'm her biological father."

"Okay." She stared at him through a dozen beats of his pounding pulse before sliding her finger beneath the seal. "This reminds me of waiting for the timer to count down when I took the home pregnancy test. Excited, nervous, anxious to see the result, scared it might be negative. I laughed and cried when it was positive."

"I wish I could've been there with you." Regret for everything he'd missed in the last seventeen months of her life tugged at his gut, but he wouldn't go back if he could. Out of all the nearly countless genetic possibilities, Daisy had been created because of their decisions and the timing.

"I've documented all of it since the day I made my first appointment at the clinic. I wanted my child to know her story." She slid the sheaf of papers from the envelope. "We can look at the pictures and read my journal together sometime."

"I'd like that." Swallowing to wet his suddenly dry throat, he let his gaze drop to the top page. "The cover letter summarizes the report. The rest of the pages detail the DNA profiles and compare the individual markers that were used to determine the results."

She adjusted the blue-framed glasses on the bridge of her nose and lifted the papers. Her expression remained impassive as her eyes skimmed back and forth, back and forth. She slowly lowered the report to her lap, looking unmoved or maybe too stunned to react. Then she exhaled like she'd forgotten how to breathe. "Wow. What are the chances?"

His heart fell to his knees. "The chances of what? I'm excluded from possible paternity, aren't I?"

*Disappointed?*

*Yeah, not even close.*

*More like devastated.*

"The letter says Sample A can't be excluded as the biological father of Sample B. The probability of paternity is within a hundred-thousandth of one hundred percent." Her softly spoken words cut through the deep sense of loss, sending his mind spinning. "I imagined Daisy and I might meet her biological father someday, but I never dreamed we'd find him next door. She's your daughter, Carson. We made her."

"She's mine? She's ours?" His voice cracked from the rush of pure joy sweeping through him, and his vision blurred with the stinging tears welling up in his eyes. He shifted Daisy to his chest, holding her close enough to breathe in her sweet baby smell. A sob and more than a few tears escaped as he kissed her chubby cheek. "I'm your daddy, Daisy. You're my little girl. Ma-ma and Ba-ba made you."

She patted his beard, a gesture that never failed to spark wonderment in his soul. "Ma-ma. Ba-ba. Ma-ma. Ba-ba."

"Yes, and Mommy should be part of this hug." After a swipe of his bicep across his wet face, he reached for the amazing woman who had made this wondrous miracle with him. "We're so lucky to have her."

"I'm lucky to have both of you." Zinnia's love and warmth surrounded him in a heartbeat. "The luckiest woman ever. I love you."

"I love you too, and I can't wait to marry you." His stomach growled, reminding how much time had passed since he'd eaten lunch. The sudden release of the stress he'd been dealing with all day would probably add to the adrenaline crash destined to hit him any minute. "How about I clean up Daisy's mess and reheat our supper while she nurses?"

She brushed her fingers across his cheek. Her lips followed, soothing the high emotions still floating downward to normal levels. "I'll take care of it while you and Daisy chill together for a few more minutes. After supper, we're going to relax on the couch and have some family time. And I think we should tell our parents about this development."

ZINNIA STEPPED IN FRONT OF CARSON ON HIS NINTH OR TENTH CIRCUIT from the kitchen to the front door to the rocking chair and back to the kitchen. He'd been pacing since they'd returned from their first-thing-in-the-morning trip to the courthouse and stop at the jewelry store. "It'll be fine."

His eyebrows dipped low and his sigh ruffled his daughter's hair as she snuggled against his chest. "I didn't expect them to drive up to meet you and Daisy and attend the wedding. They completely freaked out when I told them I'd donated my sperm to pay for college application fees. It's been a point of contention between us for a long time."

Finger-combing the hair brushing the collar of his suit coat, Zinnia rose on her tiptoes for a kiss. The tension left him the moment his lips touched hers, which had been her plan. "They wouldn't have a grandchild if you hadn't. You made the right choice for you, and it worked out perfectly in the end. Now come sit down before you make us all dizzy."

Shadows moved across the porch, and familiar and unfamiliar voices carried through the open windows.

She hugged her husband-to-be and brushed her lips over his again. "Sounds like my mom and dad intercepted them. Are you ready?"

His nod suggested he was more resigned than ready. "As I'll ever be."

With her hand wrapped around his and her dress swishing about her legs, she led him across the room and opened the door. Five visitors turned toward her, including one she hadn't talked to in nearly fifteen years. "Beryl! It's so good to see you. Mr. and Mrs. Hines, come in. I'm Zinnia and this is Daisy. Did you meet my parents, Iris and James?"

The couple between her mom and dad and her college roommate stood stock still, their gazes seemingly locked on their son and granddaughter.

Mrs. Hines finally stepped forward as Daisy stirred, the woman's blue eyes an exact match for the pair that blinked open a moment before she rested her palm on her grandchild's back. "Good to meet you, Zinnia. Hello, Daisy. You look so much like your father when he was a baby. Carson, we've missed you."

Daisy ducked her head and grabbed a handful of his beard. "Baba."

He smiled, clearly calmed by her expectation that she was safe in his arms. "Yes, Ba-ba's right here. I missed you too, Mom. Hi, Dad. Glad you could make it to the wedding. Iris. James. Why don't we go inside? We've had a slight change of plans. Zinnia and I went to get the license first thing this morning since everybody's attending the wedding. The judge will be here any minute to perform the ceremony."

Releasing his hand, Zinnia gestured their chatting families inside, taking a moment to give Beryl a hug meant to erase the years they'd lost touch with each other. "I can't believe you're here. We have so much to catch up on."

Beryl's wide grin hadn't changed a bit since their freshman year of college. "Right? Prince Charming finally got off his duff and arrived, I see. And I want the whole story, because there's definitely more to it than just a hunky geneticist sweeping you off your feet."

"A lot more. I'll fill you in later." Zinnia linked her arm through her former roommate's and walked her into the living room. "Cute dress, by the way. That shade of pink always was your best color."

"It keeps men from being intimidated by my intelligence." Beryl rolled her eyes and laughed. "And students learn very quickly not to assess the difficulty of their classes by what the professor wears."

"You—" Three sharp raps drew Zinnia's attention to the door. She spared a quick glance for Carson and smiled. "That'll be the judge. Wedding time."

While she welcomed the officiant and showed her where they planned to stand for the ceremony, Beryl coaxed a giggle from Daisy and had a short chat with Carson that looked like a protective-friend warning. That was the friend she remembered—loyal, bold, and never afraid to speak her mind.

Judge Lawson took charge, bringing order and silence by crooking a finger at Carson and clearing her throat. As soon as he stood in his designated spot, their officiant smiled. "Zinnia and Carson, I'm so excited to be part of your beautiful story of how fate, patience, and timing can lead to the happiest conclusions. We're gathered here with your families and friend to confirm your abiding love and deep commitment to each other with marriage. Carson Hines, do you take

Zinnia Trimble to be your lawfully wedded wife for as long as you both shall live?"

He slipped his hand around Zinnia's and gave it a gentle squeeze. "I do."

"And, Zinnia, do you take Carson Hines to be your lawfully wedded husband for as long as you both shall live?"

"I do." Zinnia relished the way her pulse sped up from the adoration in his expression.

"Your vows are your promises to one another as you exchange rings." The judge grinned when Daisy patted his cheek. "Your daughter's correct, Carson. You're first."

He dipped his hand into his pocket, withdrew the wedding band they'd chosen this morning, and placed it on Zinnia's finger. "Zinnia, I love you with all my heart. The moment I met you, my life changed for the better. You've given me so much more than I ever thought I could have, and I promise to devote myself to making you as happy as you make me. This ring is a symbol of my love and devotion."

The gold warmed against her skin when he slid it into place on her finger. She moved the ring she'd stowed on her thumb to his finger and met his gaze. "Carson, you are my soulmate. Fate brought us together, knowing we're meant for each other, and I'm so blessed to have you as a partner. You bring me happiness like I've never known before. We're together, as we should be, and I promise to love and treasure you always."

Judge Lawson placed her hand over theirs. "By the authority granted me by the state of Ohio, I pronounce you husband and wife. May your life together be long and filled with joy."

A chorus of congratulations and applause accompanied the firm press of Carson's lips against Zinnia's. She pulled him back for another and another as the clap of Daisy's hands and a happy squeal joined their audience.

*Happily-ever-after was absolutely worth the wait.*

# THE NERD UPSTAIRS

NERDS & BABIES #2

# CHAPTER ONE

"CALL ME AS SOON AS YOU GET THIS MESSAGE, BERYL. SERIOUSLY, it's urgent. I need to talk to you right away. *Please.*"

Dr. Beryl Drechsler leaned against the headrest, closed her eyes, and sucked in a shaky breath to fight the wave of nausea triggered by seeing Jen's name in her missed calls and voicemails for the eighteenth time in two days and then hearing her voice.

*I shouldn't have listened to her message. Why couldn't she have just sent an email? Then I could've deleted it and been done with her.*

Her cell rang in her hand, making her heart jump in her chest, and her gut correctly guessed who the caller was. How long could she avoid her friend—former friend, by necessity—before the message got through?

*Message. Maybe I can do that.*

Considering the three-hour time difference, Beryl suspected the barrage would continue until she answered. She'd moved three-quarters of the way across the country to distance herself from the woman who had been one of her closest friends for the last twelve years—for two very good reasons.

*I told you why I was leaving. That should've been enough.*

She ignored the incessant ringing and navigated to her text messages. *"Can't talk. At work."*

Technically, it wasn't a lie. Her car was still parked in the faculty lot, even if the engine was running to cool the early September heat trapped inside after a day in the bright sunshine.

*"Actually, I just can't. Please respect my choice."*

She blocked Jen's number, silenced her phone, and closed it in the center console, with the hope that out of sight, out of mind worked better for inanimate objects than people. Out of mind would never happen in this situation.

*No more favors. For anyone. Ever again.*

With her newest heavy-metal playlist turned up as loud as her ears could tolerate, she backed out of the parking spot and headed for her new home. The lavender Victorian had come on the market the same morning she'd contacted the real estate agent her department chair had recommended—during the conversation that included a job offer she couldn't refuse. A week after her closing and move-in date, she'd found out her undergrad roommate had returned to her hometown and lived two blocks away. Those were all signs she'd made the right decision to cut her ties to Jen and leave California.

Losing nearly everything she loved meant never looking back.

Beryl resisted stopping at the coffee shop across the street from campus, but no way, no how could her willpower defeat the siren song of the custard stand three doors down, especially when the drive-thru lane was empty.

Five minutes later, she flipped on her turn signal at the exit and licked round and round the mega-sized chocolate-vanilla twist, following its swirled surface from the cone to the melty curl at the top. The steady flow of traffic allowed a tasty mouthful from the peak and another swoop around the base of the mountain of soft-serve deliciousness. She'd probably ruined her appetite for supper, but being single had its perks—and she needed a whole lot of comfort to wallow in at the moment.

Somewhat soothed by her treat, she exited at a break in the line of cars and joined what constituted rush hour in the college town that was only slightly bigger than a village. It didn't require anywhere near the concentration of driving the congested roads of San Jose. The change had been good for her—personally, professionally, and financially.

She crunched into the cake cone as she turned onto her street, almost reaching the point of calm that had often evaded her the last several months. Flashes of purple showing through the thick foliage of the huge oak in her front yard triggered a sense of home. Maybe she would finally find peace here.

She followed the driveway toward the back of the house, only to have her composure destroyed. An unfamiliar luxury sedan sat in the turnaround by the garage, its driver hidden by the glare of the sun on the windshield.

In no mood for visitors, she tapped the opener button clipped to the visor and waited for the door to rise. Two new benefits to having an attached garage sprang to mind as she pulled inside, cut the engine, and pushed the button again.

*I can finish my ice cream without being interrupted and I can avoid whoever decided to ambush me on a Thursday afternoon.*

The doorbell dinged and donged before she hung up her keys inside the kitchen door. "Go. Away."

She chomped another bite of cone and deposited her computer bag on the counter on her way upstairs. Another round of Westminster chimes rang through the front parlor as she climbed the staircase, but she headed to the master bedroom, intent on changing out of her dress and pumps after a day of classes, meetings, and setting up her lab.

The ringing changed to knocking while she chewed the last bite of her treat and plugged her phone into its charger. "Oh my god, can't you take a fucking hint?"

Her Spanx bodysuit shaper landed on the floor next to the hamper, but it could stay there until laundry day for all she cared. The cheval mirror stood too close to the basket to traipse naked across the room and risk seeing her physical scars. The emotional ones challenged her enough most days.

Clad in shorts and an exercise tank, she padded barefoot along the second-floor landing to the room she'd designated her new home office

—accompanied by a new cycle of repeating chimes. Someone was persistent as hell, but she'd been practicing her stubborn skills since before she could walk and talk.

As she tore the packing tape off the top of the first box, rumbling came from below. Then the *beep-beep-beep* of a work vehicle in reverse joined more rhythmic knocking. "What now?"

The view from the window overlooking the street revealed a moving truck backing into her drive. It stopped with its nose barely out of the road. Then a burly guy jumped out from the cab on the driver's side and a burlier man rounded the front end. They both waved toward her house, even though they couldn't possibly see her through the sheer curtains she had yet to replace.

The infernal ringing and knocking finally ended, and a woman in a dark pantsuit came into view from the direction of the porch.

*You. It's about damn time you laid off the freaking doorbell.*

The intruder extended her hand, shaking the driver's hand and nodding. Then both men headed to the rear of the truck, pulling on work gloves as they walked.

"What the hell are you unloading in my driveway?" Left with no other choice, Beryl scuttled down the steps and reached her front parlor at the same moment the door chimes started up again. Donning her worst grouchy professor stare, she swung open the door. "Will you give it a rest already? You have ten seconds to state your business."

One gray-blonde eyebrow lifted and the determined lawyerly looking woman fished a business card from her jacket pocket. "Beryl Drechsler, I'm Madeleine Flanders. I represent the interests of Jennifer James in the divorce proceedings of Ms. James versus Reginald James."

*Can I peg 'em or what?*

NEVER MORE GRATEFUL FOR HAVING THE MEANS TO FLY BUSINESS class, Archer James snagged his carryon from the overhead compartment and slung the strap of his computer bag on his right shoulder. The flight attendant smiled and said something as he deboarded at the head of the line, but his brain and his body were too busy sucking down the last fumes he could muster after the five-thousand-mile trip.

He managed a polite farewell as he left the plane, focused on putting one foot in front of the other up the jetway, through customs, and finally toward baggage claim. For the first time in over three years, the trip home meant he was staying, which had necessitated packing up everything in his Tokyo apartment. Only part of his belongings would be arriving on the carousel after he descended the last escalator, but he could live with the minor inconvenience until the rest was delivered to his house a few miles outside of San Jose sometime in the next month.

As he trudged with the rest of the crowd toward the claim area, a sign with his name on it caught his eye. He moved along until a familiar face to go with the placard appeared in a hole in the scattering sea of bodies.

Archer raised his hand to catch the younger man's attention. "G'morning, Marcus. I checked the three green-and-black suitcases."

His assistant gave a curt nod. "Good morning, sir. There's a large coffee and a bacon, egg, and cheese croissant waiting for you in the car. I'll let Billie know you're on your way outside."

"You're a lifesaver. Thanks." Rolling his carryon toward the doors to the pickup lane, Archer concentrated on staying awake long enough to spot his ride and eat his late breakfast.

*Then a long nap.*

Within thirty seconds, one of the company SUVs pulled up to the sidewalk and the driver rounded the front end to open the door for him. Her motherly smile was a welcome sight. "Welcome back, Archer. I've missed you."

"It's good to be back, Billie." He slipped into the back seat while she stowed his bag in the cargo space behind him. "How are the grandkids?"

"Spoiled rotten." She grinned up at him as she gripped the handle to close the hatch. "A grammy's work is never done. You look like hell. Eat your breakfast and we'll drop by the house so you can shower before your meeting with Reggie."

"Meeting? I was supposed to go home and crash for the next twenty-four to forty-eight hours." His cell buzzed against his thigh, setting off a warning in his empty stomach. He dug his phone out of his pocket and groaned when his brother's name appeared on the screen. "Shit, that's him calling now."

"You talk. I'll drive around the loop while Marcus collects your luggage." The rear door clunked shut and she climbed behind the steering wheel while Archer called on all his patience.

As ready as he would ever be, he tapped the Answer icon and raised his phone to his ear. "Hey, big brother. I just got in. I'm heading home for—"

"Don't unpack." Reggie paused for all of half a second before his voice broke through the words that made no sense. "Check your email for a boarding pass. You're on a flight to Ohio from SFO in three and a half hours, with a layover in Denver."

Shaking his head, Archer silently cursed the inconsiderate asshole. "Absolutely not. You know I'd normally do anything for you, but I've slept about four hours in the last two days. I'm going to bed."

"Not an option, Arch. I wish it was, but... So, there's a, um, legal issue you need to deal with. Immediately."

"A legal issue?" His brother's hesitation set his brain on high alert. "What's going on? Keep it simple and to the point."

A noisy exhale carried through the phone, tipping him off that the situation was *not* good. "Jen and I are getting divorced. It was just too much—the infertility issues, multiple IVF attempts, the solution to the problem. Dealing with one newborn, we might've been able to handle. I don't know. But two? And then the nanny quit, and we said things that we'd both been thinking the whole damn time and never admitted. Sometimes, love just isn't enough. Anyway, something... An unexpected development came up during our last meeting with the lawyers."

A really bad feeling rippled through Archer's spine, especially since Reggie and Jen had been a couple since second grade. "Unexpected development. What the hell does that mean? What happened?"

"So..."

An image of Reggie rubbing the back of his neck formed in Archer's mind, amplifying the unease suddenly churning in his gut. "Spit it out."

Throat-clearing and then a noisy exhale warned him the complication was worse than any difficulty he could imagine. "Okay, so... You have to promise not to freak out."

*Fuck. Talk about a bad way to start an explanation.*

Something—a car door, maybe—clunked in the background before his brother continued. "When we started hashing out custody, the lawyers informed us that the fertility clinic mishandled the paperwork. I don't know how it could've happened, and I'm sorry, okay? But... honestly, it was kind of a relief since I've never felt like the kids were mine. Jen didn't, either, and—"

*A relief?* Rage drowned out the rest of his brother's rationalization for failing as a father—and a brother. "After the favor I did for you, you're telling me you don't want my niece and nephew?"

"They're *my* niece and nephew, little brother. They're *your* son and daughter. Biologically *and* legally."

# CHAPTER TWO

CROSSING HER ARMS UNDER HER ECSTATICALLY FREE BREASTS, BERYL blocked the entrance into her house. "The condition of Jen and Reggie's marriage has nothing to do with me. Now, if you don't mind, I have more important things to do than talk to a stranger about somebody else's personal business."

The attorney, whose business card Beryl refused to take, raised her chin. "Ms. Drechsler—"

"*Doctor* Drechsler." She aimed a glare at the pushy woman and settled in for a battle of wills. Tenacity was a trait she'd embraced decades ago.

"My apologies, Dr. Drechsler." Casting a glance toward the driveway, Flanders flexed her jaw. She gave an almost imperceptible nod before looking back toward Beryl. "I'll get straight to the point."

"Since your ten seconds have long expired, I wish you would."

The woman blinked like she was surprised by the bluntness, despite her intrusion and persistence. "My review of the documents from the fertility clinic revealed that you're the mother of Mia and Marshall James, the babies Jennifer and Reginald James have been raising as their own."

Every bit of solace from her earlier indulgence vanished in an instant. Only grief and anger remained. "We're not having this discussion. You need to leave right—"

"There was no forfeiture of parental rights form included in the signed surrogacy-insemination agreement. As such, the twins are yours, both biologically and legally." The lawyer gestured to her left, but Beryl aimed another glare at her.

"How dare—"

A red-haired woman wheeled a stroller along the sidewalk leading to the porch. A pair of sleeping babies lay side by side in the double-seated contraption.

Beryl tried to tear her gaze away from the mirage and failed.

*Wake up. This isn't real. It can't be. Wake up, damn it!*

"Since neither Jennifer nor Reginald wishes to petition the court for custody, the children are being surrendered to you. Immediately. Per a court order." Holding out a sheaf of papers, the divorce lawyer stood her ground. "Ms. James said she's been unable to reach you. You'll need to sign these documents to…"

The door moved as Beryl swayed. Her vision blurred and her legs turned to jelly.

Then a voice echoed in her head, saying her name and asking too many questions. "Who are you and why are you here?"

Why was her college roommate here?

"Beryl, can you hear me? It's Zinnia. Carson, will you get her a glass of water please? And, you, give her some space to breathe. No, she isn't subject to fainting spells."

Beryl's vision cleared as the voices continued, but her muscles still wouldn't cooperate to let her sit up. The parlor's tin ceiling and her friend's blonde hair came into focus. "What happened? How did I get inside? I was at the door, talking to…"

The lawyer, the movers, the babies in the stroller—it all rushed into her thoughts, making her lungs refuse to work and her heartbeat pound in her ears.

Zinnia frowned and squeezed her tingly fingers. "Breathe, Beryl. Slow and steady. In, two, three, four. Out, two, three, four. Again.

That's it. It's okay. I'm staying right here with you while we figure out what's going on. Can you sit up for a drink?"

A shrug was all she could manage, between the lump clogging her throat and the tears stinging her eyes. She'd never been on an emotional rollercoaster until midway through doing the favor Jen had asked of her. Since then, crying jags had become the norm and being her usual snarky self required a lot more effort than she could muster most days.

With a hand at her back, Zinnia held a glass to her lips. "Drink little sips. Carson, would you mind showing everyone to the kitchen for a few minutes? We'd like some privacy."

He leaned down and whispered something to her, earning him a hesitant smile and a nod.

"You're right." She rose from where she knelt on the floor beside the couch. "I'll let my dad know we're going to be late for dinner."

Everyone but Zin's husband trailed her out of the room before he sat in the adjacent chair. "We kind of got the gist of things from the lawyer, but I'm happy to lend a sympathetic ear if you want to talk about it."

Only knowing his experience with being a sperm donor and accidentally finding his daughter allowed Beryl to cradle her head in her hands and share the pain she'd never told anyone about. "Jen tried everything to get pregnant. IVF. Fertility treatments. The whole deal. I agreed to be inseminated and serve as a surrogate since I didn't plan to have children of my own. But I became attached. God, it was damn near impossible to let them go. I couldn't handle seeing the babies or listening to Jen talk about being a mother anymore. It hurt too much, so I left California. I didn't expect...the loss, the regret."

"I get it." Carson shifted forward in his seat and braced his elbows on his knees. "Did you know Daisy has webbed toes like me? Besides the dark hair, blue eyes, and cleft chin. I freaked out when I saw them the first time. I was cleaning her up after breakfast and took off her messy socks. All I could think about was the need to find out if she was my daughter, so I processed her DNA from a saliva sample and compared it to mine—without Zinnia's permission."

Beryl jerked her head up to really look at the man she'd accused of being a hunky geneticist who'd been too busy in his lab to find Zin and sweep off her feet. "Since when are you a rule-breaker?"

He smirked and laced his fingers together. "Then I felt guilty and couldn't look at the results. Not once in twenty years had I ever considered I might meet a child created from my sperm donation, but I adored Daisy and I wanted her to be Zinnia's and mine in every way. Luckily, she understood why I did what I did. Stress can cause us to make choices we wouldn't normally make. You did what you thought was right, even though it felt wrong. You were put in a no-win situation and those ungrateful idiots took advantage of your generosity. Your so-called friend and her husband didn't appreciate the huge sacrifice you made for them. Here's your chance to do this mom thing the way you wanted. To show your babies how much they mean to you."

So many mixed emotions escaped in a sob, made worse when he wrapped his arm around her for a side hug, but relief was the strongest. She leaned into the embrace and hoped she hadn't fallen into the deep end of delusions. "I'm telling Zin you made me cry."

His snort sparked an unwilling smile. "We both know she's more likely to believe *you* made *me* cry. Now get your shit together so you can start being a mom to your son and daughter."

She wiped her wet cheeks on his shirtsleeve, feeling hopeful for the first time in months. "My kids. I'm not dreaming, am I?"

He gave her another gentle squeeze. "Nope, but you'll be getting a lot less sleep."

DESPITE FIRST-CLASS SEATS, TWO MEALS, AND A PAIR OF NAPS ON EACH leg of his most recent flights, Archer had no desire to add another sixty miles to the shitload he'd already traveled in the last twenty hours. Exhaustion didn't begin to describe the state of his mind and body.

He was a *father*, and his almost ex-sister-in-law had shipped his son and daughter off with her lawyer to some random woman who'd served as an egg donor and surrogate. Everything about staking his legal claim to the three-month-old babies he had yet to meet promised to be a clusterfuck of epic proportions, especially working out an agreement with their biological mother.

*Find a lawyer. Hire a nanny. Buy baby furniture and have it delivered. Kick my ungrateful brother's ass into next week.*

*What a fucking shitstorm.*

His phone buzzed in the cupholder of his rental car as he took a swig of coffee. "That better not be you, Reggie. God, I'd rip your balls off if you had any."

A glance at the screen slightly eased the fury staging a riot in his brain.

He tapped the Answer button and switched to speaker. "Hang up and call me back tomorrow if it's bad news, Marcus."

His assistant cleared his throat, clearly covering a chuckle. "Just checking to see how your trip went. I kept an eye on your flights and it looked like all the departures and arrivals were on time. I upgraded your ride and arranged for a late check-in at your hotel."

"No issues. Got the car. Thanks." Buckled up and ready to go, Archer punched his destination into the SUV's GPS and adjusted the volume of the computer-generated voice coming from the speakers. "You're coming to work for me when I quit the family business and start my own company next week."

"Of course, sir."

"You can stop calling me sir now." The signs and the map on the navigation screen led him toward the airport exit. "Arch or Archer is fine with me."

"Yes, sir. Archer." Muffled sounds carried through the phone before Marcus whispered to someone that he would be there in a minute. "This situation with the twins. How are you? I mean, I had no idea, and then what your brother did. Wow. I know it's none of my business, but I can't imagine just turning my back on children I said I wanted."

Archer huffed a laugh, because venting would take more energy than he had at the moment. "Yeah. I'll be fine. Reggie's always been a people-pleaser, but this is just fucked up. I should've known better than to… Never mind. Listen, get back to playing cards with your mom. I'll message you if I need anything, like proofing my resignation letter."

"Don't bother. You could write a detailed business proposal in your sleep, and Mr. CEO wouldn't recognize a misplaced comma or a run-on sentence if it bit him on the ass. Have a safe drive. Text me when you get there so I can tell Billie you didn't fall asleep at the wheel and end up in a ditch."

A genuine smile slid across Archer's face. "You bet. Later."

Other than a few road noises and the calm voice giving him directions, silence fell as he merged onto the highway. Headlights and taillights dotted here and there in the mostly empty darkness, easing some of the tension in his neck and shoulders. It was welcome change from the endless bumper-to-bumper traffic at home that meant having a driver in order to get any work done. He'd enjoyed walking or taking public transportation almost everywhere he needed to go in Tokyo, but driving reset his thoughts—although nothing short of passing out for twelve uninterrupted hours would clear his mind of the mess his brother had created.

Tall trees grew in big broccoli-looking bunches along the roadways, and the flatlands near the airport became hillier as he followed the bypass around the city and drove south toward the town of Cradle Gorge. The dark landscape and the lack of cars eventually quieted his hyped-up nerves, but the welcome sign at the edge of town set his stomach tangling in knots again.

At the first stoplight, he tapped on the address Reggie's attorney had emailed him to pull up directions on his cell. A drive-by would only delay sleep by a minute or two and make finding the surrogate's house easier in the morning.

*Or I just need to know where Mia and Marshall are.*

*My children.*

*I'm a dad.*

The entire concept blew his mind. He hadn't planned on having kids, and only once in his life had he regretted prioritizing his career over a relationship. He and the most amazing woman he'd ever met had agreed to a one-night encounter that had rocked his world less than forty-eight hours before his three-year stint in Japan.

*Maybe I'll—*

*No, I won't. She wasn't interested in doing the marriage and motherhood thing, and she sure as hell won't want me now that I'm a single father.*

Disappointment jabbed him in the heart. No other woman he'd been attracted to had been as bold, beautiful, and brilliant as the breathtaking maid of honor at Reggie's wedding.

He turned right at the next light and refocused his thoughts on the matter at hand instead of obsessing over the impossible. That could happen over the next eighteen years of raising his children. After another right and a left, he slowed to read the numerals painted on the curb at each driveway. A flash of red, noting the end of the route, lit up his phone as the correct number caught his eye.

Half a dozen windows—four on the main floor and two on the second story—glowed pale yellow against the darker exterior of the house. An oddly shaped shadow passed behind the curtains of the lower level's biggest window, only to pivot and pace the opposite direction seconds later.

His gut urged him to stop, even though he was in no condition for a confrontation. His foot moved to the brake, like it had a mind of its own, and he tapped in a two-word message to Marcus that he'd arrived.

He pulled into the driveway, shut off the engine, and climbed out of the car without considering the consequences. Then his feet carried him to the porch while his brain fixated on the fact that his twins were inside.

A muffled cacophony of baby sobs carried through the door as the figure moved in front of the same window again, somewhat clearer this time. A person holding a baby walked toward the front door. He hesitated only a single thump of the pulse inside his skull before raising his hand to the doorbell and pressing it.

*Breathe. Stay calm.*

The cries abruptly stopped, the locks snicked, and the door swung open. A mass of unruly brown hair at the back of the surrogate's head clung to a pudgy wet cheek. Eyes the same color as his stared right at him.

*Mia?*

The woman—most likely the biological mother of his children—spoke without looking at him. "Zin, what are you doing here?"

*Zin? Who's Zin?*

She swayed back and forth. "You should be home with Carson and Daisy. I'm going to have to get used to—"

"Sorry to—"

The wild-haired person shrieked and spun around. Before she could speak, the baby—his daughter, based on the curly tufts of hair gathered in a fountain at the very top of her head—let out a wail. Then an equally unhappy sound came from beyond them. The woman groaned and somehow managed to shove her hair out of her face without losing her two-handed grip on the baby.

*Mia.*

Recognition roared through him, waking every part of his long-past tired body and mind, immediately followed by a hope that otherwise wouldn't have occurred to him in a million years. "Beryl Drechsler."

# CHAPTER THREE

BLINKING HER BLEARY EYES AT THE MAN STANDING IN HER DOORWAY AT nearly midnight, Beryl struggled to find the self-defense knowledge lost somewhere in her spent brain. How did he know her name?

He took a step forward into the arc of light from the foyer, and she took a step back. His brown hair stood on end like he'd shoved his fingers through it a dozen times in the last five minutes. Dark circles rimmed his eyes, scruff covered his jaw, and his wrinkled dress pants, button-down shirt, and loosened tie looked like he'd slept in them. The faint birthmark sticking out of his rolled-up sleeve reminded her of someone, but she couldn't place him in the current condition of her mind. Then he rubbed the bridge of his nose with his thumb and forefinger.

A memory from three years ago leapt from the jumbled mess in her head. Hours of trying to console her inconsolable children didn't staunch the sudden tremors rolling through her vaginal and uterine muscles. That memorable night with him was still the best orgasmic inspiration she'd ever had, but sex was *so* not on the table—or anywhere else—tonight. "Archer James. You're back from Japan?"

He nodded once. "Mind if I come in?"

A yawn escaped when she would've attempted a smile. She rocked back and forth from right to left, hoping Mia finally surrendered to sleep. A glance toward Marshall in the swing confirmed he was quiet only long enough to gear up for another round of making his unhappiness known. "It depends on if you can stop babies from crying. I've changed their diapers, fed them, burped them, rocked them, paced with them, and recited the elements of the periodic table and their atomic numbers. I can't carry a tune in a ten-gallon bucket, so singing's not an option. And I don't have my CD player unpacked yet."

"I'll try." Archer stepped inside, closed the door, and formed those amazing forearms into a cradle. He seemed mesmerized by her daughter, even though her cheeks were blotchy and her tiny nose was scrunched up in preparation for more yowling. "Ready."

She lowered Mia into the curve of his arms, not sure if she should wish for him to have magical powers with small humans or to be as incapable as she was at soothing her children. Her skin tingled where her hands made contact with him, but the look of utter enchantment on his face as he held her daughter turned her insides to goo. Had he changed his mind about marriage and family?

*Or maybe he met someone while he was overseas.*

*Is he a father?*

Cursing the twinge in her chest at that pointless thought, she hurried to Marshall and bent to unfasten the multi-strapped harness holding him in the seat. Her life had no room for dating or even a five-minute hookup for the foreseeable future.

Her son paused his crying to hiccup, but he restarted as she lifted him to her shoulder.

"What are you doing here?" Unwilling to apologize for her somewhat-rude question, she walked to the antique rocker she'd inherited from her grandmother and sat. All her patience belonged to her children now. Thankfully, Marshall quieted as she set the chair in motion. "You're welcome to sit if you want to."

"Thanks." He dropped into the Queen Anne chair a few feet from her, and Mia gave a last whimper before closing her eyes. "She has your mouth."

Several seconds passed before he looked up and grimaced, clearly realizing what he'd implied.

She chortled, but Marshall joined his sister in dreamland instead of bawling. "I know. I'm loud, brash, and bossy."

"I meant she looks like you. I didn't know you were the surrogate. Egg donor. Both. That was incredibly generous of you since having kids wasn't in your plans." The lines around Archer's eyes softened and he brushed his fingertips over her daughter's silky curls.

"Yes, it was." Anger pushed aside the joy of having her twins with her for the hundredth time tonight. "I'm guessing your brother told you neither he nor Jen wants to raise the babies I carried for them now that they're divorcing. She sent her lawyer here with them today. I have no idea what I'm doing, but I don't care. They're mine and I'll figure things out. I can't say the same for Reggie. He clearly didn't really want to be a father, biologically or otherwise, so no great loss there."

Archer's eyebrows dipped into a deep vee as he suddenly looked up at her. "He isn't their father."

Confusion mixed with exhaustion, making her brain short-circuit. "What do you mean? Jen specifically told me I was getting a dose of James sperm."

He leaned his head against the back of the chair and scowled toward the ceiling. After a slow exhale, he stared straight at her with a grim line where his kind smile had resided. "You got the James DNA contribution, but it wasn't Reggie's. It was mine."

BERYL'S EYES WIDENED AND HER JAW DROPPED, ALL BUT CONFIRMING she'd connected the biological dots. "You... You're... We're..."

Her near speechlessness exactly matched his shock when she'd opened her door. Given a choice, Archer wouldn't have chosen anyone else to be the mother of the children he hadn't intended to have but didn't regret.

A soft sigh came from the baby cuddled against him, and he swallowed the lump of emotion forming in his throat. "They're ours. Yours and mine. I came to get them, but—"

"You're not taking them from me." She aimed a fierce stare at him, her motherly instincts clearly on high alert since her entire body had stiffened. "I'm their mother and I have legal custody. A lawyer friend of a friend reviewed the paperwork before I signed the documents this afternoon."

"That was when I didn't have all the facts. Knowing it's you… Beryl, I promise you I'm not going to take them. Share, yes. Take, no." Their timing might have been off the first time around, but everything fit now and he had no intention of letting his second chance with her slip away. "Let's put our kids to bed and talk more tomorrow. You got thrown in the deep end today and I've spent the last day traveling halfway around the world. We're both too tired and too stressed to have this conversation right now."

The fire in her mood seemed to go out. "How can you be so rational? I feel like I've been trying to stop the twins from crying for a month."

He wanted to wrap her in a gentle hug and never let go. "Maybe we should try doing the parenting thing together for a while and see how it works out."

Her expression should've turned him to ash. "You live in California. I live here. My *job* is here. I'm not moving and we're not shipping our kids back and forth across the country. There's no way I'm agreeing to that kind of shared parent—"

"Bear, I'm willing to move or do whatever it takes to make this work for us." Ready to beg if he had to, he pushed up from the chair. "I want what's best for both of us and our children. Right now, that's sleep. I have a hotel reservation here in town, but I can stay and help with feedings and whatever we need to do tonight if you have an extra bed or a couch where I can crash. You can text me when they wake up."

The visible tension in her shoulders and jaw eased as she stood. "Thank you. I have a guest room. They had their bottles and I changed their diapers about an hour and a half ago. There's an app for the baby monitor."

"Okay. Let's put these two to bed, get the app set up, and then I'll move my car and get my suitcase." Relieved that she hadn't refused his offer, he managed a small smile. "Lead the way."

She padded out of the room and toward the curved staircase in the entryway. "The guest room is down this hall and through the library. I think the movers who brought all the baby furniture and necessities today set up the bed when they brought it down from upstairs, but I can't say for sure. I haven't had a chance to check."

"Don't worry about it. A mattress on the floor will work if it isn't." He followed her up the steps and along another hall. "Wait. Movers? Do you mean delivery guys?"

"No." Her pace slowed as she entered the first room on the right. Dim light shone from a lamp near the window, illuminating a matched set of furniture—two cribs, two dressers, a rocking chair, and a shelved piece of furniture with a short railing around the top of it. An assortment of other baby items filled a corner of the room near what was probably a closet. "All of this, plus more baby stuff in both parlors and the kitchen, is from their nursery in California."

How could Jen and Reggie throw away the children they'd begged him to help procreate without an ounce of remorse or a second thought?

Rage tried to well up inside him again, but he shoved it back down. Without their selfishness, he might never have known Beryl was their mother and she wouldn't have gotten this chance.

*I wouldn't, either.*

The situation had righted itself.

He walked to the bed opposite the one Beryl stood next to and took a moment to simply study the baby in his arms—his daughter. Her long eyelashes brushed the tops of her cheekbones. Curls framed her delicate ears, and her adorable chin wiggled up and down from the sucking motion she made with her tiny mouth.

His heart broke for her and Marshall, for how they'd been nothing more than possessions to his brother, possessions that could be discarded when they didn't suit a purpose in his life anymore. *Some-how, I'll make up for allowing that mistake.* "I'll always be here for you, Mia. Always."

A faint sniffle drew his attention to Beryl. She'd placed their son in his crib and ran her fingertip over his little fist. "I think they prefer to sleep in the same bed. They were happier when I put them together earlier so I could wash my hands. If you give me your phone, I'll add the monitor app and log you in after you put her next to Marshall."

"Makes sense. They lived in the same space before they were born." He closed the short distance between them and lowered Mia onto the mattress beside her brother. His kids turned their heads toward each other and shared a pair of contented-sounding sighs. "Look at that. Mommy's a smart cookie."

She blinked up at him and sniffled again. "Book smart. I'm so scared of screwing up."

"We won't be perfect, but we'll do the best we can, just like all new parents who love their kids." He held out his cell and waited while she set up the app.

Within two minutes, she completed the task, including showing him how the monitor worked. "I'll text myself from your phone so you have my number too."

"Good thinking. Then you can let me know if and when you need my help." Slipping his cell in his pocket and his hand around hers, he led her to what seemed to be the master bedroom next door. Damn, he wanted to climb into bed with her, to make love to her and hold her while they slept. Instead, he pressed his lips to her forehead as he released her hand. "We made those beautiful babies and that's pretty fucking amazing. The rest is learn as we go. First up is getting as much sleep as we can. Goodnight, Bear. Sweet dreams."

# CHAPTER FOUR

THE MONOTONOUS *BUZZ-BUZZ-BUZZ* OF HER ALARM PULLED BERYL from the best dream she'd had in at least a year. The weight of her lover's arm around her waist as he slowly rocked in and out of her from behind had seemed so real—a repeat of the night she'd spent tangled up with Archer James. His body heat had seeped into her skin and his mouth had explored every inch of her body. The memories of connecting with him were still as vivid as the regret-filled hours and days after they'd parted ways.

She groaned as she reached toward her nightstand to shut off the obnoxious noise in the early morning dusk. A self-induced orgasm in the shower might take the edge off, but it never brought the same satisfaction as sex with her one-time lover.

The ache to be touched pulsing through her breasts and clit cut off mid sensation at the sudden unhappy cries emanating from her phone.

"The babies. Shit!" Shoving away the sheet, she scrambled out of bed. How could she have slept through the nighttime feedings and diaper changes? What kind of mother forgot about her children?

She was almost out the bedroom door when Archer's calm voice carried to her ears in stereo. "Let's try not to wake up Mommy, okay? She needs her rest. According to the calendar down in the kitchen, she has class and meetings today. I know you're hungry, but everything I've read says to do diaper changes before bottles. You're next, Mia. Give me a minute to finish with your brother."

Drowning in relief and blinking back tears, Beryl hurried into the room next to hers. Her guilt amplified when he glanced her direction with exhaustion written all over his face. "I'm so sorry. I should've taken care of the twins last night and let you sleep."

His biceps flexed against the sleeves of his t-shirt as he fastened the second tape at Marshall's waist and snapped the onesie over the diaper. "I was awake anyway. Too wired. It's going to take a few days to adjust to living in a drastically different time zone. Besides, you had a really stressful day yesterday, and life isn't going to slow down for you to catch up. I'll nap when you get home from work this afternoon. Go grab a shower while I handle their liquid breakfast."

His willingness to share responsibilities with her eased the feelings of being overwhelmed and failing at parenthood.

"Thank you." She kissed her daughter on the cheek as she picked her up and then waited for Archer to be ready for the next baby in the assembly line.

"You're welcome." His tired eyes didn't dim his genuine-looking smile. "We're in this together, Bear, and I'm glad I'm here to help. There's nowhere else I'd rather be."

His words sparked much more than a sexual response from her body. Her heart recognized this man and yearned for more than a single night, even though she had never wanted or needed a romantic relationship to be happy.

After a quick swap, she cuddled her son while Archer finished his job. The whole context gave her vibes of partnership, an aspect of marriage she'd seldom witnessed until seeing Zinnia and Carson together. Her parents had lived separate lives and left her to fend for herself. "I'm glad you're here too."

"Can you watch her while I wash my hands? She fusses up a storm if I put her back in the crib." At her nod, he disposed of the diapers and headed across the hall to the bathroom. He returned in less than a minute, settled Mia into the crook of his left arm, and extended his right arm. "Drop Marshall in. The bottles and bouncer seats are ready in the kitchen and I'll have coffee brewing before you're out of the shower."

She bit her lower lip to stop the telltale tickle in her nose that warned her the waterworks were threatening again, but a tear leaked out and dribbled along her cheek. Ducking her head, she placed their son in his father's capable hold. Her stubbornness and independent streak might've been enough to survive caring for their twins on her own, but having Archer's support made it better.

"Hey, Bear, are you okay?" His softly spoken question almost wrung a sob from her. "This is a lot to deal with. I'm here if you need to talk, to sleep, to be held and reassured. Anything. All you have to do is tell me what you need, and I'm on it."

She snagged a tissue from the changing table and forced a slow breath to keep any more tears from falling. "I've been really emotional for a while. Letting them go was so much harder than I expected. What you're doing to help while I process everything... You have no idea how much I appreciate it."

He touched his forehead to hers. "You're worth it. Do you need to take the day off work? Or would you rather stick to your regular routine? What's best for you right now?"

Guilt crowded in again for the answer that shouted the loudest. "Am I a bad mother for wanting to teach my class and go to my meetings?"

"No, absolutely not." His quick response didn't truly convince her, and he must've seen it in her expression. "Why do you want to go to work today?"

"Because those are things I can control." That truth came easily.

"And when you come home, will you focus on your job or our kids?" His eyebrow rose, like he was challenging her to convince him she wouldn't prioritize the twins at least part of the time.

She stuck out her tongue at him. "I know it isn't logical, but..."

He laughed and pressed his lips to hers in a mostly chaste but instantly lust-inducing kiss. "I get it. Emotions aren't logical, and I know you'll talk me down when the time comes."

Considering her racing pulse and the sudden wish for the traditional life she'd deliberately chosen to steer clear of before, his declaration was the understatement of the year.

*IT'S NOT IMPULSIVE.*

Archer reread the resignation letter he'd written during Marshall's and Mia's first nap of the morning and after his second cup of coffee for the final time. Instead of making his personal reasons sound more professional with each pass, he'd given his outrage and disgust free rein. The callousness his jackass of a brother and inconsiderate wife had exhibited toward the twins and Beryl crossed a line that no apology could make up for.

The Send button coaxed his mouse arrow closer until he finally clicked on it. With his business ties to Reggie severed, he could direct his energy toward his own interests.

*And raising my kids.*

*And creating a future with Beryl.*

Simply seeing her again had convinced him to rethink his focus on the career he'd loved the last fifteen years. The impromptu kiss he'd given her in the twins' room this morning had rekindled the fire that had never gone out into a roaring flame.

*That wasn't impulsive, either.*

She'd been living in his mind since the unforgettable night they'd shared in her bed. Phenomenal chemistry aside, he'd liked her, her honesty, and her tendency to say exactly what she thought. She never half-assed or faked anything.

Looking into the face of forty only reinforced his unwillingness to waste time dancing around his feelings.

*This is the real thing.*

A soft coo broke the steady hum of the refrigerator, pulling him back to the present. Another slightly louder voice—his daughter's if he had to venture a guess—joined the first, but neither sounded distressed.

The twins seemed to be carrying on a private discussion in some language only they shared.

After a check of the clock, Archer closed his laptop and gathered the supplies to prep formula for the next feeding. His kids were content, and he wasn't about to throw a wrench into the peaceful moment. Their lives had been disrupted even more than his.

His phone dinged and lit up on the kitchen counter as he filled the second bottle. A surprised-face emoji popped up under his assistant's name, triggering a bark of laughter. Marcus had obviously read the email he'd been blind-copied on roughly ten minutes ago.

Another message followed the first. *"He's going to shit a million-dollar brick."*

Archer snickered as he tightened the ring-nipple-cap combo and set aside the bottle. *"Not my problem. Give me the weekend to come up with a business plan. Gotta go rescue the twins. It's feeding time again."*

He pocketed his cell on the way up the back stairs from the kitchen, listening in on the happy noises coming through the monitor app until he arrived in the upstairs hallway. The pair's voices met him near the master bedroom doorway and grew louder as he approached the nursery. Had Reggie ever marveled at the way Marshall and Mia interacted?

*Yeah, right. He probably couldn't tell them apart by their personalities, either.*

As he entered the room, his daughter reached for her brother and rolled sideways enough to pull him into what looked like a hug. Touched by their incredible connection, he snapped a picture at the same time his cell alerted him to another text message, this one from Beryl.

*"1:00 meeting canceled. Should be home by noon. Everything going okay?"*

Both babies looked his direction, but they didn't let go of each other.

He grinned at them. "Mommy's checking to see how we're getting along. She said she'll be home soon. Do you think she misses us?"

Mia smiled, melting his heart into a mushy ball of affection.

Having to navigate from his messages to the camera, he missed the photo op by at least a full second. "You have to promise you'll smile for her later. I'll send her the hug pic for now."

The three bouncing dots appeared as soon as the photo showed up into the conversation. Then a heart, a big smile, and a sobbing face popped into a new bubble. *"So sweet. Thank you."*

*"You're welcome, Bear. See you soon."* He would've liked to have added kissing lips, but moving too fast might make him lose more ground than he'd gained since last night and early this morning. If he could be patient in business, he could do the same for the mother of his children—the woman he'd fallen for.

# CHAPTER FIVE

SHIFTING THE STRAP OF HER COMPUTER BAG HIGHER ON HER SHOULDER, Beryl skittered down the steps outside the biology building faster than she'd moved in months. With any luck, her babies would be doing cute stuff this afternoon—instead of crying the way they had most of yesterday after everyone had left. Her heart still hurt from being unable to soothe them. Jen and Reggie had upended their lives overnight.

*I'm glad they're too little to know and remember what happened.*

Although anger surged through her on their behalf, the custard stand didn't tempt her in the slightest as she turned out of the parking lot. She had a reason to hurry home, and leaving work early meant less traffic to get there.

When she pulled into the garage, Archer's rental sat in the space to the left. The last instance of a man parking his vehicle out of sight from her neighbors had happened when they'd hooked up after his brother's wedding reception. Having him here with the twins invited her to pretend their night together had resulted in an unplanned pregnancy neither of them regretted. In spite of her plan to remain unmarried and childless, the scenario was far more palatable than reality.

The door into the kitchen opened as she approached, and he

appeared on the top step. "Perfect timing. Our little huggers have dry diapers again and everybody's lunch is ready."

In awe of his efficiency and thoughtfulness, she followed him into the house and wrapped her arms around him before she overthought the action. "Thank you. For being here and making lunch and sending the picture. For volunteering to handle parental duties while I recharged and went to work. All of it. I don't know what I would've done without your help."

He hugged her against him, reminding her of the tight embrace they'd shared before parting ways three years ago. "You would've figured it out, but I'm glad I'm here for this—and for you. It isn't temporary, either. I quit my job today. I'll start thinking about what I want to do next over the weekend. My loyalties and priorities have shifted."

A familiar mix of sensations raced along her skin with the firm yet gentle touch of his lips on her ear. Desire, connection, and something more—all the things she'd felt with him last time—made her pulse speed up, urging her to hold on tight to him and never let go. "Stay-at-home dad?"

"Maybe work-from-home dad, but I need to sleep on it." He eased back a few inches and entwined his fingers with hers. "We should feed these two before they stage a mutiny."

The instant camaraderie that had led to their hookup struck again. The easy meshing of the current moment of their lives sucked her feelings into a doubt-filled spiral about why she'd chosen to stay independent rather than compromising on everything she wanted for herself.

She walked with him to the swings he'd moved to the kitchen, savoring the ways they fit together. "I missed you."

As he bent to unbuckle Marshall, Archer glanced up at her. "I think they missed you too. They tried to grab my hair when I was holding them, but their little fingers yanked on the ones the barber keeps trimmed on my neck instead. Evidently, I'm in need of a haircut."

"Ouch." Taking advantage of the time he needed to unfasten and lift their son out of the seat, she gave herself a metaphorical kick in the ass. If she expected total honesty from him, she had to reciprocate. "I missed the babies while I was at work, but I was talking about you during the last three years."

He jerked his gaze back to hers, his mouth curving into a wide smile. The look in his eyes made her insides melt. "I thought about you pretty much every day while I was gone. I didn't really have a choice about leaving at the time, even though I was excited to go. The thing is, I've always wondered if things would've been different if I'd stayed. Those what ifs never stopped."

The seemingly effortless way he handed off Marshall to her and moved to release her daughter from the other swing sparked a wave of lust.

*I think my aging ovaries just exploded.*

Since when were dad skills an attractive trait?

She pressed a kiss to her son's forehead, reached for his lunchtime helping of formula, and stuck it in his mouth before he could complain that she wasn't fast enough. "I wondered what you were doing in Tokyo for months, and I didn't like that you were a big distraction when I was supposed to be focusing on my research. Not that any of this is your fault, but I agreed to be Jen's surrogate to get you out of my head."

With Mia cradled in his left arm, he picked up the second bottle on the table and pulled out the chair beside her by hooking his foot around its leg. "I worked sixteen-hour days, usually seven days a week to forget you. It didn't help much. I had a lot of very realistic dreams. My first thought when I landed in San Jose was that I wanted to see you again, but I also figured nothing had changed with your job. Knowing where we are today, would you change what happened if you could?"

"No." The answer didn't require a pros and cons list or even a moment's hesitation. The days, weeks, and months of crying—hers— didn't matter anymore. "They're here. You're here. I'll take the gift and be happy with it."

"A gift." He nodded and smoothed his palm over their daughter's messy curls. "That's the perfect word for this situation. So, I have a proposition. And I want you to promise to think about it before you say yes or no."

SUFFERING FROM EXTREME EXHAUSTION PROBABLY WASN'T THE BEST state to be in while making a once-in-a-lifetime proposal, but a golden opportunity had landed in his lap and Archer refused to let it pass him by. "Do you agree to listen and consider my idea?"

Beryl studied him with a stern expression that reminded him of how damn smart she was. The gears in her scientific brain were obviously working to formulate all possible outcomes. "Yes."

He took a deep breath to give his thought process a boost so he could form a coherent and convincing argument. "From what we've said, I think we're on the same page as far as wanting to reconnect and explore our relationship. We both want to parent our kids, and doing it alone isn't something either of us can easily do. I definitely have no desire to end up in a custody battle."

She raised an eyebrow at him. "You don't have to pussyfoot around me. Just state what's on your mind."

"Okay. I want our current living and parenting arrangement to continue while we get to know each other better and work toward marriage, or some kind of permanent commitment. We'll have equal access to the twins and shared responsibilities—meaning neither of us has to sacrifice our careers. We can also consult with each other on how to handle their medical care, education, and all that stuff." Her almost imperceptible nod gave him the confidence to continue. "Since I'd like us to focus on creating a good relationship example for them to follow, I think we should—"

"No." Her narrowed-eye glare almost drew a chuckle from him. "If we want to have sex, we're allowed to have sex. I'm not agreeing to some puritanical bullsh—bull hockey—made up by a bunch of misogynistic do-as-I-say-not-as-I-do idiots."

He surrendered to a full-bellied laugh at her quick save. "That was never an option. I'm not sacrificing sex with you when we already know we're compatible in that area. I was going to say we should lay some ground rules about how we conduct healthy discussions. No screaming and yelling. No going to bed mad. Those kinds of things. I don't want to screw this up—for us or for them."

"I didn't realize you're such a planner." She frowned, but something in the way she looked at him said she was teasing. "That might cause some friction."

"Friction is good when applied at the right time and in the right place. If I didn't need a twelve-hour nap, I'd show you just how good friction can be." The slow grin that slid across her face told him he'd read her thoughts correctly. The promise there went straight to his dick. "Seriously, Bear, I know we can do this and I want you to be just as sure before you agree."

As she opened her mouth, chimes rang through the house at the same time her phone dinged on the table. She looked down and then pushed back her chair. "I'll get it. Zinnia's at the door."

He pushed to his feet to follow her, pretty sure he'd drift off to sleep if he didn't. "There are flowers at the door?"

"No, my friend Zinnia. The women in her family have flower names. Her mom is Iris and her daughter is Daisy." With Marshall's bottle propped up with her chin, she opened the front door.

A blonde with glasses rimmed with the same color as her orange shirt and the trim on her bike shorts stood on the porch, a dark-haired baby perched on her hip. "Carson said he saw you on campus a little while ago. Is everything okay with the— Who are you?"

"Archer, Zinnia. Zinnia, Archer. Mia's and Marshall's *actual* father. Long story." The woman instantly morphed into someone far more dangerous-looking than a slightly nerdy mom, but Beryl waved her inside with an elbow. She'd clearly confided in her friend, at least in part, about the clusterfuck his brother and sister-in-law had managed to generate.

The little girl clapped her hands. "Bee-bee! Bana."

"Hello to you too, Daisy. I'll have to check the fruit basket for bananas. Didn't Ba-ba let you have one for breakfast?" Beryl headed toward the kitchen.

"Ba-ba bee-bee bana ma-ma." An infectious giggle showed off several of Daisy's front teeth.

He smiled at their guests, not the least bit embarrassed by the fact that he'd fathered the twins. "Nice to meet you. I'd shake your hand if mine weren't busy."

Zinnia's cautious nod implied a bit of a protective streak where Beryl was concerned. "You're Reggie's brother, aren't you?"

"Yes." Unable to think of anything expletive-free to say about his only sibling, he kept his mouth shut on that topic as he walked with Beryl's friend along the hallway. "I had groceries delivered this morning, including bananas, if Daisy's allowed to have one."

"Bana bana!" Daisy's enthusiastic grin widened when Beryl plucked a banana from the basket on the counter.

Zinnia looked directly at him, distrust radiating from her tell-the-truth-or-else stare. "Did you babysit this morning?"

After shifting Marshall to her shoulder, Beryl sat and gestured with the piece of fruit for her friend to do the same. "He did. Well, sort of, if you can call it that. Remember how I said Reggie was the babies' father? It seems Jen misled me. Archer donated the swimmers I was inseminated with, and the paperwork he signed was missing the same form mine was. I guess you could say he fulfilled some fatherly duties while I was working."

"No way." Zinnia dropped into the chair across from him, her gaze drilling deeper. "You better not fight Beryl for custody after what she's gone through."

Beryl rolled her eyes as she rubbed Marshall back. "Stand down, Zin. He isn't the enemy."

Somewhat entertained by their exchange, he counted to fifteen to see if they had anything else to say about him before he interjected.

Before he got to the last number, Daisy broke the silence. "Bee-bee, bana. Bee-bee, bana."

He set aside Mia's bottle and crossed his fingers he didn't end up having to change shirts again from burping her. What constituted frequent spitting up was on the list of questions he'd started for the pediatrician they had yet to research and engage. "Do you just peel it and Daisy takes bites? Or should I get a plate and silverware?"

"A plate, a knife, and a spoon please." Zinnia huffed out a sigh. "Aren't you going to defend yourself?"

Pushing away from the table, he shrugged. "Why should I? Bear's doing a great job of it so far."

# CHAPTER SIX

PAYING CLOSE ATTENTION TO THE POSITION OF THE TOWEL, BERYL reached for a clean diaper on the shelf below her son and crossed her fingers Marshall didn't give himself a shower again. At least he'd mostly missed her and the wall, which had made cleanup somewhat easier since she hadn't disposed of his bathwater before it happened.

"You still haven't answered my question." Zinnia walked into her peripheral vision with a freshly bathed and dressed Mia nestled in her arms. "What are you going to do if—"

"We'll make it work." Everything at the ready, Beryl flipped the towel out of the way and hurried through fitting the diaper into place. "Archer and Reggie are really close, but he's really angry with his brother right now for dropping this bomb on him out of nowhere. He wants to be a father and we've talked some about our future. His and mine. Mostly, he talked and then you interrupted when you stopped by at lunchtime. I trust him not to suddenly disappear—with or without the babies—or sue for custody."

Zinnia's eyebrows rose at least an inch. "How can you know that? You're talking about the future like you plan to get married or something. That seems kind of drastic for a shared parenting arrangement when you hardly know each other."

The argument made sense if not for one little fact.

Beryl hoped the heat creeping up her neck didn't show as she finished dressing Marshall. She had nothing to be embarrassed about, but admitting to herself she'd never really moved on after the hookup was a doozy of revelation. "So...we sort of have a past. He was Reggie's best man and I was Jen's maid of honor. We may have had our own wedding-night sex-fest, without the legal or emotional ties."

"May have, huh? Wow." Zinnia paced toward the window. "That explains the happy-family vibes I was getting. A one-night stand that didn't result in an accidental pregnancy but still led to the two of you becoming parents. Is it awkward? It doesn't feel like it is. In fact, you and Archer seem to have settled into domesticity rather well."

"The chemistry's still there, and we get along really well. I like him, Zin. A lot."

"Okay. He seems like a decent guy. And he's much more comfortable around the twins than Carson was around Daisy at first." Her friend nuzzled Mia's cheek. "You look so much like your mommy, especially your mouth and chin. That nose is all your daddy, though."

"Their eyes too." Finally finished diapering and dressing her son, Beryl picked him up and breathed in the scents of baby wash and shampoo. "Hey, little man, are you ready to swing while the adults in the house eat supper?"

His tiny smile and soft coo made her fall more in love with this child she'd created.

Mia answered her brother with more baby sounds.

Grinning, Zin stepped out of the nursery and into the hall. "I love how they talk to each other. It's like they have their own language."

"They do. We've been putting them in the same crib to nap because they're much happier when they're together. Talking and hugging and holding hands. I could watch them for hours." Beryl trailed after her friend to the kitchen, where Carson checked on something in the oven and Daisy sat in one of the pair of matching high chairs from the moving truck.

He looked up as they entered. "Perfect timing. Everything'll be ready in five minutes. That gives us some time to chat. So, I was thinking, Bee-bee. Two of my collaborators still need to learn to use my new equipment. Would you mind if we collected samples from you, the babies, and Archer to analyze? I've never run DNA analysis on different-gendered fraternal twins before, and definitely not under these circumstances."

The image of a needle popped into her head, making his wide line-backer shoulders weave and blur. "What kind of samples?"

Had her voice squeaked?

"Blood would be ideal, but we can use swab samples—saliva—instead. No need to poke the babies and cause them pain." His outline grew larger. "Hey, are you okay? You look a little pale. Oh, needles. I sometimes forget they bother a lot of people. Nobody has to get stabbed if they don't want to."

Hands on her shoulders guided her into a chair and then a phenomenal ass appeared next to her at eye level, partially blocking her view of the instigator of her wooziness. Had their voices or the smell of food awakened Archer?

He glanced down at her with a concerned frown. "She has a major aversion to anything related to what you mentioned, including the verbs you used. Will our samples and information be used for any other purpose than the training? And will we receive a copy of the report?"

"You must be the sperm donor. Archer James, right? The jerk's brother." Zin's husband took a step toward them with his hand extended. "Carson Hines."

Instead of accepting the greeting, Archer slid his fingers under Beryl's hair and caressed her neck, inciting goose bumps along her skin. "I don't like the term 'sperm donor.' I'm Mia's and Marshall's father in every way."

Carson chuckled and moved back toward the stove. "No offense intended. I'm a sperm-donor dad too. Beryl says you're voluntarily stepping into the official role. Legally and parentally. Have you—"

"Knock it off." Feeling more like her usual self, Beryl shifted closer to Archer, hoping he got the hint to keep touching her. "If anybody's conducting an inquisition, it's me. How soon do you need samples and do we need to go to your lab?"

The timer beeped and Carson donned a pair of oven mitts she didn't recognize. Had she unpacked hers yet?

He checked behind and beside him before opening the door and lifting out a huge casserole dish. The mouthwatering aromas of garlic, Italian seasonings, and tomatoes filled the kitchen. "Ideally, you'd come to the lab so we can minimize contamination of the samples. Does Monday morning before your class work for you? Or Wednesday. The earlier, the better. Processing the samples takes roughly ten hours. With four of you, the report will be a little more complex."

She raised her gaze to check with Archer—something that struck her as unsettling since she rarely found herself in a position to consult with someone else before making a personal decision. "You're an early riser, but I don't know what you have going on Wednesday morning."

Lips that had touched nearly every part of her body three years ago curved upward as he looked at her. "Other than talking to my assistant about my new business plan at some point, the next week will consist of taking care of M and M. We should have the feeding schedule under control by then."

SITTING IN THE A-FRAME SWING WITH HIS SON TUCKED IN HIS RIGHT arm and his daughter in his left, Archer rocked his foot on the ground to continue the slow back-and-forth motion. "I'm pretty sure you've heard my sperm-donor dad story. Tell me yours."

With Daisy crashed on his chest, Carson grinned from the patio chair a few feet away. His gaze drifted toward the door leading into Beryl's less formal parlor, where the mothers of their kids were going through several tote bags of outgrown baby clothes. "I donated at a fertility clinic in Pittsburgh when I was eighteen—for the money and to see what the process was like because I planned to study genetics in college. Twenty years later, I came here from California as part of a semester-long visiting scholar swap. I fell head over heels in love with my landlord neighbor and discovered by accident that she was the recipient of my donation. We got married after knowing each other eighteen days and celebrated our one-week anniversary on Tuesday."

"Wow, that was fast. Congratulations." *Maybe the plans that formed out of nowhere aren't so crazy after all.*

"Thanks. I've been invited to stay another semester and apply for a faculty position that's open. Now we're working on a change for the birth certificate. Life is very good from where I stand. Or sit."

"Birth certificate. Bear and I need to take care of that at some point." Laughter carried through the open window, adding to the serenity that had settled over Archer, despite needing a lot more sleep. "I still can't believe my brother and his wife—almost ex-wife— thought it was okay to return the twins like they're a pair of pants that didn't fit. I'm not sure I'll ever forgive him, not after he begged me for help."

"It was a pretty crappy thing to do." Carson smoothed his hand over his daughter's hair and kissed her forehead. "If I had to guess, I'd say they were already having problems and expected a baby to fix what was wrong with their marriage."

"I was out of the country, so I didn't see what was going on with them." The hum of cicadas reminded him of fall hikes with Reggie when they were younger, so Archer pushed to his feet and paced to work off the anger trying to build inside him again. They'd been best friends as well as siblings all their lives, not at odds over his brother's disregard for a selfless favor. "It's weird. In some ways, I'm grateful, even though I hate what they did—especially now that I know the effect it had on Beryl."

"Watching her struggle to accept that she wasn't dreaming yesterday made me see a vulnerable side of her I didn't think existed. Beneath her tough exterior is a woman with profound feelings."

Giving a nod, Archer sank onto the seat again. "It tears me up to think of her suffering alone through all of it. I'm here to support her however she needs me, and I'm glad you and Zinnia have her back."

"You're staying then?" The question sounded like a challenge from a protective friend.

"Yes."

"For how long? A week? A month?" The geneticist's hard stare didn't waver for a second.

"I have these beautiful kids and a chance to make a future with the woman I haven't been able to get out of my head for three years. Did she tell you about how we clicked at Reggie and Jen's wedding?" A second too late, the reality that she may have referred to their night together as a hookup or a one-night stand registered in his brain. "The timing was off then. It isn't now."

Carson's grunt didn't sound like he agreed with the idea of rushing into a relationship, in spite of meeting Zinnia less than a month ago. "You better not hurt her. She deserves happiness after what she went through."

"I couldn't agree more. An occasional offer from you to babysit for a couple hours will help us focus on our relationship, beyond parenting these two. My end goals are to make her happy and be a good father."

Carson's tight jaw seemed to relax and his chuckle assured Archer he'd convinced him his motives were on the up and up. "Let us know when you're ready for some adult time, and we'll work out the details."

The click of the patio door opening drew their attention, and Beryl stepped onto the deck with Zinnia right behind her. "Hey, Ba-ba, are you done giving Archer the third degree? It's time to say goodnight. Eight o'clock is the new midnight, and we need to recharge while the babies are sleeping."

"Just making sure he's not a jerk, Bee-bee." Shifting Daisy in his arms, Carson stood. "Since my wife and I have been told to go home, it was good to meet you, Archer. See you Monday morning, if not before when we're out for a walk through the neighborhood."

More farewells followed as Beryl escorted their guests to the front door. When they set off along the sidewalk with a stroller, she locked up, looking almost as tired as Archer felt. "Do you want me to carry Mia and Marshall upstairs? I'm sure you're even more ready to go to sleep than I am."

He shook his head, enjoying the taste of fatherhood. "I'll carry them up since you offered to feed them solo tonight. Besides, I'd like for us to put them to bed together when we can. Family time."

"Okay." The hopefulness in her eyes hit him straight in the heart and traveled southward.

His gaze strayed to the hypnotizing sway of her hips as she climbed the stairs and led him into the twins' room. Even though he was dead on his feet, desire thrummed through him. He wasn't willing to act on it yet, not before she was ready.

After a gentle press of his lips on his children's foreheads, he passed them to their mother one at a time. "Call, text, or come get me if you need help tonight. I'm a fairly light sleeper."

"I remember." She settled Marshall into the crib beside his sister and smiled. "Thanks. I may take you up on it if they cry. You know, you could sleep in the master bedroom with me, just in case."

# CHAPTER SEVEN

BERYL DRANK THE LAST SWALLOW OF HER COFFEE AND SHOVED DOWN the feelings of rejection still trying to get a rise out of her. The brew left a far less bitter taste in her mouth than the insecurities that came with a body ravaged by pregnancy.

So what if Archer had made the assumption her motive for wanting to sleep with him was sex?

It had been—for both of them—in the past. He didn't need to know how much the past year had changed her outlook on life, and wishing he'd been around to help soothe her battered emotions was too much to admit to him right now.

*Battered. Something deep-fried sure would hit the spot. Oh, what I wouldn't give for a double order of onion rings.*

Too bad her stomach disagreed. Luckily, turning forty-three last month hadn't put coffee on her must-avoid list.

She lowered her foot to the ground and set the swing gently moving back and forth, grateful for a few minutes' downtime before another busy day started.

*I wouldn't trade it for all the fried food and ice cream in the world.*

The monitor app on her phone stayed silent as she savored another swallow of coffee, but Mia and Marshall would wake soon.

*My babies.*

Her nose tickled and tears welled in her eyes. For the first time since the positive pregnancy test, she wanted to happy-cry instead of letting loose a tidal wave of angst and regret.

A blurry silhouette in the kitchen window added to the joy trying to escape.

Then Archer appeared in the doorway, his hand wrapped around a mug and his hair sticking out every which way. Slightly baggy boxers and nothing else showed off his trim runner's body. A similar memory from three years ago rushed forward as he stepped onto the patio. "Morning. Good coffee. Mind if I join you?"

Fairly certain her voice would give away how much she longed to touch him, she gestured to the empty half of the swing and shook her head. Her damp hair shifted with the motion, almost hiding him from view.

He padded across the pavers in his bare feet, set his mug on the ground by the frame, and sat beside her. The swing set a new rhythm, one that wasn't as smooth as before. "I only heard the kids once last night. They must be getting used to all the changes."

"Mm-hm." With her empty cup poised at her lips, she pretended to take a drink. The weight of his gaze tempted her to look at him, but she focused on the colorful blooms in her flowerbed as she set aside her mug. If he wanted to address the elephant in her backyard, he could do it on his own.

"You're not mad at me, are you? About last night?" He blew out a noisy sigh. "I want you. Don't ever doubt that. I just… I'm serious about us having a future together, and I have no experience with a commitment like that. Plus, I hadn't had enough sleep to make a rational decision about our physical relationship."

"I was disappointed, not mad. I've felt so alone through all of what happened and I wanted someone to lean on for a little while." The words tumbled out, even though she'd stifled her lack-of-filter tendencies more often lately.

His eyebrows dipped to match his sudden grimace. "I'm sorry for assuming it was about sex. You can lean on me whenever you want or need to. Like right here, right now."

Slipping under his raised arm, she nestled against him. His chest rose and fell as she enjoyed the feel of his bare skin on her cheek. The familiar scent of his deodorant brought back a dozen memories of their lone night together. "Sex may have been low on the priority list, but it *was* on the list—somewhere after support and sleep. Do you need to get tested before—if—we take that step?"

"Nope. I haven't been with anyone since we were together." He touched his lips to her forehead, leaving behind a gentle kiss, and his voice softened. "That night stuck with me. I haven't wanted any other woman. Only you."

"I'm different now." She closed her eyes to immerse herself in being held by him. "I have stretch marks and a C-section scar. My stomach and my boobs look like a two-year-old drew a road map all over them."

"Not surprising, since you carried our twins inside you for nine months."

"Thirty-three weeks and four days." She'd missed out on roughly a month and a half of being a mother because her blood pressure had skyrocketed for no apparent reason—except the stress of knowing they would no longer be hers to love and care for.

"That's a long time to have your skin stretched out to accommodate two babies. Your body still makes me horny, but it isn't what I remember most about you. I loved the way you spoke your mind and the way you laughed when you found something truly funny. You were always honest and straightforward. That's what sucked me in from the moment I met you." He tightened his arm around her, making her feel treasured. "You're the most genuine person I've ever known. And you're beautiful to me, no matter how many scars you have. Inside or out."

The intimation that he recognized the hell she'd experienced broke through the feeble wall she'd built around her emotions. Tears stung her eyes, dripping faster than she could blink them away.

"You can cry on me anytime. It isn't going to scare me away." He tipped up her chin with his free hand and wiped at the trails on her cheeks. The compassion in his eyes tempered his slight smirk. "Is it okay if I kiss you like I mean it?"

His question—the same one he'd asked her three years ago—reignited the need to physically connect with him and to surrender to the feelings that had lingered in her body and soul. She barely managed a nod before he lowered his lips to hers in light caress after light caress.

*I mean it too.*

A whimper slipped out as he teased the seam with his tongue and then dove in when she opened to him. Desire rushed through her in an instant, the way it had the first time they'd kissed. The sensations amplified with the rough groan that accompanied him lifting her onto his lap.

Her palms followed the contours of his upper back as she savored the feel of his skin beneath her fingertips. His erection pressed into her thigh, and his hand slid under the hem of her tank top, feathering along the waistband of her shorts. Every touch drew her deeper into the blissful haven they'd created what seemed a lifetime ago and only yesterday.

The needy moans she couldn't hold in were suddenly upstaged by harmonizing baby cries.

Archer eased away and rested his forehead against hers, his breathing rough and unsteady. "They stopped us from giving the neighbors a free show. How about if we pick up where we left off at the next naptime?"

*COCK-BLOCKED BY MY THREE-MONTH-OLD TWINS.*

The possibility would never have occurred to Archer a week ago, but life was damn good, even if his kids had stifled every opportunity for him to give and take pleasure with Beryl and her gorgeous body all day. He wouldn't refuse to share her bed tonight. In fact, he'd beg her for the chance if she didn't offer it.

He grinned and shook his head as he followed her into the kitchen for M and M's evening feeding. The dishwasher hummed and the counters were clean except where he'd prepped the bottles. Leftover lasagna had sufficed for supper after a day of entertaining the pair who'd decided they didn't want or need to nap most of the day. The whole scenario reminded him of his near-perfect childhood, of close-knit family, of his parents' strong and happy marriage.

*I want that for us.*

He adjusted his hold on his daughter, snagged both bottles, and trailed Beryl outside to the swing. The setting sun cast hints of copper highlights in her wavy brown hair, something he hadn't noticed during their brief encounter in California. Discovering all the ways to satisfy her had been his sole intention. They still had a lot to learn about each other, despite the parental and sexual connections they shared.

As soon as she settled Marshall into feeding position and he did the same with Mia, he draped his arm around her shoulders. "We're getting the hang of this parenting thing. Or they're trying to lull us into thinking we are."

Her uninhibited laughter sounded more like the Beryl he'd been drawn to and less like the shell-shocked woman who'd been in mourning for most of the past year. "Probably the latter. I wouldn't have a clue what to do without Zinnia's help. She's such a natural mother. She always has been, even when we were roommates in college."

"You're doing great. Do you have family you can ask to come help for a few days while we—"

"I don't have any family, not by blood anyway, except the babies." She tensed against him for half a second and then seemed to relax again. "I guess you deserve to know my story so you know what you're getting into. My mom died when I was two. I lived with an aunt until she died when I was seven. Then I went into the foster system. Nobody wanted a little girl whose mouth was as smart as her brain. The group home wasn't much better, but nobody expected much and I aged out after three years. Oh, and before you ask, I never knew my father. He left after my mom told him she was pregnant. At least that's what my aunt said."

His insides tied themselves in a knot for the childhood she'd lived. He smoothed his hand over her bare arm and kissed her hair, hoping to convey support rather than pity. "His loss. You're an amazing woman. Strong, intelligent, determined. I know sharing this wasn't easy, so I feel privileged that you trust me with your story."

She shrugged as she looked up at him. "I decided a long time ago not to let it define me, so thanks for not telling me you're sorry. I'm not. It helped me work harder to be self-reliant."

The woman was a badass queen and he wouldn't change a damn thing about her.

Unable to resist the call of her irresistible mouth, he pressed his lips to hers. "As sexy as your independence is, I'd like to take care of you. Or at least help you take care of yourself. Will you let me?"

"As long as you aren't bossy about it." A playful smirk lit up her face and went straight to his dick. "Except in bed. We can both be bossy there."

God, he loved her honesty.

*Maybe I love her?*

The prospect didn't make him want to warn her he wasn't up for a long-term relationship—and run the other direction, just in case. Diving right in seemed like the best approach and completely natural.

He waggled his eyebrows at her and grinned. "Is that another invitation? Because I'm ready to say yes this time."

"Are you now?"

"I am. In fact, I'm willing to ask instead of waiting to be invited." Meeting her gaze, he focused on conveying his feelings for her in a single look. "May I share your bed tonight? I'd like to show you how much I missed you and thought about you over the last three years. I want to explore a partnership with you."

She rolled her eyes at him as she eased the bottle from their son's mouth. Then she lifted him to her shoulder. "If that was supposed to be a marriage proposal, you need to work on your delivery. It sounded like a business proposition."

Thrilled to have gotten a positive reaction out of her, he laughed. "You'll know if and when I ask you to marry me. I don't need a piece of paper to commit to you if you're opposed to getting married. We can do this whatever way is comfortable for us. For the time being, one step at a time is good. No rush."

"I'm holding you to those terms. Moving across the country, buying a house, and starting a new job on top of suddenly having the babies... I don't have the brain capacity to decide what I want from our relationship or how I want it to progress after all that's happened." Her words fit the bold woman who'd mesmerized him in California, but they didn't bite quite as hard as they once would have. Maybe the deepening twilight had softened them.

"I promise not to pressure you. We're both adapting to a lot of changes." Their daughter's eyelids drifted shut and the bottle slipped from her mouth, signaling what he hoped was bedtime. "Mia conked out. Is Marshall done?"

"Mm-hm." Cradling their son against her chest, she pushed to her feet. "Come on. We both need some stress relief in the master bedroom and a few uninterrupted hours of sleep."

With effort, he managed to keep his chuckle from becoming an all-out bark of laughter as he followed her toward the door. "Is that what we're going to say instead of sex when the kids are in listening range? Right behind you, Bear."

"Lock up please. Presumptuous, aren't you? Maybe I want a massage or a sparring match." She stopped at the sink and twisted the top off the empty bottle. The running water and one-handed washing gadget he'd ordered online yesterday didn't draw a peep from either twin.

He turned the deadbolt and locked the knob, never taking his eyes off the up-and-down motion of her hand as she moved it over the sudsy brush. "Hmm. Those sound like euphemisms for something much more fun and satisfying, although I won't argue with giving you a massage. I remember touching every inch of you."

"I remember it too, so hurry up with your half of cleanup." After propping the disassembled bottle in the drainer and drying her hand, she wiggled her ass on her way toward the foyer. "I'll meet you upstairs."

Two minutes later, he pulled the nursery door closed behind him and tried to tame his nerves as he walked into her space. Not much was different from the bedroom they'd shared in her townhouse the one night they spent together—same brightly colored accents against a pale gray background.

She lay stretched out on her stomach across the disheveled covers, her tank top and shorts no longer covering the body he wanted to intimately reacquaint himself with. Her dips and curves were a work of art, her breasts and hips a little fuller than before but still perfect. The defiant tilt of her chin suggested she wasn't as confident in her own skin as she used to be and expected him to point out what she considered faults.

He crossed to the bed and shed his clothes, determined to prove her worth. "It seems like I've waited forever to be with you again. You're so fucking beautiful and I want to be inside you."

Instead of rolling over and spreading her thighs, she raised her amazing ass in the air. "Condoms are in the nightstand drawer."

The combination of the position and a layer of latex between them rubbed him the wrong way. No way in hell would he let her put up those walls now.

*One step is better than a standoff. Compromise.*

He could handle not being face to face with her this time if she conceded on the condom. "I had a vasectomy after my brother told me the insemination was successful. Is it okay if we go without protection?"

The weight of the decision showed in the way she nibbled on her lower lip as she stared at him. "I'm not having any more children, even if I somehow get pregnant."

"It won't happen. I would never ask you to take that risk." Running his fingertips over her hips, he climbed onto the mattress and knelt behind her. She tensed beneath him, triggering more than a little doubt about taking this step. "If you're not ready, we can hold each other tonight. I missed that part just as much."

She nodded and relaxed into his touch. "I thought... It's too much too fast."

He guided her onto her side and curved around her, his hand at her waist and lips near her ear. The need to comfort her nearly over- whelmed him. "It's okay. We'll get there when we're ready."

She sniffled and pulled in a shaky breath, breaking his heart. "Thank you."

"You're—" The ringtone for his mother cut him off, and a surge of panic raced through him. "My mom. I need to answer."

# CHAPTER EIGHT

COMPUTER BAG CLUTCHED IN HER HAND, BERYL SCUTTLED DOWN THE stairs outside the biology building, prioritizing her to-do list. Spending an hour with Mia and Marshall came first, even if she had to combine it with a walk through the neighborhood to keep her butt in shape.

*Grade labs and quizzes.*

*Write one section of the new paper and send it to my collaborators.*

*Check and respond to emails.*

*Get over my damn self and let Archer give me an orgasm.*

*Have dinner with his parents.*

Thankfully, they'd arranged for a rental car so no one had to pick them up from the airport and suffer through an hour or more of awkward silence.

"Beryl, do you have a minute?"

Casting a glance over her shoulder, she slowed and smiled at Zinnia's mom, the woman who'd always treated her like a daughter rather than her daughter's friend. "It's good to see you, Dr. Needleman —Iris. A minute is about all I have these days."

"I can imagine. Let's walk and talk. It's what I do best." The older woman fell into step beside her. She seemed to take everything in stride, including the news Beryl had shared with her Monday morning after the stop in Carson's DNA lab. "I wanted to check on you. How are you adjusting to your new job and motherhood? Lots of changes all at once."

A laugh escaped. Luckily, it didn't sound too hysterical. "What an understatement. The babies are sleeping most of the night for now, thank god, and Archer has been pulling his weight and then some—even when he's starting a new business. So far, I'm keeping up with teaching, grading, and writing the paper I've been working on. Being able to recycle content from my previous position is helping a lot. Did Zin tell you Mia and Marshall's grandparents are coming for a visit?"

Dr. Needleman grinned as they turned toward the faculty parking lot. "Zinnia referred to them as your possible future in-laws when she mentioned they were flying in today and have open-ended plans. She says Archer looks at you like a man in love. But don't you let him rush you into anything, young lady."

"Rush? Hardly. We've been sleeping mostly naked together for going on a week and haven't had sex since our one-nighter three years ago. No petting. No nothing. A kiss now and then when we're not in bed. I think he owns stock in patience." Beryl sighed and ignored the filter that sometimes failed her. "Will I ever feel sexy again?"

Stopping in her tracks, Zin's mother pulled her into a tight hug. "Sweetheart, you've been through so much turmoil. Give yourself a break. The scars—physical and emotional—are part of having kids, living, and loving, even without the trauma you've experienced." Iris eased back and grabbed Beryl's hands. "Besides being gorgeous, you're strong, intelligent, and resilient. The life you've lived proves it. Remember who you are and let your feelings for Archer guide you. In this case, a little introspection is usually a good thing. If he's half as smart as you are, he'll wait as long as it takes for you to heal, and he'll help you get there."

Tears streaked down Beryl's face before the sting in her eyes registered. Trying not to blubber like a fool, she swallowed against the lump in her throat. "But I'm not good at feelings."

"Having so many of them at once doesn't mean you're not good at them. It means you're more sensitive than you thought you were.

There's nothing wrong with that." After a gentle squeeze of her fingers, Iris handed her a tissue. "Go home and take a few minutes for yourself and for the two of you before Archer's parents arrive. Tell him how you feel—about yourself, about him, about you as a couple. Maybe talk to a professional to work through the tough stuff. That's your honorary mom talking, not the dean and not your friend's mother."

Grateful for the sympathetic ear, Beryl nodded. "I hope Zinnia knows how lucky she is to have you. Thanks for talking me through the meltdown. I seem to need it a lot lately."

"You're doing great, and you're welcome to stop by the house or my office any time you need a reminder of it." Dr. Needleman pivoted toward the center of campus and back again. "Speaking of the house, James and I would love to have you to dinner sometime soon. And the babies and Archer, of course. He bought a cookbook at the library sale and is anxious to try out some new recipes. Let him know what day is good for you. Gotta go. Meeting in five minutes. Kiss Mia and Marshall for me."

The woman took off at her usual full-speed pace, waving at and greeting every person she saw as she headed toward the building that housed her office.

*Can I be like her when I grow up?*

Scoffing at the possibility, Beryl set off across the parking lot to her car. She would never have the temperament of a saint or the charisma to charm everyone from wealthy donors to mouthy undergrads who could've been a terrible influence on her only child.

As she exited the faculty lot, an incoming call from Archer popped up on her GPS screen. Her insides tingled and trembled, a sure sign he was far more than a one-time hookup and the biological father of her kids. She tapped the button on her steering wheel to connect. "Hi. I'm just leaving campus. Do you need me to go to the store on my way home?"

"I had groceries delivered this morning so you wouldn't have to stop. The babies are sleeping and my parents texted that they landed a few minutes ago and should make it to the hotel about five thirty. I was thinking we could sit on the swing and enjoy a few minutes' downtime in the sunshine before you start grading papers. M and M will probably nap until my mom and dad get here."

The tentative tone in his suggestion brought a wave of guilt. He'd been so damn patient with her.

She flipped on her turn signal and waited for several cars to pass while she repeated Iris's words in her head. "I'd like that. Give me five minutes to decompress and change clothes when I get there."

"Take ten if you need it." He sounded happier, less uncertain about how she might react to spending time with him. "See you soon, Bear. Safe drive home."

Instead of feeling the urge to fling a defensive comeback at him, she embraced the true meaning of his words—that he'd missed her and didn't want her to be involved in an accident. Maybe she didn't have to hide her insecurities from him.

*But can I let go of them?*

TEN MINUTES HAD PASSED A WHILE AGO, BUT ARCHER IGNORED THE clock on the microwave and rinsed another handful of blueberries. Something was going on with Beryl, but nagging her to confide in him would make her less likely to share whatever it was. His business strategy focused on the long game. She and their relationship deserved the same thought and consideration.

Footsteps on the stairs sent his heart thumping and his nerves jumping. In his entire thirty-nine years, he'd told three women he loved them—his mom and both his grandmothers. He'd never come close to falling in love prior to meeting Beryl Drechsler. Looking back to his brother's wedding weekend, the truth was clear. A one-night stand with the woman who'd gained and held his attention hadn't been all he had hoped for during their wedding-party dance. She'd owned his soul from the first second, and leaving the country had given him a convenient excuse to discount the obvious facts.

The instant she entered the kitchen, her presence touched him, soothing and caressing his wired nerves. "It's been forty minutes. My neck was stiff, so I stretched out on the bed to work the kinks out and accidentally fell asleep. I'm so sorry."

He picked up the dishtowel to dry his hands after adding the final handful to the bowl of fruit salad. "You have nothing to apologize for. Taking care of yourself is good. Ready to come outside and sit with me until M and M wake up?"

She nodded and reached for him, suggesting she might be ready for his declaration. "I have some things to tell you."

"Me too." The fit of her hand in his bigger one reinforced the decision to share his feelings with her. He led her outside and sat without relinquishing their connection. "Do you want to go first?"

"Yeah. Probably." Her fingers flexed, but she didn't pull away. "I don't know how to describe what I'm feeling, other than I've become very self-conscious about my body since the babies were born. Not just because of the stretch marks and Caesarean scar. My hormones and self-esteem feel out of whack, and I'm not the same woman I used to be. I don't feel sexy, even though I want you and I know you want me. I've tried, but I don't know how to become the old me again, at least sexually. I think I need to see a therapist."

He swallowed the immediate impulse to refute how she saw herself, to tell her she was perfect in his eyes. Only her opinion of herself mattered. "What can I do to help? Do you want me to go with you? Because, honestly, I'm feeling a little out of my depth with everything that's going on, but I want to be strong for you. I can help you research who's available in the area."

She leaned into him, the tension draining from her muscles where they touched. "That would be great. It's been a lot to deal with, and I'm grateful you're here. I don't know how I would've survived the last week without your help. Thank you for staying."

Her admission made him adore and respect her all the more. It also relieved some of the stress he'd been burying since Reggie's phone call. He brought their joined hands to his lips and kissed her knuckles. "I'm glad you agreed to let me stay. This may have been the hardest week of my life, but it's also been the best. Do you know why?"

"Because of the babies?" She glanced over at him with a slight frown. "It isn't because we're having sex."

He shook his head and hoped he put his feelings into the right words. "The kids are a bonus, just like our physical relationship will be. The best part has been spending it with you and seeing how well we work together as partners and parents. I don't have a problem with continuing to take things one step at a time, if that's what you need, but I want you to understand something very important. I love you. You— the woman who's been doing her best, in spite of how difficult the past year has been. I'm not going anywhere, whether we have sex tonight or six months from now. We'll get there. Together."

Tears welled in her eyes, making her brown eyes shine like the highlights glinting in her hair. One big drop spilled past her eyelashes and rolled along the side of her nose. "Okay. It's all a little over-whelming right now, so I really appreciate your patience. And for the record, I think I might love you too."

A swell of contentedness lightened his heart and soul, even though they still had obstacles to overcome. He tugged her onto his lap and wrapped his arms around her. "It's a good thing I know you wouldn't lie to spare my feelings."

"Of course not." She laughed against his ear as faint chimes and a peep in Marshall's tiny voice rang through both their phones. "The babies are awake, and your mom and dad must be here. Are we ready for this?"

"Absolutely, as long as we support each other." He lifted her to her feet, grasped her hand again, and walked with her through the kitchen and toward the front door. "Let's answer the door first since M and M are happy for the moment."

Her slow breath in and breathy exhale were her only signs of nervousness.

He hoped his worst-case-scenario visualizations didn't come true. However, he wasn't sure what to expect after the brief text exchange with his parents yesterday morning when they'd informed him they were flying out today. Why would they question his choice to walk away from the company business?

*They have to know I won't shirk my responsibilities to Mia and Marshall.*

As Beryl opened the door, he vowed not to jump to conclusions and judgments without a discussion.

His mom immediately stepped forward and pulled her into a brief hug. "It's good to see you again, Beryl. This house is just lovely. It suits you so well. How have you been? Do you like your new job? You're next, Archer."

Although he wanted to step into protector mode, Beryl seemed relaxed, so he stood his ground.

She moved aside and gestured for his parents to come into the foyer as more baby noises carried through the monitor app. "Thanks. It's good to see you too, Mrs. James. Mr. James. I'm still settling in, but I like it here."

A broad smile instantly replaced the fatigue on his father's face. "Call us Lorna and Phil. I'm glad to see you're doing well for yourself. Arch, I want to hear all about your stay in Tokyo. Our grandchildren. Is it okay if we see them?"

His mom nodded. "Yes. We had no idea Reggie planned to give them up. I realize the divorce has been hard on him, but I don't understand what prompted him to completely cut ties with his own flesh and blood."

Warning bells went off in Archer's gut, enough to stop him mid turn toward the stairs. "You do know he's not their biological father, right?"

Matching confused expressions twisted the knot in his stomach tighter. A second later, his mom's wide-eyed stare suggested the correct lightbulb had lit up in her mind.

# CHAPTER NINE

BEING THE QUEEN OF BLUNTNESS IN NO WAY PREPARED BERYL FOR THE tension swirling around the Jameses. Reggie had evidently decided to pass off the babies as his own rather than telling his parents that Archer had donated the sperm she'd been inseminated with.

*Just like Jen kept the truth from me. Or did he lie to her too?*

She slid her fingers through Archer's and squeezed, hoping the contact conveyed her support. "Why don't we go get the babies up from their nap? Phil and Lorna, would you like to come with us?"

Mrs. James' eager response eased some of the awkwardness. "We'd love to. I bet they've changed so much since we babysat before our anniversary getaway. I can't believe it's been almost three weeks. The boys grew so fast at that age."

Archer gave a curt nod. "They change every day."

Since avoidance of the revelation seemed to be working best for everyone, Beryl led the way upstairs and to the twins' bedroom. Marshall and his sister lay cuddled together, their favored position upon waking. They smiled up at her, triggering a fuzzy feeling in her heart.

She reached over the side rail to loosen Mia's curled fingers from her brother's hair. "Hi there. I missed you while I was at work."

Her daughter cooed and her son echoed the sweet hello.

Their grandparents moved closer to the crib, obviously far more attached to the babies than Reggie and Jen had ever been. Lorna sighed. "They look so happy. I don't understand why—"

An unfamiliar ringtone interrupted whatever she'd planned to say and caused her husband to frown. Phil pulled his cell phone from his pocket and tapped the screen twice. He opened his mouth, but the caller's voice came through the speaker before he spoke.

"Hey, Dad, what are you and Mom doing in Ohio? We were supposed to have dinner tonight."

Wearing a disapproving frown, Mr. James shook his head. "We're about to visit with our grandchildren at their mother's house."

"Oh." After a long pause, Reggie cleared his throat. "I sent Arch to make sure all the legalities were taken care of with Beryl. Are you still at the hotel? You haven't seen him, have you?"

Archer rolled his eyes. "I'm standing right here. We just started a discussion about how you're not actually—"

"What's the matter with you, brother? You haven't responded to my emails, I still need your final assessment of the Tokyo project, and I'm not accepting your resignation. Marcus's either." What sounded like a car door clunking shut carried through the phone and then doorbells chimed in stereo through the house and the speaker. "I'm at Beryl's house to talk to you, Arch. Are you on your way over?"

Beryl swallowed a growl and picked up Mia. Keeping her tone calm proved difficult after all he and Jen had put them through. "We're all here, Reggie, and you're not welcome."

A huffy exhale filled the quiet room. "Shit. Beryl, let me in. Please. I can explain."

"Watch your language, Reginald." The frown Mr. James aimed at his cell assured her the man was *not* pleased with his oldest son's actions. "Little ears, mixed company, and very disappointed parents. You have a lot more than explaining to do."

"You're right, Dad. Can I come in and talk to you?"

Only the calming presence of her daughter's tiny fingers in her hair kept Beryl from demanding the intruder leave. "Only if your parents feel like listening."

After several moments of muffled conversation, a different voice came through the line. "Beryl, it's Carson. I have the copies of the report you asked for. If now's a bad time, I can bring them by your office tomorrow morning."

"Now's fine." She kissed her daughter's cheek and handed the baby to Archer so she could text Zinnia's husband. *"Come to the patio door. Be there in a few minutes. And don't let the jerk on the front porch follow you."*

A thumbs-up popped up a few seconds later. *"The brother, right? You okay, Bee-bee?"*

*"Yep."* Since the word answered both questions, she set aside her phone and lifted Marshall to her shoulder. "The verdict, Phil? Lorna?"

A whole conversation seemed to pass in the look Mrs. James shared with her husband. Then she gave a curt nod. "This is Beryl's home, Reggie, and we won't disrespect her by going against her wishes. You've put her and this family in a very distressing situation. Your father and I will meet you on the sidewalk at the street."

"Okay. Thanks, Mom." Although Archer's brother sounded repentant, Beryl had no idea when she would be ready to forgive him, let alone forget what he'd done.

Mr. James tapped the screen again and stuffed the device in his pants pocket. "Do you mind if we say a quick hello to the twins before we head outside?"

WATCHING HIS PARENTS SMOTHER MIA AND MARSHALL WITH attention made a lump form in Archer's throat. He'd purposely kept his distance since the babies were born, not wanting to be the interloper among his brother's family and his mom and dad. None of his expectations of the situation matched reality, and his hopes had the potential to soar to startling heights—or crash to the ground.

Doubts had crept into his mind with Carson's carefully chosen words. What if the DNA profile showed he wasn't the twins' biological father? How could he trust anything Reggie said after his brother had kept secrets from their close-knit family?

Beryl rubbed back and forth across his lower back, distracting him from his worries for a few seconds. "We should head downstairs since Carson probably stopped on his way home from work. Daisy gets a wee bit upset when her daddy's late for supper."

He barely managed a nod, the possibility of a negative result still swirling in his thoughts.

After a quick swap of the babies, his mom and dad descended the stairs to the foyer with the family of his own he'd never planned on having. He brought up the rear, following Beryl when she turned toward the kitchen.

A few steps from the door to the patio, he hesitated. "Bear, I want you to know, no matter what the report says, I'm willing to raise M and M as my kids and partner with you in whatever way you need."

"Why would you—" Her eyebrows dipped into a deep vee and a frown curved her beautiful mouth downward. Then she blinked at him, clearly running every scenario through her mind. "Do you think Reggie used his sperm instead of yours and didn't tell anybody? Because it doesn't mean sh— Crap. I love you. The babies love you. You're a thousand-times-better father than he could ever aspire to be. And you know what? We're not reading the report, at least not until after we decide how we're moving forward as a couple. And, make no mistake, we *are* a couple. For the long haul."

Her confidence in their relationship sealed his fate—a future with her and their children.

He choked back the raw emotion filling his chest as he wrapped her in a one-armed hug. "I love you too. Will you think about us getting married?"

She raised an eyebrow and scrunched up her nose. "I *have* been thinking about it—since you showed up here a week ago wanting to share responsibilities and work toward marriage or a marriage-like commitment. I guess I should've proposed instead of trying to be subtle and encouraging."

The lack of pretense in her reaction didn't surprise him, but her solution did. "What if I want to ask you?"

"Too late." She used her free hand to cover his mouth. "Say you'll marry me, Archer. This weekend, so your mom and dad can be at the ceremony."

Unable to keep from grinning against the fingers at her demand, he let go of the uncertainties. "Mm-hm."

"Right answer." She smirked back at him as she replaced her fingers with a light brush of her lips. "Time to take care of this business with Carson. Oh! I bet he knows what we have to do to make sure everything's legal."

Pleasant tingles spread through his entire body at the touch. "Okay. Let's do this."

The only other sperm-donor dad he'd ever met greeted them with a nod when he opened the door. Although the large envelope drew his attention, Archer forced his gaze to the man's serious expression. "You look like you're delivering bad news."

Carson blinked and then shook his head. "Sorry. I was just remembering how anxious I was about finding out if I was Daisy's biological father. Getting the results of DNA analysis is a lot less stressful when you're only confirming what you already know. So, congratulations and thanks again for allowing me to use your samples for training my colleagues. Hey there, Marshall. Hi, Mia."

Relief tried to crowd out concern, but Archer forced it aside. "I have reason to believe my brother may have lied about the insemination. Is it possible for him to be Mia and Marshall's father and the DNA test to show that I am?"

A furrow formed in the taller man's forehead. "Offspring share roughly fifty percent of their DNA with their father, so determining paternity with brothers can be a little trickier. It would've been better to know it upfront and include his sample in the analysis, but we can do it after the fact if we need to. We'll look at blood types as a first step. I already have all of yours since my protocol is to always include it in the processing and report. Do you know your brother's?"

Archer swallowed to wet his dry throat. "Yes. We donated blood together during a company-wide drive a few years ago. I'm type B. He's AB."

Carson pulled the sheaf of papers from the envelope and shuffled through them like he knew exactly where to find what he needed. He stopped at the second to last sheet and ran his index finger down the page. "Beryl, you're O and the babies are both O. Reggie can't have fathered them. O and AB blood types can only produce A and B children. O and B parents produce O and B children."

The weight lifted from Archer's body, releasing far more tension and triggering far more elation than he would've thought possible. "I'm their biological father. They're our kids—Bear's and mine."

"That's a very reasonable conclusion, as there's well over a ninety-nine-point-nine percent probability." Carson punctuated his science-y statement with a chuckle while he returned the papers to the envelope. "Zinnia wants to know when you two are tying the knot so she can put it on her calendar. A foregone conclusion, she called it. Of course, I don't disagree."

Beryl sighed. "You had to ruin our news, didn't you? Mr. and Mrs. James don't even know yet. Keep Saturday and Sunday open until we work out the details."

Carson's belly laugh made Marshall jump. "Congratulations on your upcoming nuptials. I promise not to tell anyone but Zin."

"And I need a favor." She snagged the report and tucked it under her arm. "Tell me what we have to do to get married. We have to have a license, don't we? Where do we go to get one?"

Her enthusiasm calmed Archer in a way he never would've dreamed before he'd met her. His world had finally righted itself after three years of wishing for more with this amazing woman.

A ping sounded as Carson pulled his phone from the inside pocket of his sport coat. "Gotta go. I'll text you the link and the name of the officiant we had on my walk home."

His gaze shifted to the right of Archer at the same moment Beryl stepped backward toward the door. Her jaw tightened.

"Arch. Beryl." Reggie's voice scraped across Archer's last nerve. "I owe you both an apology."

# CHAPTER TEN

BERYL SLIPPED UNDER THE SHEET AND SCOOCHED TOWARD THE MIDDLE
of the bed to lay her leg over Archer's. The contact sparked a current
that zinged along her skin from the point of contact to every erogenous
zone in her body. Rather than acting on it like she had during their first
time together, with passionate kisses and an urgent need for sexual
connection, she rested her hand near his belly button. "You're not
obligated to forgive him. Apology or not, your brother violated your
trust and you get to decide if and when he's earned it back."

Her life experiences with family had taught her to hold back and
protect herself so she would never again be abandoned and forced to
live with strangers. After a lifetime of having reliable relatives, he had
to be struggling to understand the selfish reasons for his brother's
deceptions.

His warm lips touched her forehead, inciting more tingles. "I'm
definitely going to make him grovel for a while. I get that he didn't
want to be seen as less than perfect, but he lied to Jen and our parents
until he got caught. I can't blame her for leaving him, and Dad's plan
for atonement is pretty fitting."

She closed her eyes and breathed in his familiar scent—baby
wipes, baby wash, and new diapers with an underlying hint of soap and

his deodorant. "A temporary demotion to intern should remind him even a perfectionist is allowed to be human. I was thinking I might call Jen in a few days, after things settle down a bit. She didn't deserve to be shut down."

"No guilt. You did what you needed to do for you at the time." He draped his arm around her back and tugged her closer still. "The whole thing was a clusterfuck, but I don't regret reconnecting with you or being a father. Right place. Right time. Right everything."

"Almost." Levering up on her elbow, she nibbled a path from his pec to his neck, determined to give and take what she'd refused to consider three years ago. "I want to make love. Not a hookup. Not one night. Not great sex."

His teasing grin held so much love. "Sex will always be great between us."

"Okay, that last one didn't come out right, but I finally believe in my heart I can have more with you. You and the babies are the family I never thought I could have." She pushed to her knees and dragged her tank top over her head, certain he saw beyond her scars. Her pajama shorts followed her shirt over the side of the bed soon after. Instead of trying to hide from him, she straddled his hips and perched her fists on her hips. "Will you let me love you?"

"Always." He cradled her face in his palms and met her halfway for a barely there kiss. "Will you let me love you?"

"Yes." Her voice broke over the word, but she didn't pull away to fight the rush of emotion. She braced her palms on his chest and went back for another kiss, a deeper one that didn't trigger a flight response.

His tongue danced with hers in smooth and gentle sweeps, inspiring a different but no less potent passion than before. A soft groan vibrated through her jaw as his fingertips traced a path past her collarbone to the valley between her breasts. He explored every inch of her skin around her nipples, circling closer and closer without making contact with them, before moving to her ribs and her abdomen.

He eased his mouth from hers, making his rough breaths feather along her jaw. His soft lips and slightly scratchy day's worth of beard stubble heightened the sensations his fingers had created as he kissed his way to one of the puckered buds he'd neglected. He flicked his tongue across it, setting off an achy need in her clit. The instant she tried to grind herself against his abs, he grasped her hips, halting the movement. "Wouldn't you rather ride my face?"

Another wave of desire zipped along her nerve endings, causing a whimper to escape. She wiggled and bowed against him, hoping to reach the orgasm only a few strokes away. "Yes."

His eyes darkened as he guided her toward his mouth. "I can't wait to taste you."

Two pounding beats of her heart later, he cupped her breasts and licked along her folds. When his thumbs brushed the tips and his tongue arrived at her clit, the world shattered into a million bright sparks. Her muscles pulsed, making her feel truly alive.

Then she was flat on her back, with her future husband staring down at her. His entire focus seemed to be centered on her. "Are you still okay with this? We can stop any time."

"Don't you dare stop." She shoved his boxers past his ass and spread her thighs. "I need you, Archer."

"I need you too, Bear." He glided inside her, stretching and filling her until they were each other's beginning and end. "So perfect. You take my breath away. This is where I belong."

She nodded, awed by the connection that hadn't faded. If anything, it was stronger—strong enough to endure anything. "It is."

Every synchronized rock and sway carried her to new heights of pleasure, beyond where she'd gone with him before. Memories of their one night of sexual bliss dimmed as she jumped off the edge again, knowing he would always be beside her, catching her every time.

# THE NERD DOWNSTAIRS

## NERDS & BABIES #3

# CHAPTER ONE

"One Mississippi. Two Mississippi. Three Mississippi."

Right on cue, son number one joined his sister's demand for breakfast. Son number two would, no doubt, create a three-part harmony any second now.

"Okay, Mommy's almost done. I guess I'm skipping conditioner again this morning." Grabbing the towel from the hook, Henley Langston stepped out of the shower. Two and a half weeks had passed since she'd managed a complete shampoo, wash, and condition routine, but it was what it was. "I'm a mother. I wanted to be a mother. Triplets are a blessing."

*And I don't have any regrets.*

Her heart smarted, making its difference of opinion known. Their father had made his choice and she'd made hers. In their case, love hadn't been enough to overcome life's challenges.

Another hungry cry added to the stereophonic fussing coming through the monitor app on her phone.

She buried the persistent ache still echoing in her soul, like she had for the last fifteen months. "There's my patient one."

Tripp had been the third to arrive and seemed to take his minutes-older siblings' more assertive personalities in stride.

After drying the essential parts of her body, she twirled the towel around her hair, slapped on a quick swipe of deodorant under each arm, and grabbed her cell. The trio of little voices grew louder as she shrugged on her robe and passed the former living room—now the master bedroom slash nursery.

Halfway through prepping two bottles, her phone buzzed with a text alert against the kitchen counter, but she didn't bother to even glance at it. "If this is an emergency, please hang up and dial 9-1-1. Otherwise, you're going to have to wait. The doctor is currently busy."

Armed with formula for the boys, she paused for a deep breath at the doorway and then hurried into the communal bedroom. Three sets of big brown eyes turned toward her as their owners' lungs probably geared up for another round of hunger-driven cries. Thankfully, smiles appeared, brightening her Monday morning.

"Who's ready to celebrate being six months old?" She set both bottles on the changing table and scooped up Tripp from the double-wide crib. Since the babies had all awakened in the very early hours of morning, she chose to forego his diaper change until the crew was fed. A snuggle and a kiss on his pudgy cheek distracted her from the lingering heartache that continued to haunt her. "Let's get you set up in your bouncy seat so your brother and sister can eat too."

He tipped up the bottle she handed to him, freeing her to repeat the same procedure with Reid. By the time he was settled with his break-fast, Glynnis had rolled and shimmied her way to the railing. Her girl clearly planned to follow in her mother's footsteps of blazing her own path and to hell with the consequences.

"Up you go." Henley sat in the rocker facing her boys so Glyn could nurse. The lactation specialist's suggestion to implement a breastfeeding rotation schedule had been a godsend after a week that had consisted of alternating between feeding her children and grabbing cat naps. Laundry, cooking, and showering had fallen through the cracks until she'd hired her first part-time nanny. Unfortunately, the fifth one had quit last month, days before the fall semester started. Caring for triplets wasn't for the faint-hearted. Thankfully, three spots had been available at the daycare center on campus.

Her mind settled with the beautiful serenity of contented babies. "Here's the plan for today. Breakfast and then everybody gets dressed. I have assignments to grade this morning and classes to teach at eleven and two while you're at daycare. Reid, I'll drop by at twelve fifteen for you to nurse while two of the helpers feed Glyn and Tripp. At three thirty, we'll leave to go visit the grandparents and have supper with them. Do you want pears, peaches, or applesauce for dessert tonight? Okay, I'll bring all three since it's a special occasion. Tripp, you can nurse at suppertime while Grandma and Grandpa feed your sister and brother. It's supposed to be a nice day, so let's walk to campus today."

Glynnis stopped nursing long enough to smile—one that made her look so much like the daddy who'd chosen his job and a promotion over moving with Henley across the country.

"Maybe I'll tell him about you someday, but it still hurts too much." Their wedding plans had imploded after he'd suggested they take a break to cool off, like she was going to change her mind about accepting her dream faculty position and living closer to her aging parents. *Not after Dad's health scare.* She probably shouldn't have retaliated by having the last of their frozen embryos implanted before she left Seattle, but their other attempts at IVF had failed and destroying their last connection meant giving up all hope of love and motherhood. "I never expected it to work. Not that you're only a consolation. I won't ever regret having you. I just wish…"

She pushed away the impractical thought. Wishes rarely came true, and true love had proven unreliable at best and counterfeit at worst.

Determined to stay positive about the good things in her life and to ignore the disappointments, she hummed Beethoven's *Ode to Joy*. It had always been one of her favorites, and she'd chosen the classical collection she'd listened to during her pregnancy because of it. Her audience didn't seem to care that she couldn't carry a tune in a bucket.

Diaper and jammies-to-jumpsuit changes followed bottles and burps, a piece of toast and a glass of juice, and a quick comb-out with plenty of detangler. Fairly certain the chances of a spit-up or blow-out mishap were low, she finally swapped her robe for a button-down blouse and her last clean skirt.

As she picked up her phone to add laundry to her must-do list, the message she'd disregarded earlier popped up.

*"Good morning, Dr. Langston. I have a lead on a potential tenant for your upstairs apartment. New university employee. Hoping to schedule a showing this afternoon. Will let you know if/when the lease is signed."*

Considering she'd asked her real estate agent to handle renting out the second floor of the house barely a week ago, Henley wanted to cheer. *"Thank you so much for the update. The cleaning service was here on Friday, so move-in is immediate."*

Her phone buzzed in her hand before she could tuck it into her purse. *"Perfect!"*

Hopefully, the candidate would agree to the non-negotiable stipulations she'd insisted be written into the contract. Unless her renters enjoyed hearing babies cry at all hours of the day and night, they'd better adhere to her rules about quiet hours, no loud music, and no wild parties.

She finally laced up her tennis shoes, stowed her pumps in the storage pouch at the back of the stroller wagon, and loaded her precious cargo. "Would you look at that? We're ready on time. I think we're finally getting the hang of this."

As she maneuvered today's mode of transportation through the back door and down the ramp she'd had installed, she sang the birthday song.

She finished at the sidewalk. "…dear Glyn, Reid, and Tri-ipp. Happy birthday to you."

A howl came from across the street before she hit the final out-of-tune note.

$$\&$$

GARRETT WELLS COMPLETED THE LAST OF THE FORMS FROM THE Employee Benefits page links he'd received and clicked Submit. His new employer seemed far more organized and forward-thinking than his previous one, not that he would've stayed at his old job, even after he'd been cleared of the embezzlement charges. His predecessor's dodgy bookkeeping had also screwed over nearly half the staff under his command. Everything in Garrett's life had gone to hell when he'd decided to accept that damn promotion.

He pulled in a deep breath and slowly exhaled. Moving to Cradle Gorge, Ohio, and becoming the university's Grants and Contracts Director were the first two steps in fixing his biggest mistake.

Several quick raps on the door frame of his office brought his attention to the woman standing there. She'd been on the video call during his second-round remote interview. "Hello, Mr. Wells. I'm not interrupting, am I?"

*What was her name?*

*Needle-something. Iris Needleman. Dean of the College of Sciences and Humanities.*

He shook his head as he stood to greet her. "Dr. Needleman. Please come in. Just taking a break from filling out all the requisite paperwork."

Her chuckle put him at ease, and she reached across his desk to shake his hand. "I hope it doesn't send you running for the hills. We need someone with your expertise in charge of the G&C office. Do you have a few minutes?"

"Sure. Have a seat." He gestured to the chair opposite him and waited for her to sit. "What can I do for you?"

She smiled, looking far more approachable than he'd expected of an administrator. "First, I want to officially welcome you to campus. The search committee really appreciates how quickly you were able to start the position."

With a nod, he relaxed into his own chair. "Thanks. I'm glad to be here."

Her expression took on a more serious tone. "I would imagine you were anxious to move on after what happened in Seattle. Second, you and I will be working closely together since so many departments in my college rely heavily on external grants for financial support of their research. I want you to know you can communicate with me directly if you have questions as you're getting up to speed on disbursement of those funds. No need to go through my secretary."

He made a mental note to add her name to his go-to list. "That'll be very helpful. Knowing who to ask for clarification is usually half the challenge, especially in a new position."

"The other deans and I want to make the transition as smooth as possible." She snapped a business card onto his desk. "I also understand you're currently staying in a hotel since the timeline didn't allow you to find housing yet. A real estate agent I know and trust said she knows of an apartment that's available to rent when I mentioned a new hire. I believe it's ready to move in and thought you might want to take a look."

Considering the movers were supposed to arrive with his belongings later today, the timing couldn't be better. A storage unit had been his only option until now. "Thanks for the heads-up. I'll give her a call right away."

"Excellent." She popped out of her seat with another bright smile aimed his direction. "I'd better get back to my dean duties. Please let me know if you need anything. See you again soon."

He barely got out a thanks and a goodbye before she was out the door. Her energy made him feel like a slug, but she seemed like a decent person to work with.

The prospect of sleeping in his own bed drew his attention to the business card. Not willing to risk forgetting to contact the agent during his lunch break, he tapped the number into his cell phone.

"Hello, this is Fran Arbogast. Can I help you find your new home today?"

"I hope so, Ms. Arbogast. This is Garrett Wells. Dr. Needleman told me you know of an apartment for rent. If it's still available, I'd like to take a look at it as soon as possible." He slid the notepad and pen toward him from near the landline, in case she rattled off specifics about the place.

"Mr. Wells, it's so good to hear from you. Welcome to Cradle Gorge, and please call me Fran. Yes, Iris said you're new to the area and in need of a rental until you familiarize yourself with the town. It's the second floor of a century home. Bedroom, office or small second bedroom, one full bath, living room, kitchen. Stacked laundry in the pantry. Outside entry. Fresh paint throughout and the owner had it professionally cleaned last week, so it's all set for a tenant. Are you free around lunchtime for a tour? Or I have an opening after four."

Fairly certain he wouldn't find anything else available today without hours of research, he picked up the pen. "Twelve thirty works for me. What's the address? I can meet you there."

"Good, good." She recited the address. "It's just a few blocks from the north side of campus. Look for the light gray house with a peach front door and white trim. I'll have the lease with me if you decide to sign right away, and we can go over a couple of little details about quiet hours and such."

A warning shiver wiggled up his spine. "Is this a student rental? Because I'm not interested in—"

"Goodness, no! It's residential neighborhood made up almost entirely of single-family homes. The owner plans to return the house to its original layout at some point, but she isn't in a position to do so right now."

"Okay. I'll meet you there in about an hour." He crossed his fingers he wasn't being misled.

"Looking forward to it. Bye now."

He ended the call and opened his maps app. A quick check of the walking time to the address she'd shared advised him he had forty minutes to check his email and unpack a box or two.

The former took half an hour, and the box on the top of the stack was a painful reminder of his mistakes. Once he got settled, he needed to apologize for the worst one and see if he could right his wrongs. For now, the box stayed sealed.

At twelve fifteen, he shed his suitcoat and headed outside with his phone in hand. The mild late-September temperature and bright sunshine were a nice change from the Pacific Northwest. The leaves on the trees left rippling shadows on the sidewalk, clearing his mind as he exited the building that housed the Grants office.

Across the green space, a woman with dark brown hair caught his attention and sent his heart into a tailspin. Her quick and confident stride toward the steps of the student center buried him in regret. The similarities with his ex-fiancée ended there. Damn, she'd deserved so much better from him, especially after all they'd been through together.

He followed the other woman's progress until she disappeared behind the glass doors she entered. She wasn't the love he'd let go. Her hair flowed loose and wild to the middle of her back instead of landing at her shoulders and being tamed in a stylish cut. The stranger's curves were more pronounced, despite her thinner stature.

*God, I wish you were her.*

*I should've tried to find a compromise.*

*What's done is done. I'll find a way to win her back. Whatever it takes.*

The walk to his probable apartment didn't give him anywhere near enough time to come up with a plan, but the cross-country drive hadn't sparked any brilliant ideas, either, other than telling her the truth and begging for forgiveness.

He made the final turn from the directions on his phone and let his thoughts wander to the fantasy he'd created during his twenty-five-hundred-mile trek. Any of the houses on this street would work for his dream of marrying the love of his life and living happily-ever-after with her.

A silver sedan sat in the driveway leading behind the gray and peach house, and a tall gray-haired woman waved at him from beside it as he walked toward her. "Mr. Wells, it's a pleasure to meet you. Let's go take a look."

# CHAPTER TWO

HENLEY BRUSHED HER LIPS AGAINST REID'S CHEEK BEFORE SHE LAID him in the crib, savoring every moment she spent with each of her children. Her older son smiled up at her from the space he shared with his siblings. Beside him, Glyn kicked her tiny legs and Tripp yawned. "I'll be back at three thirty so we can go to Grandma and Grandpa's for a visit. I love you."

Leaving them hadn't gotten any easier, but she forced herself to walk to the check-in station to sign out. Then she hurried back to the physical and life sciences complex across the quad.

Her phone buzzed against her hip from inside her purse as she ascended the exterior stairs.

When she slid her cell from the outside pocket, Fran's name popped up. *"Lease is signed and your new tenant is moving in this afternoon!"*

She navigated to her messages, and another appeared.

*"Deposit and first month's rent are paid. I'll email copies of the paperwork as soon as I get to the office. Let me know if you have any questions."*

Grateful for having someone to manage the rental and for the passive income to put toward college savings, Henley stopped at the first-floor elevator to tap in a response. *"Thanks so much. I appreciate your help more than I can say. Hope you have a terrific day!"*

*"My pleasure. You too! Talk soon."*

A small amount of tension drained from her shoulders with that particular task done. "Only a million other things on my to-do list."

"You and me both." The woman who'd joined her at the elevator unnoticed grinned. "Hi. Beryl Drechsler. Chemistry. Judging by the dark circles and frazzled expression, I'm guessing sleep is at the top of the list."

Henley shrugged. "I have six-month-old triplets. I'm a realist, so a fifteen-minute power nap is about number twelve. Henley Langston. Physics."

The doors swished apart and her new acquaintance chuckled and gestured for her to enter. "I can totally relate. My twins are a little over three months old and starting to teethe. Which floor?"

"Four. Thanks. Teething is the worst." She caught a glimpse of her reflection in the stainless-steel walls and cringed. "I swear I combed my hair this morning."

Beryl's knowing laugh triggered the urge to hide. "I've decided that's the least of my worries. Want to meet for lunch sometime? And a friend and I get together once a week for mom's night out if you'd like to join us. Everybody deserves a break now and then."

The possibility of friendship deflated at the reminder she didn't have the kind of support system that allowed for casual adult socialization, especially since she refused to intrude on her parents' retirement freedom. "Single mom, and I've gone through five part-time nannies since the babies were born. The thought of attempting to find a babysitter for a night out? There's just no way. Lunch sounds great, though."

"Holy cow, woman. You need some downtime. Bring the kids and we'll make it a playdate instead. Seriously." Beryl dug a business card from her computer bag and handed it to Henley. "Email me this week. I mean it."

Biting her lower lip, Henley willed away the stinging in her eyes and nodded. Crying didn't solve anything, not even happy tears. She'd learned that lesson the hard way in the months following her breakup and during the early stages of pregnancy. Bawling certainly hadn't healed her heart when she'd held her special deliveries upon their arrival. She had always imagined sharing that amazing experience with their father.

Luckily, the doors whooshed open again, saving her from further conversation. She forced a smile at Beryl and stepped into the corridor. "Thank you."

"I'm coming to find you if I don't hear from you by Friday." The lighthearted warning colored Beryl's words, but sympathy and commiseration came across stronger.

The elevator doors slid shut, leaving Henley mostly alone in the hallway housing her department. She tucked the card in her purse as she passed the main office and continued to her own. Accepting the invitation would entail moving on with her life, acknowledging that the man she'd planned to marry wasn't going to suddenly contact her or show up. The piece of her heart he'd broken would stay that way and she would have to explain why he didn't participate in their children's upbringing.

Then the judgment would come.

How could she have had the last of their embryos implanted without telling him? How could she have had a successful procedure and not told him? How could she have delivered three babies with half his DNA and kept them from him?

She'd asked herself those same questions a hundred times, but her only answer was to point her finger at him.

What choice had he given her?

Coming in second place to his job had made her question whether he had ever loved her. Or maybe multiple unsuccessful IVF procedures were the real reason he'd chosen to stay in Seattle. For all she knew, he had met someone else and was married with a baby of his own by now.

She dropped into the chair behind her desk, wishing the thought hadn't carved another hole in her heart. "It doesn't matter, and I don't want to know."

The alarm on her phone sounded, alerting her to the thirty-minute countdown for her two o'clock class. She switched to professor mode and shoved her feelings into the box she hoped would someday stay closed forever.

❧

GARRETT BLINKED AT THE NUMBERS ON HIS CELL PHONE AND FLOPPED back on the mattress. Quiet hours evidently didn't apply to the first-floor residents since the only clear digit was a five—all the way to the left. A baby had been crying for at least the last six minutes and another had joined in about a minute ago.

As he rolled over to bury his head under the pillow, a different little wail merged in perfect harmony with the other two. Mrs. Arbogast had given him fair warning about the triplets living downstairs, but he hadn't expected a rude awakening not much more than half a day after he'd moved in.

Swallowing a groan, he pushed aside the covers and stumbled toward the bathroom. Partway there, a faint offkey rendition of "Mary Had a Little Lamb" carried through the fancy metal grate in the wall outside his bedroom. The woman could benefit from voice lessons, but the tearful trio had finally quieted.

His heart didn't, however. The out-of-tune song reminded him of the love of his life.

*Doesn't everything?*

*I'll find her and fix this. I have to.*

He turned on the shower and crossed his fingers for more consis-tent hot water than his hotel room. Steam escaped past the tiled wall a minute later, so he made a quick adjustment and stepped under the spray. The steady deluge massaging his back and shoulders blocked out the mother's singing and whatever noises came from below, but the best part was water pressure that flowed harder than a light spring rain.

*This is worth a few concessions, and I don't have to listen to people walk on the ceiling and bang their headboard on the wall at all hours of the night.*

After a leisurely wash, he took his time drying, trimming his beard and moustache, and getting dressed for the second day of his new job. The scent of brewing coffee greeted him as he entered his kitchen. It was as close to feeling like home since he'd packed up the remains of the house he'd shared with the woman who should've been his wife right now.

*At least I'm not living as far from her as I was last week.*

He typed her mom's name into the browser search bar on his phone as he sipped his coffee, determined to take the first step in contacting her. She hadn't gotten to the details of her offer before he'd interrupted her about his own job opportunity, inciting their relationship-ending argument. By the time he'd arrived home that evening, she had removed almost every sign of her presence from his house. Seeing her engagement ring on his nightstand had gutted him. If she could walk away from two and a half years together, their days had been numbered —in his self-righteous mind anyway.

God, he'd been stupid not to call her, go after her, find some way to repair the damage.

Now he had only the vaguest idea where she lived. Although her plan had been to move within easy visiting distance of her parents, that could mean she lived ten minutes away or an hour from Cradle Gorge and her family.

A news story about Rita Langston landed at the top of the search results, but it only stated the retired nursing professor still resided in the college town and was active in her community as of last fall. Her husband Frank had recently sold his flooring store, due to health issues. The article didn't mention their daughter Henley, and Garrett hadn't worked up the courage to scour the internet for information about her yet.

The possibility that she might've found someone else to make her happy set his stomach roiling and tumbling, and he pushed away from the counter to dig through the open moving box in the corner that contained cereals, pasta, and other nonperishables. He would need to venture out to a grocery store at some point today, but he couldn't put off his purpose for choosing this place much longer.

After several handfuls of dry Frosted Flakes, a granola bar, and the rest of his coffee, he brushed his teeth and sat at the desk in his home office to research the couple who should've been his in-laws by now. He'd liked them and they'd seemed to approve of him for their daughter, but their opinion of him had likely changed since the breakup.

*With good reason.*

A deep breath did little to calm his nerves as he braved a new search on his laptop. Dozens of entries filled the screen, but the most current at the top of the list sparked true hope after so many months of regret.

"She's here. I can't believe she's *here*."

Maybe he would be able to right his mistake without either of them having to sacrifice anything else. Thankfully, none of the results included a wedding announcement.

He clicked on the link for the Physics Department and scrolled past the header and several alphabetically organized faculty members to her picture. She looked the same as the photos he had on his phone, except her easy smile seemed forced.

His heart beat stronger than it had since the last time he'd awakened beside her.

"Please don't let it be too late."

He navigated to the campus map he'd bookmarked the day of the job offer two weeks ago. The building housing her department, as well as Chemistry and Earth Sciences, resided in the complex that included Biology, Genetics, and more life sciences on the opposite end. His office sat at the other side of the green space, approximately a quarter of a mile away.

The chances of eventually crossing paths with her were fairly high since the university wasn't large and her work in astrophysics depended on grants. Still, seeking her out seemed like a better choice than waiting for a random meeting—and the sooner, the better.

A glance at the time on the computer screen challenged his patience, but knocking on her office door at six thirty-five was pointless, even if she taught an eight-o'clock class on Tuesdays. Mornings had never been her favorite time of day.

*She loves the night sky.*

He created a new note on his phone, added her office information, and tapped in the things he wanted to say to her. "I love you" and "I'm sorry" tied for the top spot, though neither conveyed the depth of his feelings.

*"I've never stopped loving you. Can you forgive me for being an idiot?"*

That was definitely more accurate.

*"I can't change the things I said or the decision I made, but I regret them every day. You're always on my mind. Losing you still cuts as deep as it did at the beginning—and even deeper because it didn't have to happen. I was too stubborn to compromise, to apologize, to recognize that you were more important than any job. I felt threatened by your success, and that's all on me. You supported me and you deserved my support in return. I was stronger and better with you. I know I'm sorry isn't enough, so I'm willing to spend the rest of my life making up for letting you go and earning back your love and your trust."*

After saving the words he hoped to say to her in the very near future, he headed to his bedroom for his wallet, keys, and suitcoat. The framed picture on the dresser from the day he'd proposed to her drew his attention, as it always did. The happiness in her smile and her eyes was a reminder of his failure. With luck, he would finally repair the damage in the next few days.

# CHAPTER THREE

HENLEY SMILED DOWN AT HER CHILDREN AS SHE COLLAPSED THE three-seat stroller wagon and stowed it near their crib. "I love you. I'll see you at lunchtime. Be good for Mrs. Parker and her helpers."

Glynnis and Reid giggled while Tripp cooed a goodbye, tempting her to stay longer. Unfortunately, she had a meeting in twenty minutes.

After a reluctant wave, she hurried through signing out of the daycare center and headed across the quad to her office to change shoes and drop off her computer bag. A familiar face waited for the elevator. *Name, name, name. Mineral. Gemstone. Aha!* "Beryl, hi. Good to see you again."

The chemist's right eyebrow rose. "You haven't emailed me yet."

Henley scrunched up her nose and entered the elevator behind her colleague. "Sorry. I had labs to grade and a mountain of laundry to do yesterday. Thank god for work-from-home Tuesdays. Then I hit a wall after bath time and went to bed at eight with the babies."

"Smart move." Beryl grinned and offered a high five. "What's on your schedule for tomorrow? Besides the usual stuff."

"Thursday. I have class from ten to twelve." Some other important event niggled at Henley's brain. "Oh! We have an appointment for the babies' six-month-old pictures at four."

The doors eased open and Beryl stuck her arm out to stop Henley's exit. She rattled off an address and then repeated it. "Six o'clock. Supper at my house. No need to bring anything except yourself, your kids, and the diaper bag."

Fairly certain her new acquaintance would hunt her down if she didn't show up, Henley nodded as she stepped into the hallway. Two nights in less than a week of not having to cook for one person and clean up for four would be a mini vacation. "Okay. And thank you."

"You're welcome. See you tomorrow." Beryl gave a triumphant fist pump as the doors closed again.

Surrendering to a giddy smile, Henley shifted into work mode and set off for her office. Maybe she could make room in her busy life for friends after all—if they didn't ask too many questions.

After a quick swap of tennis shoes for pumps and her computer bag for the file on her desk, she retraced her steps out of the building. As she followed the sidewalk toward the building that housed the college dean's office, the Office of Academic Research, and the Grants and Contracts offices, steady footsteps sounded behind her.

"Dr. Langston!"

The cheery greeting relieved the stress of possibly arriving late to her meeting. She paused at the steps and turned to smile at the Dean. "Good morning, Dr. Needleman."

The older woman stopped, leaving several armlengths between them. "Good morning. Looks like we're both trying to beat the clock. Let's walk and talk instead of going inside since the sun is shining."

Glad for the more relaxed setting for their meeting, Henley closed the distance between them and matched Dr. Needleman's pace as she walked toward the far end of the green space. "It won't be long before winter and cold weather will be here."

"Your usual mode of transportation to campus might have to change. How are those adorable triplets? Is the daycare center working out for you?" The woman's questions came as no surprise. She always seemed to start off conversations by showing interest in faculty's personal lives and offering help when a problem arose. Her maternal approach had made the transition from new hire to unexpectedly pregnant to single mom a bit easier.

Henley nodded. "Mrs. Parker and the staff have been amazing with the babies. They're a handful, but I wouldn't trade them for the world. I can't believe they're six months old already. Your granddaughter is just a few months older, isn't she?"

The woman's smile widened. "They do grow up fast. Daisy's ten months old this week and such a daddy's girl. You've met her father, I think. My son-in-law. Carson Hines? Genetics?"

"I have." She racked her brain for where and when. Unfortunately, that information was lost in the haze of motherhood. "He's a visiting scholar, right?"

A moment of hesitation suggested otherwise. "Yes, he is, but he'll be staying for at least the spring semester too. Did you see the email about the fall picnic at my house in two weeks? Zinnia—my daughter—and Daisy will be there with Carson. Beryl Drechsler from Chemistry and her husband, Archer, are coming with their three-month-old twins. You'll have plenty of help with Glynnis, Reid, and Tripp."

The prospect of being the only single mother cast a shadow over any excitement related to actually socializing with grownups who weren't her parents. However, the invitation didn't seem like one she should decline. "I'm hoping to come."

"Terrific. Oh, and I also mentioned a new hire looking for a rental to Fran Arbogast on Monday. Did she get in touch with you?" Dr. Needleman followed the sidewalk past the Business building, still maintaining a steady pace. "I'm sure you've been anxious to find a tenant."

"Lease signed, sealed, and delivered Monday afternoon, although I haven't met him yet. It's on my to-do list for this weekend. I really appreciate your referral." Since they were nearly three-quarters of the way around the quad, she handed the file she carried to her companion. "Here are my notes and a rough draft of the abstract for the proposal I'm working on. The submission deadline is the second week of November."

"I'll take a look when I get back to my office and have feedback for you by the end of the day." Dr. Needleman smiled and waved to a group of students gathered outside the Fine Arts building. Did she know every person on campus? "I know how difficult balancing work and motherhood can be. I'm glad you're finding your way."

*What other choice have I had?*

"You've been very accommodating, and I appreciate it." As they closed in on her boss's destination, Henley prepared to turn toward the science complex. "More than I can ever express. Thank you."

"You're very welcome, Dr. Langston." Dean Needleman patted her arm and slowed near the entrance to the building. "I'd like to set up a meeting with my top researchers, the grant reviewers, and the new Grants and Contracts Director for early next week. Will Monday or Wednesday morning work for you?"

GARRETT'S STOMACH GROWLED AS HE GLANCED AT THE UPPER-RIGHT corner of his computer monitor.

*How can it be one already?*

The morning had flown by while he'd familiarized himself with the current external grants, including one whose principal investigator had been a major part of his life a year and a half ago. His mind had wandered for a solid twenty minutes before he'd regained his focus.

He pushed away from his desk and stood, stretching to ease the tension in his back and neck. A trip to the student center for lunch was a much better plan than going to Henley's office. He wouldn't disrupt her workday, despite his need to reconnect with her.

*I can survive until Friday afternoon.*

He probably shouldn't have used his administrative access to look up her class schedule, but dropping in on her at an inopportune time wouldn't gain him any points. The possibility that she might refuse to talk to him at all had poked at his hopes since the day he'd accepted a job offer more than halfway across the country.

Patting his pockets for his wallet, keys, and phone, he left his office and headed down the corridor to the elevator. At the last second, he continued to the stairway instead of pushing the down arrow on the wall. The extra exercise would do his brain and his body good.

Bright sunshine and a clear sky met him at the exit, instantly reenergizing him. The weather in Cradle Gorge sure beat the gloom and drizzle of his former home this time of year.

As he filled his lungs with fall air, a flash of dark pink snagged his attention at the far end of the science complex. The same woman with dark-brown hair he'd noticed on Monday hurried toward the double doors.

*Could that be her?*

Henley had often worn a skirt that same shade of pink, and she might've changed her hairstyle. He hadn't seen her in over a year after all.

Something shiny glinted on or in her left hand, sending his gut into a spiraling maelstrom. His heart tried to pound out of his chest, and dancing spots appeared in his vision. The urge to follow her hit hard, even though he'd resolved to wait.

*What if...*

What if the woman was Henley?

What if she'd fallen in love with someone else?

What if he was too late?

Then she was gone—inside, out of sight but not out of mind. She never left his thoughts.

He inhaled again and forced his leaden legs into motion. Jumping to conclusions wouldn't help or alter the situation. If she'd moved on, he would have to accept reality and do the same, no matter how impossible.

*For all I know, it wasn't even her.*

God, he hoped he hadn't screwed up his entire future with that single decision one year, two months, and twenty-seven days ago.

The weight of his regret pressed down harder with every step, testing him as much today as it had in the weeks after their breakup.

"Garrett? Garrett Wells?"

He jerked his attention to the present and came face to face with a bearded guy with a football-player build. Familiar blue eyes stared back at him. "Carson?"

"That's Dr. Hines to you, dude." His neighbor down the hall for two years of grad school grinned. They'd commiserated about their crappy apartments over burgers and beers at least once a week. "What are you doing in Ohio? I thought you were still crunching numbers out in Portland. No, Seattle. How have you been?"

Shoving his unpleasant mood aside, he shook the man's hand and ignored the last question. "I just moved here last week. New director of Grants and Contracts as of Monday. Weren't you in California?"

"Not anymore." Carson waved toward the entrance to the student center. "Do you have time for coffee and the whole story?"

Garrett sidestepped a group of students coming out of the door and then held it open. "About an hour. I was headed here to grab a sandwich or something. Late lunch."

"Sounds great." His old friend slipped his phone from his pocket as he walked through the first set of doors. He paused at the second set to tap on the screen. Then he headed inside and veered toward the selection of pre-made subs, wraps, and salads. His phone chimed halfway there. "Got plans for supper tomorrow? My wife and I are grilling with friends. Chemistry professor and her husband. Our kids."

Garrett snagged a turkey wrap, an apple, and a bottled water, doing his best to bury the sting of jealousy. "You? Married with kids? Not something I ever pictured. Double helixes were practically your life."

"One kid. A baby girl. Priorities change with the right circumstances." Hands full and looking like he'd decoded the origins of the human species, Hines strolled toward the checkout line. "How about you? Wife? Any little Garretts running around?"

A shake of his head was all Garrett could manage. He paid for his lunch and headed for an empty table in the corner, not that he had an appetite anymore. His plans had gone up in smoke with Henley's departure.

"Hey, sorry if I hit a sore spot." Carson sat across from him and spread out his lunch. "I just always pictured you as the guy with the perfect marriage, two point five kids, and a house in the suburbs. All that picket fence stuff. Rough divorce?"

Swallowing past the ache in his throat, Garrett willed his emotions into hiding. They didn't budge. "I was engaged last year. A promotion came up. I decided to accept it, but she had a job opportunity in a different part of the country. We argued, she left, and…" He shrugged and peeled the cellophane from his wrap. "Maybe because we'd been trying to get pregnant and not even IVF was working. We both wanted kids, and she was already over forty. Everything fell apart. The wedding plans. Our relationship. I didn't try to fix it. I let her go without a fight."

*I screwed up.*

"Ouch. Regrets suck." With his sandwich raised almost to his mouth, Carson furrowed his eyebrows. "You obviously still have feelings for her. It's not too late to try to make amends as long as you're both breathing."

"Easier said than done. What if she's with someone else now?" Putting his worst fear into words triggered more churning in his stomach.

"You won't know unless you talk to her. I know about guilt and making up for not doing the right thing. Want to hear about how I found out I was a dad?" The way his friend scratched at his beard and grimaced suggested it was a hell of a story.

Garrett gave a curt nod. "Sure."

A devious smirk slid across Carson's face. "Then you better say you're coming to the cookout tomorrow night."

# CHAPTER FOUR

*A HUNDRED ONE.*

No sooner did Henley remove the temporal thermometer from son number two's forehead than Reid let out a wail. She picked up Tripp and trudged to the kitchen. "Mommy's coming."

Their sister hadn't made a peep so far, but it was only a matter of time before she joined her feverish and fussy siblings' bout with the virus they'd probably picked up at daycare sometime over the last week.

A bleary-eyed glance at the microwave clock as she headed back to the communal bedroom told her the sun wouldn't rise for another five hours. She likely wouldn't get any sleep between now and then, either. At least she had a backup plan for her ten-o'clock lab. Their outing to Beryl Drechsler's for supper, on the other hand, was a no-go—as was their portrait session.

Son number one moved on to a gut-wrenching sob as she measured a dose of medicine in the dropper for Tripp. A quarter of it dribbled out of his mouth, down his chin, and into the folds of his neck.

"Darn it." She grabbed for the nearest burp cloth and wiped away as much as she could in a single swipe. "Let's sit you in your bouncy seat for a couple minutes so I can take care of your brother."

After she rushed to rinse the dropper, prep a small batch of formula, and hand off one of the three bottles she returned with, she crossed the dimly lit room to Reid in the swing. He quieted when she lifted him to her shoulder, but Glynnis chose that moment to wake and make her displeasure known.

"I need a clone. A pair would be even better." Hoping to comfort her daughter, Henley shuffled to the crib and rubbed Glyn's back through the slats. About eight seconds of silence passed before her efforts failed. "Mommy's right here. I guess I should've bought the twin carrier when I saw it. Hindsight and all that."

A heavy clunk sounded from Tripp's direction, pulling her attention into thirds. His bottle rolled back and forth on the floor and his adorable face scrunched up for another round of crying.

"This too shall pass. They're only little once. They grow up so fast." The age-old adages didn't console her sick children—or her. "Shall we try the recliner and some offkey ballads?"

Arranging three babies and herself in the chair wedged into the barely sufficient spot by the fireplace took several minutes. Then she hummed the opening strains of "Desperado" soft enough to avoid disturbing her tenant any more than she probably already had.

Her left arm tingled and pins prickled her right hand after "Imagine," "Bridge Over Troubled Water," and "Comfortably Numb," but her children had zonked out. She closed her eyes, savoring the peacefulness, even though it probably wouldn't last for long.

The synchronized breathing of the trio in her arms and on her chest lulled her deeper toward sleep. Their father appeared in her mind, his kind brown eyes and sweet smile welcoming her into dreamland. The shadowy stubble of his early morning pre-shaven jaw tickled her fingertips as she cradled his cheek and leaned in to kiss him. He wrapped his arms around her, bringing them skin to skin from head to toe under the covers.

His whisper against her lips still sparked a rush of endorphins. "I love you. Now and always."

"I—"

*Bang!*

A squeak escaped her throat as her eyes flew open and her heart hammered against her chest. Then three cries resumed, dragging her fully awake.

The floor above them creaked and a groan carried over the miserable sobs surrounding her. Heavy footsteps moved across the ceiling, assuring her the upstairs resident wasn't getting any more rest than anyone else in the house.

She focused on staying calm. Giving in to the tears the dream tried to trigger would only make her nose stuffy. Being a single mother of sick triplets was already difficult enough. "Mommy's here. Should we try some Joan Jett this time? Or would you prefer Kansas? Hm, maybe not. That might be too depressing. I can't hate myself for loving your daddy and everything crumbled to dust with him. I thought we were stronger than that, but I guess not. How about a show tune instead? Something from *Paint Your Wagon*? I watched it at least a dozen times with Grandma and Grandpa while I was growing up."

Reid's and Tripp's unhappy sounds tapered off, but Glyn continued fussing, a sure sign she'd succumbed to whatever germs had come home with them. The thermometer sat on the end table beside the chair, but a major shift would be required to reach it, pick it up, or use it.

Leaning forward, Henley touched her cheek to her daughter's forehead. "Feels like you decided to join the party. We're going to have to play musical chairs to get the medicine."

She shimmied her arm from around Tripp without waking him, but Reid frowned and whimpered with the first sign of movement. Any chance of an uneventful exchange hopeless, she freed her other arm and stood with Glyn.

The chorus of crying began again before she buckled the final victim of the latest illness into the swing. After securing the boys in the crib, she doled out another dose of acetaminophen. Thankfully, Glyn swallowed more of it than her brother had, but one suck from her bottle was evidently all she wanted. It narrowly missed landing on Henley's toes.

"Okay, we'll try your pacifier. It's still in the diaper bag. Back in a minute. I have to wash the dropper again and find the backup supply of pain reliever too." She slowly inhaled and exhaled on her errand to the kitchen, hoping to loosen the tightness in her neck and shoulders. The emergency stash of her mom's homemade truffles in the freezer called her name as she detoured toward the bathroom, but she nixed stopping for an emergency chocolate fix. Her bladder thanked her for taking advantage of the quick break, even though she would've preferred a truffle. "I can do this."

Tonight wasn't the first time she'd dealt with sick children on her own and it wouldn't be the last.

Fighting a yawn and seriously considering canceling his plans with Carson, Garrett trudged up the exterior staircase to his apartment. He needed a twelve-hour nap a lot more than he needed to eat. Of course, the minute he fell asleep, the triplets downstairs would undoubtedly start crying again.

A tiny stab of guilt poked at his conscience. He was partially to blame for the round of tears at three in the morning. It would certainly teach him not to let his obsession with reconnecting with Henley make him leave his gym bag on the foot of his bed. The heavy thunk had been loud enough to jar the neighbors awake when he accidentally kicked it in his restless fits of sleep.

He dug his keys from his pocket as he arrived at the landing by his door. A sheet of paper was taped above the doorknob. He unfolded it while he inserted the key in the lock. "God, if this is an eviction notice for—"

*"My apologies for last night's disturbances. The babies are sick and I tried everything to soothe them. They usually sleep 6-7 hours at night, so I promise it won't be a regular occurrence. Again, I'm sorry for any inconvenience we've caused."*

At least his landlord felt some remorse for his lack of sleep. If he crossed paths with her, he would offer his own apology for his contribution to the crying.

His phone buzzed against his thigh when he stepped inside. The message from Carson triggered a chuckle.

*"We're upgrading from greasy burgers and fries to filet mignon and baked potatoes. Casual attire since my daughter likes to play in the dirt. Don't be late!"*

He tapped in the only suitable response. *"Will be there in 20 minutes. Or less. :D"*

*"Come around to the back of the house when you get here."*

The promise of real food for the first time in over a week was incentive enough to revive him. A thumbs-up emoji sufficed while he swapped his suit and wingtips for shorts, a short-sleeved button-down shirt, and his hiking shoes.

Sixteen minutes later, he walked up the driveway of a pale-purple Victorian. Laughter, voices, and the aroma of grilling food drew him along the stone path leading around the side of the porch.

As he rounded the back corner, two women came out of a set of doors, each toting a baby. Before they took two steps, a guy rose from the bench at the edge of the patio and crossed to take the bundle from the blonde.

Garrett's chest squeezed from the unfulfilled dream he and Henley had shared—marriage and children.

"Hey, Garrett! Glad you could make it." Carson popped up from where he squatted near a little girl sitting in a turtle-shaped sandbox. He shoved out his hand and did the shake-to-man-hug thing. "How about we get introductions out of the way? My wife, Zinnia."

The blonde smiled and waved. "Nice to meet you, Garrett."

The brunette beside her adjusted her armload. "I'm Beryl and this is my husband, Archer. Welcome to Cradle Gorge. I hear you're the new director of the Grants and Contracts office. I'm sure we'll see each other around. I'm new Chemistry faculty. The twins are Mia and Marshall."

Carson ran his palm over the dark-haired girl's curls. "And this is my daughter, Daisy. Daisy, can you say hi to my friend Garrett?"

Bright blue eyes that matched her dad's met Garrett's, and she showed off several tiny teeth with a wide grin. Then she patted Carson's leg, opened and closed her cute fingers in the air, and returned her attention to the plastic shovel at her side. "Ba-ba. Ma-ma. Bee-bee. Ach-oo. Em-em. Wet."

His friend's belly laugh sparked giggles from his kid. "Sorry about that, Garrett, but you've been dubbed Wet by the ruler of names."

Despite the deep ache in his soul, Garrett chuckled. "I've been called worse. Good to meet everybody."

Carson kissed Daisy on the forehead and redirected the hand headed toward her face. "The sand goes in the bucket. Banana goes in the mouth."

"Bana!" She smacked the shovel on the gritty pile at her feet, sending sand flying every which way. "Bana!"

"Supper'll be ready soon." He scooped her up and brushed off her ruffly-bottomed shorts. "How about a ride in the swing? What can I get you to drink, Wells?"

"Wet." Daisy dove toward Garrett, her little arms outstretched. "Wet."

Panic mode hit, and he grabbed for her before she could fall. "Whoa! That was scary."

She pressed her fingers into his beard as her dad held onto her legs. "Wet."

Carson's left eyebrow rose. "Want to hold her? She likes beards."

"Um, yeah. Sure." Although his plans for fatherhood were probably shot to hell, he still liked children, so he lifted Daisy to his chest and braced his forearm under her bottom. "I bet you keep your mommy and daddy on their toes. Want to swing while he gets me something to drink? And he stills owes me a story about how he found out he was a dad."

Beryl snorted and handed off the other twin to Carson before turning toward the door. "It's far better than anything you can imagine. You'll never guess what happened in a million years. Iced tea, lemonade, water, milk, juice?"

"Iced tea, thanks." Intrigued by the teaser, he cast a glance at Zinnia. "You don't mind if he shares his epic adventure?"

The blonde's relaxed expression suggested it wasn't anywhere near as fascinating as her husband claimed it was. "No. It's actually a pretty amazing story. Of course, Beryl and Archer's saga is even more interesting."

The man in question swayed back and forth with the sleeping baby he held. His tight jaw hinted their journey to parenthood had been painful. "This is true, but it's more her story to tell than mine—if she wants to."

With the infant cradled against his chest, Carson rubbed circles on Mia's back. "I'll go first since theirs is an impossible act to follow. I made a one-time sperm donation when I was eighteen. Zinnia wanted a baby and chose my profile twenty years later. Daisy was born nine months later. Then I came to Cradle Gorge for a visiting scholar position last month, moved into her rental house, and fell in love with both of them. I accidentally discovered Daisy Mae has webbed toes like me, besides having the same eye and hair color. Hope and panic made me do a somewhat unethical DNA test with my new lab equipment, and we came back with a match. Luckily, my amazing wife forgave me for doing it without her permission. We're celebrating our one-month wedding anniversary on Friday, and I couldn't be happier."

"No way." Garrett weighed the odds of something like that happening and came up nearly empty-handed. A look at Zinnia confirmed the story. "That's crazy. I mean, what are the chances?"

Switching his son from his right arm to his left, Archer grinned. "One in something, because it's clearly possible."

His wife reappeared with a glass in one hand and a platter in the other. "Meat grilling time, Zin. Here's your tea, Garrett. Get ready for your jaw to hit the ground. I offered to be a surrogate for a close friend. My eggs. My uterus. Her husband's sperm via artificial insemination. Except it wasn't. The husband asked his brother to donate sperm for the procedure without telling the wife. Two babies and one divorce later, Arch and I became the legal parents of our twins."

Garrett slipped Daisy into the toddler swing hanging from a wooden A-frame and buckled her in as he sorted through the tangle of information. Thankfully, the baby released his beard without a fight. "So...let me get this straight. You're the biological mother of Mia and

Marshall. Archer is the biological father. And…you both thought you were doing a favor for his brother and sister-in-law, but she didn't know about the sperm donation. Neither did you, but Archer did. Obviously. But…you and Archer. You're married, right? Did you know each other before the whole fiasco? I'm having a hard time wrapping my brain around all of it."

The filets sizzled as the woman wielding the oven mitts and tongs transferred them to the hot grill. "It's pretty mind-boggling, isn't it? They met at his brother's wedding. Best man and maid of honor. Instant attraction and connection. But she wasn't interested in a serious relationship and he was leaving the country for work, so they went their separate ways. Fate knew better than they did."

He gave the swing a gentle push, inciting more giggles from Carson's daughter. The sound inspired a smile, even though his thoughts wandered through the memories of trying to conceive with Henley. "My fiancée and I—ex-fiancée—went through a year and a half of fertility treatments and IVF. That was difficult enough. Surrogacy…and then getting the babies back after giving them up and finding out they were Archer's. Wow. That had to be really tough."

Beryl nodded, sharing a look with her husband, who had draped a protective arm around her shoulders. "It was. But we're together now and working on dealing with the damage it caused. Did you split up because of the stress from the conception issues?"

Another surge of regret washed over him. "Not on my side. I chose a work promotion over her dream-job opportunity and a move across the country. Biggest mistake I've ever made, but I'm hoping to fix it."

She aimed a slightly judgmental glare at him. "I guess it's a good thing the other guest I invited couldn't make it. Sick kids. Not that I was trying to play matchmaker, but I wouldn't want Henley to think I was trying to set her up with you."

"Henley? *Kids*?" Nausea swelled in his gut and his vision blurred.

Beryl's voice sounded like she was talking into a cave. "Yeah. Triplets."

# CHAPTER FIVE

FEELING MORE LIKE A STUDENT THAN THE PROFESSOR, HENLEY counted down the minutes until her two-o'clock class was over. They crawled by as she waited for the last four people to finish their quizzes so she could go home for the weekend and catch up on her sleep. Roughly three hours in two days had caught up with her before her morning class.

Finally, the seats emptied one by one, leaving her to gather her laptop and head to her office.

While she walked, she tapped in a message to her mom. *"Done with class. Home in about half an hour. Any new symptoms? Have their temperatures gone down yet? Do I need to call the pediatrician?"*

God, she hoped they didn't need a trip to the doctor. Her energy level had fallen into the negative range at lunchtime.

Her phone buzzed at the same time she unlocked her office door.

*"All below 100 at 1:00. They're napping. Looks like the worst is over. Soup is cooking in the crockpot so you won't have to make supper. See you soon."*

Placing her laptop and the stack of quizzes on her desk, she dropped into the chair. *"Thank goodness! You're a lifesaver! Love you!"*

She may have gone overboard on the exclamation points, but recovering children and a ready-made meal were cause for celebration. The news gave her the boost she needed to retrieve her purse, pack her computer bag, and change into her tennis shoes so she could stagger down the corridor toward home. Then the elevator doors slid apart when she reached out to push the down button, adding another improvement to the end of a long week.

Fresh air and a mix of blue sky and fluffy clouds greeted her as she exited the building, and she paused for a deep breath with her face turned upward to the sunlight filtering through the trees.

"Am I their father?"

She jerked her gaze in the direction of the voice that haunted her dreams—waking and sleeping. The man seated on the bench at the bottom of the steps stared up at her. His brown eyes matched those of her former fiancé, but the facial hair was new. He flexed his fingers on the edge of the seat and huffed out a breath. More than anything, she wanted to rush into his arms to confirm that he was real, not some figment of her imagination.

"Are they mine? Ours?" He looked every bit as shellshocked as she felt.

Then his words registered.

*He knows about the babies. How?*

"Is that why you're here?" The question escaped before she could censor her thoughts, and disappointment roared through her body. Hope had ballooned without her permission at the sight of him, even though he hadn't tried to contact her since she'd moved out of his house.

"Yes. No. I don't know." He scrubbed his hands through his hair, exactly like he had whenever he felt out of his element for the two and a half years they'd been together. Shaking his head, he pushed to his feet. "Walk with me?"

Walking and talking had been his go-to method of clearing his head and organizing his thoughts. How many times had she accompanied him on a lap around their block while he hashed out whatever was on his mind?

*A few dozen? A hundred?*

She used the railing to steady herself as she descended the concrete stairs, too exhausted from life to run and too afraid of another rejection to outright agree to his request. "I need to go home."

"Okay. Lead the way." He fell into step beside her when she followed the sidewalk to the left and then to the right to take the shortcut across the quad. Silence reigned until they passed the student center. "I know about the triplets."

She nodded at his obvious statement and swallowed to ease the lump in her throat. "I planned to tell you."

"When?" The anguish and judgment in that single word stung.

Tears threatened, but she blinked them away. "I don't know."

A full block passed under their feet before he spoke again. "I'm their father then?"

Faced with finally telling him the truth or outright lying, she forced her focus to each seam in the sidewalk. "Yes. I had the last of our embryos implanted a few days before I left Seattle."

He showed no sign of responding, which seemed like the kind of judgment she'd always imagined.

Caught between wanting to be swallowed up by a blackhole and needing to fill the empty space with words, she chose the latter. "I was so devastated by your choice to stay. Maybe it doesn't justify what I did, but they were all I had left of you, and the reminder of that hurt too much. I wanted them gone if I couldn't have you. And the possibility of it actually working never entered my mind, not after all those failures. My body... I didn't expect..."

The steady footfalls beside her didn't slow or speed up, reminding her of the even keel he had always conveyed during their relationship —until the end. He'd been her rock-solid partner before their lone argument that had destroyed it all.

Another block came and went.

"It wasn't your fault. For whatever reasons, the IVF didn't take when we tried it. I'm sorry if I said or implied that you were to blame. You weren't." At the stop sign several doors down from her new home, he paused, looking left and right before he crossed the street. "Where are we going?"

She attributed his gruff tone to the secrets she'd kept from him. Only one atonement fit. She pointed to the third driveway from where they stood. "The gray house with peach and white trim. Would you like to meet them?"

He quickened his pace and shoved his hands through his hair again. "*Triplets*. God. They were... All week I thought about trying to contact you, and you were right under my feet. I don't believe this. I heard them...and you. Every night. More like early morning, I guess."

"I don't understand. Heard? What do you—" She nearly barreled into him when he stopped at the end of her drive.

He caught her, bringing her body to life for the few seconds before she righted herself and stepped away from him. With his mouth in a stern line and his eyebrows dipping low, he pointed toward the second-floor windows. "You're my landlord."

Her stomach wobbled and her brain fought to process the newest revelation. His dark mood made sense now. He probably hadn't gotten much more sleep than she had all week.

"I didn't know. I haven't had time to look at the documents Fran emailed me, and she signed as my representative." She managed to make her rubbery legs carry her up the paved walkway, along the side of the house, and through the gate into the backyard.

The kitchen door opened as she approached it, revealing her father and his only granddaughter. He looked past Henley and frowned. "Everything okay, Hen?"

Her voice abandoned her for several seconds, so she nodded and swallowed to wet her parched throat. *I owe him at least this much.* "I, uh... Garrett, you know my dad, and this is Glynnis. Our daughter."

GARRETT'S BREATH CAUGHT IN HIS LUNGS AND HIS HEART HAMMERED out a beat of at least a hundred miles an hour.

*Our daughter.*

*Glynnis.*

She blinked at him, her long dark lashes framing eyes the same color as his and her mother's. Wispy dark-brown curls curved around her delicate ears. As she smiled and ducked her head against her grandfather's chest, dimples formed in her cheeks. The curve of her lips was like looking in a mirror or leafing through the pictures in his baby book.

His initial reaction to Beryl's bombshell last night had been anger and disbelief, but it had given way to other emotions, along with the realization that he'd chosen to let Henley go. Part of searching her out was telling her all the feelings he'd typed into his phone only a few days ago.

Determined not to screw up this opportunity to reconnect, he extended his hand to the man who should've been his father-in-law. "It's good to see you again, Frank."

Mr. Langston held onto his guarded expression and gave a single shake before he moved his hand to Glynnis's back and gave a noncommittal grunt. Then he turned his attention toward his daughter. "I have a doctor's appointment at three fifteen, but I can reschedule if you need us to stay."

"It's fine, Dad." She leaned in to kiss their daughter's cheek. "How are you feeling, Glyn?"

The baby reached for Henley, wrapping her little fingers in her mother's hair.

"Mommy missed you too." She slid her computer bag off her shoulder and let Frank swap it for Glynnis. "Grandma says your temperature is almost back to normal. Let's go inside and see how your brothers are doing."

*Brothers. We have two sons and a daughter.*

The stinging sensation in his eyes that had struck upon seeing his child for the first time returned with a vengeance.

Henley walked into the house, looking back at him as she entered her kitchen. "You're welcome to come in."

He followed, even though his eyes were swimming and his muscles didn't want to cooperate. Biting the inside of his lower lip worked to keep his emotions in check, at least for now.

Mrs. Langston lifted the lid from the crockpot on the counter, but she stalled midair when her gaze landed on him. Then she looked toward the pair of babies in the double swing a few feet away. "Garrett? Wh—"

"Mom, it's okay." Stopping to give her mother a side hug, Henley whispered something he couldn't hear. "You and Dad should get going so you're on time for his appointment."

Mrs. Langston's curt nod made her seem anything but convinced, although he could hardly blame her for being protective. "If you're sure. I washed all the sheets and remade the beds this afternoon."

"Thanks. You're the best." After another quick hug, Henley continued to their sons. "And thanks for babysitting and supper. I'll call or text if I need anything."

After another nod, Mrs. Langston dropped a round of kisses on her grandchildren and then picked up her purse from the table. Her expression stated loud and clear that she didn't trust him as she neared the door.

Changing her mind probably wasn't even a remote possibility at the moment, so he forced a smile. "I hope to see you again soon, Rita."

Although the chill dissipated when the Langstons left, awkwardness and distance remained. He had a huge rift to mend.

"This is Reid. Second to arrive." Henley brushed her fingertips over the unruly thatch springing from the head of the baby on the left.

*My hair stood on end just like that when I was his age.*

Garrett tried to move closer, but his feet refused to budge and his mouth wouldn't form words.

Reid's nearly toothless grin turned into a giggle, and happiness glowed in his mother's smile. "We'll have a cuddle as soon as Mommy takes off her shoes."

*Can I hold them?*

"And Tripp. Last but never least." She let the baby on the right curl his fist around her finger and brought it to her lips. He cooed up at her, showing off a dimple in his cheek to match his sister's. "Mommy loves you too."

*My flesh and blood. The kids we tried to have when we were together.*

What if he'd moved with her? Would they have attempted IVF with the last of their embryos prior to leaving Seattle? Or had the procedure worked because he'd stayed and she'd gone?

In any case, he'd lost what he should've shared with her—celebrating the successful implantation, navigating the pregnancy, witnessing the birth, experiencing months of his children's existence.

*I don't even know when they were born.*

All that he'd missed ran unchecked over Garrett, stealing what little control he possessed. He slumped onto the closest chair and buried his face in his hands. The tears he'd staunched flowed freely, and his mistakes became a weight too heavy to bear.

He could've been part of his children's lives if he'd supported the woman he loved and made a small sacrifice to prove it. She wouldn't have had to introduce him to their kids, like the total stranger he was. They would be a family now.

A chair scraped across the floor, and her knees bumped into his. Fingers tangled in his hair, tugging on his sideburns. "Touch nicely, Glynnis. Gently please. We don't want to hurt Daddy."

*Daddy.*

Henley's soft words penetrated his soul-deep pain, tempting him to look at her, to drink in her presence before she disappeared. The kindness in her hesitant expression soothed some of his remorse, as did the pure innocence in their daughter's eyes, but the ache still occupied every inch of his soul. "She's beautiful, just like her mommy."

Henley grasped his hand and squeezed, a few stray tears streaking down her cheeks. "I'm so sorry I didn't tell you, Garrett. No matter the reasons, it doesn't excuse my actions. Or inaction. You deserved to know."

He couldn't argue that, but his transgression had put the entire situation in motion. "It's my fault. If I hadn't... If I could take back the things I said... I never should've accepted the promotion. You were more important."

"We both made choices. Things we can't change. It's done. We can only live with our mistakes and move on." Her soft voice hinted that she harbored as many regrets as he did, but her realistic slant also suggested she had no interest in resurrecting their relationship. "Would you like to hold Glyn while I get Reid and Tripp?"

Despite the emptiness her words brought, he swiped at the wetness on his face, determined to accept whatever terms she offered—for now. "She won't be uncomfortable since she doesn't know me?"

She shook her head. "She won't mind."

Glynnis reached toward him, inciting a brief moment of panic, but he tucked his hands under her arms and lifted her onto his lap. She smiled up at him with such trust that his doubts about her wanting to be held by a stranger vanished.

His heart melted. "Hello, Glynnis. It's great to meet you. I'm your daddy."

A faint blush crept up Henley's neck to her cheeks. "I've shown them pictures of you and sometimes I play an old message on my phone so they can hear your voice."

Maybe his wish for a reconciliation wasn't hopeless after all.

# CHAPTER SIX

WITH HER BACK TO GARRETT, HENLEY PRESSED HER PALM TO HER chest, but it did nothing to calm her galloping pulse. Sharing the same space with him after so many months apart reawakened the dreams she'd had in the earliest days after their breakup.

*He's here about the babies, even if he thinks he made the wrong decision. It's too late for us.*

She winced from the pain that realization sparked and covered it by bending over to untie her shoes and set them on the rug near the door. Forcing slow inhales and exhales, she crossed to the double swing and released the clip securing Reid in his seat. "Were you a sweet boy for Grandma and Grandpa? Of course, you were."

He raised his arms in the universal pick-me-up gesture and blew slobbery bubbles when she scooped him up.

"How old are they?" Garrett's quiet question sent her pulse skipping again.

She padded to the freezer for a teething ring, hoping to distract herself from the bewildering mix of emotions coursing through her veins. "Six months on Monday. Born March twenty-seventh. Your birthday. We were supposed to have pictures taken yesterday, but they were sick, so I've rescheduled for Tuesday afternoon. Do you want to go? You should have your picture taken with them. Oh, and I have extra copies of the hospital photos and every month since they were born. I saved them for you."

*Stop babbling.*

A stretch of silence enticed her to look at him. More than likely, he was wondering when she'd planned to give them to him since she didn't know when she would've told him he was a father.

*His distrust is justified, the same as mine.*

The chair creaked and Glyn cooed behind her as she handed Reid the teether.

"Thank you. For the pictures and for inviting me." His rough voice seemed to consist of fifteen months' worth of lost time and opportunities, adding to her guilt. "What time on Tuesday? I'll clear my schedule."

"Four o'clock." *My schedule. My landlord.* Her brain kicked into high gear, creating a dozen different reasons why he would've said those things. "How long will you be here?"

The question slipped out before she could stop it. She didn't need another disappointment, but knowing the length of his stay might prevent her from getting too attached.

"I—"

A half-hearted cry came from Glyn, signaling the fast approach of afternoon-feeding time.

"What's wrong? Do you think she's still sick?" He sounded panicked, completely out of his element, which shouldn't be surprising given his lack of experience with triplets. "She was happy a second ago."

"Dinnertime." She opened the pantry cabinet next to the fridge to retrieve the box of baby cereal and a jar of applesauce. "She isn't shy about letting everybody know when she's hungry. Are you ready for trial by fire?"

Footsteps warned her he'd stood and was moving toward her. "I'm willing to do whatever it takes to be a good father. What's first?"

*Breathe.*

She focused on gathering bowls and spoons instead of the goose bumps from his determination to be an involved parent and his prox-imity to her. "Step one is checking to see if a diaper change is neces-sary. If it's wet or messy, you'll need to take her to the changing table in the bedroom. All the supplies are on the lower shelf. She likes to kick her legs, so you have to make sure you get the diaper positioned correctly and snug enough."

"Checking. How do I do that?" He sounded no less resolute. "My friend Carson pulled the diaper away from his daughter's back and looked inside last night—after what his wife called the sniff test. I'm all ears if you have a better way."

"*Carson*? Carson Hines?" Reid scrunched up his nose in his usual precursor to crying at her shriller-than-normal tone, so she hugged him closer and swayed back and forth. "I'm sorry. Mommy didn't mean to scare you. All better? The geneticist who's a visiting scholar? That Carson Hines?"

"Yeah. We lived in the same apartment building during grad school. I saw him on campus yesterday and…" His long pause put her senses on high alert. "He invited me to his house for supper last night. His wife and daughter were there and another couple with their twins. A Chemistry professor."

He had to be talking about Beryl Drechsler. Not once in their lives had she ever been thankful for her children being sick, but they'd saved her from a very awkward situation this time.

*Oh.*

Was he hinting that he knew she was supposed to be a guest at their cookout? Or had Beryl unknowingly mentioned her name and the fact that her children were sick?

Remorse surged through her conscience again. She pressed a kiss to Reid's forehead and resumed her meal prep. "The babies and I were supposed to be there."

"I know." The feel of his presence vanished with more footsteps and his tone gave nothing away. "I'll go change Glynnis's diaper. Then Tripp's and Reid's. Where's their bedroom? Never mind. I'll find it."

Before she could analyze his short responses, he carried their daughter out of the kitchen.

Was he angry? Overwhelmed? Simply willing to help?

His behavior confused her, even if it wasn't unexpected. They had, however, always been so in tune with each other, rarely disagreeing and never outright arguing—except over their divergent career paths. That connection was gone now and she couldn't read his shuttered moods anymore.

Less than ten seconds later, he reappeared. His expression said it all. He'd discovered the communal bedroom where the living room should be.

She finished measuring a helping of cereal into the first bowl. "If you're planning to judge the layout of my house, keep it to yourself please. Three babies require a lot of time and attention. When they're sleeping through the night more regularly, we'll move into the bedrooms. For now, this is my life and I'm doing what works most efficiently."

Hating the defensiveness in her tone, she focused on preparing the next serving with one hand—the way she did most things at home.

The weight of his gaze grew heavier. "I wasn't going to... You could've asked me for help."

She spun around to face him, but she reined in the noisy part of her anger and hurt that wanted out to avoid scaring her children. "Like I asked you to come with me to Ohio? We both know how that turned out."

He flinched and opened his mouth like he had something to say. Then he closed it without speaking and headed back toward the living room she'd commandeered for baby central.

GARRETT KEPT ONE HAND ON HIS DAUGHTER'S BELLY AND SNAGGED A diaper from the shelf below. The crash course Carson had given him on baby care had come after his friend had talked him out of confronting Henley last night—definitely a good thing. The woman he'd known didn't have a snarky bone in her body, but she had clearly changed since their breakup.

*And it's my fault.*

An apology wasn't near enough to make amends—for either of them.

He muddled his way through the steps he'd learned, satisfied with the end result when he fastened the second tape. Glynnis didn't complain, so he counted it as a major win. "Let's see if we can put your pants on without twisting them in a knot."

She smiled at him and kicked her legs.

"Are you going to give me a hard time?" He wiggled his tie at her, hoping for a successful distraction. "You'll get to eat sooner if you cooperate. Plus, I still need to take care of your brothers' diaper changes. That's better. Almost done. What do you think? Not half bad, huh?"

Her cute little giggles hit him straight in the heart as he picked her up.

Pushing aside the reminder of how much he'd missed in six months, he returned to the kitchen and strapped her into the closest high chair. A toy was suction-cupped to the tray, so he twirled the brightly colored wheel at the top. "I'll be back in a few minutes."

Tripp still sat in the swing, obviously content to watch and wait for the moment, and Henley stood at the counter with a row of baby bottles. Reid grabbed for the pitcher in her hand.

Scooping him from her arm, Garrett steeled his feelings for another attack as he executed his escape plan. "Hi there, Reid. Daddy's here. Diaper time."

Wide eyes stared him up on the quick walk to the changing table, but his son didn't seem inclined to cry. A tiny frown formed when Garrett laid him down.

"You're a curious little guy, aren't you? I don't think Mommy would appreciate having a spill to clean up, so we need to find some-thing else to occupy your attention." He repeated his previous actions, taking care to keep things covered while he worked, as he'd been fore-warned by Beryl and Archer. "How about putting in a good word for me to your mom? I'd like to spend as much time with you and your brother and sister as I can. It doesn't seem like I stand a chance with her, but I'm not giving up yet."

Reid grinned, like he understood the assignment and agreed to be an accomplice.

"Deal." He picked up the older of his boys, still not quite believing he was the father of triplets. The what-ifs that had gone through his mind after Henley's departure asserted themselves again. What if one of their earlier IVF attempts had been successful? What if she'd declined the job offer here? What if she had stayed in Seattle with him? "The past can't be changed, but I can do my darnedest to fix it. The first step is proving I can be a good father and a reliable partner."

A sad cry carried from the kitchen, one that didn't sound like Glynnis. Henley's gentle voice followed up before he and Reid finished crossing the makeshift bedroom to the doorway to the kitchen. "You're hungry, aren't you? Mommy's almost done. Grandma texted me that you went for a walk with Grandpa this afternoon. Did you see the doggy across the street? She likes to bark, doesn't she? Woof-woof."

Garrett couldn't help but smile at her attempt to entertain their son. A deep breath as he re-entered the kitchen only partially fortified him to be in the same room with her again. He kissed the top of Reid's head and secured him in the high chair farthest from the table. "Almost there, Tripp. Gotta be sure your brother can't reach anything."

A huff of nearly silent laughter came from Henley's direction and he almost missed her murmured words. "Fast learner."

Glynnis smacked her palm on the tray and squealed as he passed, so he paused to smooth his hand over her curls. "Food's almost ready, Glynnis. A little patience goes a long way. Here I come, Tripp."

The serious look that greeted him told him everything he needed to know about his younger boy. This kid was an observer, always watching and hoping to avoid confrontation instead of creating it. He popped his index and middle fingers of his right hand into his mouth in the same way Garrett had as a baby.

He bent to unfasten the buckle to free Tripp, amazed by how each of his and Henley's kids possessed a different mix of their physical and personality traits. "I'm your daddy, and I'm so happy to meet you. You seem a little shy. Is it okay if I pick you up? We'll go get you a clean diaper so you'll be comfortable while you're eating. Does that sound okay?"

After a few more seconds of a stare-down, Tripp extended his left arm.

Taking the action as confirmation, Garrett lifted him from the seat and kissed his chubby cheek. Tripp rested his head on Garrett's shoulder as soon as he positioned his forearm under his son's bottom. "Not enough sleep last night? Me either."

The final diaper change moved along a bit faster than the first two, especially since the third recipient didn't wiggle or kick. Within a few minutes, he was fully dressed again and still looking up at Garrett like he hadn't decided if he approved of the man claiming to be his father.

"It's the beard, isn't it? Do you think I should shave it off? Maybe you'll recognize me then." He leaned down to let Tripp touch his facial hair if he wanted to. "It's sort of prickly today since I trimmed it this morning."

A hint of a smile curved his son's mouth, revealing the faint indentation of a dimple that matched his sister's. Then he reached upward until his fingers brushed the whiskers. The sweet laugh that followed made Garrett's heart swell, but he didn't dare move for fear of ending the memorable moment.

The rattle of what was probably his daughter banging on her tray made them both jump. "I bet your sister is going to be a handful when she gets older. Let's go see if your dinner is ready and I need to wash my hands."

Henley set a pair of bottles on the table next to a trio of bowls as he carried number three of three to the empty high chair. After he buckled in their son, she fastened a bib in place. "Thank you for changing their diapers. I can take it from here if you need to go."

Her belief that he would skip out on the hard work of taking care his children cut deep, but now wasn't the time to tackle that discussion. "Unless you don't want me to help, I'd like to stay."

# CHAPTER SEVEN

*I'D LIKE TO STAY.*

Henley tried and failed to keep her attention from straying to Garrett as he fed another bite of cereal and applesauce to their middle child. The concentration and then triumph when he successfully managed to hit his moving target and get most of the contents to stay in Reid's mouth announced loud and clear that he would've been a good father—not that she'd ever doubted it.

He hadn't, however, answered her question about how long he planned to stay. The month-to-month rent payment was probably a lot cheaper than staying in a hotel for a week or two if he figured in meals. The cost to her babies would be much higher. The longer he stayed, the more attached they would become.

*And what if he wants to share custody?*

Shipping Glyn, Reid, and Tripp more than halfway across the country for weeks or months at a time would destroy her. Of course, traveling with them to Seattle and seeing Garrett every day wouldn't do her heart any good, either.

*But how can I deny him contact with our children?*

A disgruntled cry pulled her from her wandering thoughts, and she offered her daughter another spoonful. As usual, Tripp waited patiently, his attention seemingly focused on his father.

Garrett moved the spoon from the orange dish toward their youngest triplet, rocking the sexy dad look with his tie loosened and his shirt sleeves rolled up to reveal his forearms. "Are you ready for more?"

Tripp's mouth opened, as did Garrett's.

Reid leaned forward with his arm outstretched, narrowly missing the spoon on its return to the bowl.

"Sorry, buddy, you ate all of yours already. You'll have to ask your mom about second helpings, but I think the answer might be no." His easy camaraderie with the boys sparked as much resentment as relief. He fed Tripp the last bite and set aside the spoon. "Cleanup before bottles?"

Henley nodded as she scooped the remains of her daughter's mouthful from her chin and tried again. "There are washcloths in the second drawer down next to the stove. The bottles are for Reid and Glyn. It's Tripp's turn to nurse."

"I hadn't thought about a rotating schedule. Makes sense. Breast-feeding all three at every meal sounds exhausting. Is it okay if I handle the bottle-feeding?" He carried the dishes to the sink and put them to soak before starting the fun task of wiping messy hands and faces.

*What are his expectations? To be able to just step right into a parenthood role?*

She stifled a frown at her unjustified pettiness, especially since his sudden appearance was more her fault than his. That discussion could wait until later. "Normally, I set up two with bottles in their bouncy seats and nurse the third, but you're welcome to help. They'll enjoy the extra cuddling."

With his back to her, he rinsed the washcloth, wrung it out, and refolded it. His muscles bunched and relaxed under his shirt, drawing her attention again. "I appreciate it. We should talk about...*things* once the kids are done and napping—or whatever they do when they're done eating. I have no idea what their schedule's like."

His lack of being in the loop amplified the guilt of not having told him about the conception, the pregnancy, and the birth. He might not have been willing to move for her, but he would go out of his way for their children. The truth of that particular realization reopened the wounds that had never healed.

She nodded since the pain radiating through her body refused to recede. No matter how long his stay in Cradle Gorge lasted, she owed him an opportunity to fully air his grievances against her and negotiate for restitution.

Two minutes later, she settled in the rocking chair, draped Tripp's favorite blanket over her shoulder, and bared her breast so he could latch on. Covering herself seemed strange, considering the intimacy of her past relationship with Garrett, but the layer also acted as a protective barrier around her feelings.

He sat in the recliner on the other side of her bed, Glyn cradled in his left arm and Reid nestled in his right. His wondrous expression as he held them cracked her heart into a million pieces all over again. They'd made so many plans for their future family, and all of it had vanished in minutes from a single decision.

She turned her cheek toward the blanket to wipe away the tear escaping from the outside corner of her eye. The loss hurt deeper than she could ever have imagined, even after so many months apart. She'd been too caught up in living moment to moment to really feel how broken she was without him.

The rare quiet should've calmed her, but her mind continued to spin.

How would she survive the next seventeen and a half years of co-parenting?

He deserved to know and raise the babies he'd helped create, but every time she saw him, she would lose more of herself.

The weight of his gaze lured her to glance his direction.

His eyebrows dipped low and his smile had been replaced by a concerned line. "Are you okay?"

She turned her focus back to Tripp and shrugged. "I don't know, but life goes on, doesn't it?"

"If you can call it living." He released a heavy sigh. "Mostly, I've been surviving since you left. Just barely. Everything fell apart."

"You got the promotion you'd been wanting." She managed to keep most of the resentment from her voice, but not all of it.

His snort said the job he'd chosen over her hadn't lived up to his expectations. "Among other things. Larry Johnson had been skimming money off some of the accounts and moving it around for the three years I was the assistant financial officer. He made it look like several of us in the office were the perpetrators so nobody would be the wiser when he retired. Then the discrepancies came to light a few months later and embezzlement charges were filed. It took another ten months to follow the trail and clear our names."

A new pang set her stomach churning. "Oh, wow. I'm sorry. That must've been difficult."

He nodded. "It was, and the doubts I had about my choice after you left proved I made a huge mistake. Unfortunately, by then, the person who mattered most to me was gone."

The satisfaction she might've gotten last year didn't materialize. As payback went, being falsely accused of embezzlement exceeded anything she would've considered appropriate punishment.

Tripp's gentle pat on her chest redirected her thoughts of justice and injustice to the present.

The blanket slipped away as she shifted him from one side to the other, and she caught Garrett's less than surreptitious stare toward her bared breast.

He didn't look away, reigniting the sexual fire she'd thought dead after the birth of their children.

NURSING WASN'T SUPPOSED TO BE A TURN-ON, BUT GARRETT COULDN'T tear his eyes from Henley's puckered nipples and fuller breasts. He'd always been a brains guy, even if he appreciated nice legs and a sweet smile. She had been the embodiment of everything he wanted in a woman from day one.

Now she represented so much more—physically, sexually, emotionally, maternally.

Her gaze dropped to their son as she re-situated him and covered herself with the blanket. "You didn't try to get in touch with me."

"I know it doesn't excuse staying silent, but my life was a mess by the time I realized how badly I'd screwed up. I was on paid leave during the investigation and spent most of my time talking to lawyers and investigators. When I wasn't being interrogated, I was doing all I could to prepare for the possibility of not being able to prove my innocence and that of the three others in the office who had targets on their backs. It wasn't fair to ask for your forgiveness while that craziness was going on." Residual panic and fear welled up in his gut, but he let his focus drift to the babies in his arms. "Between my state of mind and how slow the discovery process moved, I was in no shape to help or support you in any way if you'd told me you were pregnant. Honestly, I'm lucky I didn't end up in jail. Larry did a pretty thorough job of covering his tracks and putting ours there instead."

She finally looked up at him again. "Karma needs to do its thing to him for an exceptionally long time. How could he destroy other people's lives without any remorse? That's just plain evil. Are you working again now that you've been exonerated? I hope it's going well."

The impulse to keep his drastic changes under wraps for another day or two occurred to him and vanished in an instant. If he truly wanted a second chance with her, he had to tell her everything that had happened. "It is, but I have a new job. I needed to do something different and I couldn't see myself going back after what happened. A few weeks ago, I saw an advertisement for a university position— Director of Grants and Contracts. It sounded like a great opportunity in the perfect location, so I applied. The search committee conducted a remote interview shortly thereafter, and the offer came the next day. It required a big move in a bigger hurry, and I'm slowly getting settled in. I started on Monday. The biggest surprise was finding an apartment to rent above you, not that I knew it at the time."

Several seconds passed before her eyes widened. Her jaw dropped and rose twice before her mouth stayed shut. Evidently, he'd left her speechless.

A bottle landed near his feet on the rug, but he didn't take his eyes off of her. "It doesn't make up for my actions, but I really hope this means I've been given a chance to fix my mistakes. I'll grovel, beg, whatever it takes."

She looked away, like she wasn't quite ready to trust his words. "I'm glad to hear you were cleared of the embezzlement charges. You're welcome to stay until their bedtime if you want to. There's plenty of soup in the crockpot for both of us plus leftovers. We can talk about our schedules for the weekend so you can spend more time with the babies."

He tried not to let his disappointment show. Getting to know his children ranked almost as high as a reconciliation, now that he knew about them. Giving her the space to decide what she wanted from and with him, if anything, took precedence over everything else. "That means a lot to me. Thank you."

"You're welcome." Her lack of eye contact warned him not to push for a discussion of their relationship outside of sharing parenting responsibilities.

He had no choice but to accept her misgivings and hope that time and patience would rebuild what they'd lost.

Another bottle fell, this one into his lap, freeing Glynnis and Reid to carry on a conversation in a language of their own. As they made baby noises, they pedaled their little legs and wiggled against him. Soft coos and indecipherable babbling then joined them from the other side of the bed.

Thankful for the break in the tension creeping into his shoulders and neck, Garrett grinned down at the pair in his arms. "Do they talk to each other like this often? Beryl said her and Archer's twins hug and chatter a lot when they're in their crib or the stroller together."

"They just started being more vocal a few weeks ago, but they've always loved being close while they sleep, and Glyn and Reid are very protective of Tripp. They prefer when he's in the middle so they can both reach him." Rustling suggested their younger son had finished nursing and Henley was in the process of adjusting her clothing. "When the weather's nice, we usually go for a walk around the neighborhood when they're done eating. If you'd rather stay in and hang out in the playroom, that's okay too."

Was she afraid her neighbors would speculate if she was seen with him? Or was his imagination working overtime?

"Keeping to the regular schedule is fine, unless you're tired from last night's lack of sleep and you need some downtime. Whatever works for you works for me." Maybe shifting the decision back to her made him seem like a suck-up, but he wasn't here as her guest and she hadn't invited him back into her life beyond today. Even then, she probably only tolerated his presence for the sake of their kids.

She stood and hitched Tripp against her waist. "You're right. I'm too exhausted for a walk. They haven't been outside since Wednesday afternoon, so let's spread out a blanket in the backyard and they can play there."

"Sounds good." Analyzing the logistics of picking up the contents on his lap and retrieving the other from the floor while also holding two babies, he scooted forward in the recliner. Lifting his daughter to his shoulder, he managed to snag the empty bottle braced between his thighs.

"I have a free hand. I'll get the other one." She bent to pick it up before he rose with his armloads, putting her well within touching range.

Despite her being close enough to catch the familiar scent of her shampoo, he shoved down the temptation to inhale and move in closer still. "Once we're set up outside, I'll rinse the bottles."

Although he couldn't see her expression, the sudden stiffness in her jaw as she straightened said she didn't like his offer to help. "You don't have to do that. I can take care of it when we come in for supper."

Launching another standoff didn't appeal to him, but accepting his help would benefit them both. "You've been doing almost all of this by yourself for six months, so you've earned a break. We used to share household chores, and there's no reason to change that."

Her curt nod was a win in his book. "Okay. Thank you."

# CHAPTER EIGHT

THE GLOWING NUMBERS SWITCHED FOR THE FIFTH TIME SINCE HENLEY had rolled to face the clock on the nightstand, only ten minutes after she'd flopped the other direction.

*12:13am.*

Even as tired as she was, sleep eluded her. Closing her eyes brought back images of Garrett caring for and interacting with their children. He'd held them, fed them, talked to them, played with them, relished his newfound role. In turn, memories flooded her mind—the past imaginings of their perfect family. His ease stepping into the reality of being a father, once the initial shock had worn off, sparked so many doubts about not immediately telling him she'd made a final visit to the IVF clinic.

*Would he have left Seattle for our babies?*

The answer—yes—stung, because she didn't doubt it for a second. He would've had to return for the ridiculous charges, but it didn't change his reason for sacrificing his promotion. She surely wasn't it.

Tripp's soft cry distracted her from that pointless thought spiral. Glyn and Reid followed up seconds later, triggering the stinging sensation that signaled oncoming waterworks of her own. The bucketloads of tears she'd already cried over Garrett were enough to last the rest of her life.

She shoved away the covers and swung her feet to the floor, thankful for the nightlight in the hall that illuminated her slippers. Resigned to another night of no sleep, she grabbed her robe from the end of the bed and shrugged it on. "Mommy's here. It's not feeding time and you shouldn't need diaper changes yet. Your fevers didn't come back, did they?"

As his brother's and sister's cries grew louder, Tripp let out a wail that rivaled theirs.

"Something's definitely wrong." Giving up on the hope of a quick fix, she flicked on the lamp as she shuffled to the crib. A brief touch of her wrist to his forehead put to rest the fever assumption since his skin was only slightly warm. She frowned and picked him up, sifting through the long list of possible explanations. "What's going on? Do you have a tummy ache?"

He tangled his fingers in her hair, but his crying continued.

"What did I eat?" She alternately rubbed and patted his back as she tried to recall every crumb she'd eaten in the last twenty-four hours, which was nearly impossible with two more sobbing babies calling for her attention. "Grandma's vegetable soup. Did I eat toast or yogurt for breakfast? Lunch. I don't remember if I even ate lunch yesterday. No garlic or spicy peppers. Nothing out of the ordinary."

Another six minutes passed with a rendition of *Bohemian Rhapsody* and no stomach-related relief—gas, hunger, or messy diaper.

"Okay, let's try a teether." She swapped Tripp for Glyn and then trudged to the kitchen. Knocking made her heart nearly jump out of her chest as she closed the freezer.

The security light on the garage lit up half of a man's face on the other side of the door. A dark beard and moustache lined the lower half and mussed hair topped his head. Then muffled words carried through the glass. "It's me. Garrett. Are the babies okay? I can help if you want me to."

Their daughter instantly fell silent, sparking a fleeting moment of parental jealousy, but a happy baby eclipsed everything.

Henley unlocked the door and waved him inside. Lifting the teething ring to Glyn's mouth, she turned toward the communal bedroom. Instead of biting down on the cold teether, Glyn reached toward her father.

Moving closer, he pushed up the sleeves of his faded sweatshirt, one Henley recognized from their two and a half years together. It was his favorite, along with the equally age-worn sweatpants he wore. She'd given him the slippers on his feet for his birthday two months after she had moved in with him. Did he think of her when he wore them?

*Can my feelings get any more complicated?*

Handing off their oldest-by-minutes child, Henley sighed. "Sorry about the disruption again. I'm not sure what's wrong tonight. No fevers. No gassy bellies. No wet or poopy diapers. Not teething pain. Not hungry. Sometimes they just need to cry, I guess."

He lifted their daughter to his shoulder and she immediately laid down her head. "It's okay. I couldn't sleep anyway. What's going on, Glynnis? You and your brothers are supposed to be sleeping."

The boys quieted at the sound of his voice, bringing on another twinge in Henley's gut.

She led him into the bedroom, determined not to take the slight personally. Her children had evidently missed their other parent after he'd gone upstairs to his apartment for the night. Who would've thought they would bond with him so quickly?

Not sure how to handle the situation, she walked to the crib and scooped up Reid. He leaned toward Garrett, making her current obsolescence clear. "Make yourself comfortable in the recliner. We have triplets who decided they didn't get enough of Daddy tonight. Would you like something to drink? Tea? Water?"

He shook his head, but it didn't hide the stubborn set of his jaw she knew well from their time together. "My hands are going to be too full to hold anything but babies, and you should get all the sleep you can instead of waiting on me. Seriously, I still can't wrap my head around you taking care of them by yourself for six months. And working. Who's taking care of you?"

She handed off Reid, shrugged, and returned to the crib for Tripp. "I stayed with my mom and dad for the first couple weeks, and they're on call if I need them. Like today, I mean yesterday, when the kids were sick and I had classes. We eat supper at their house once or twice a week and they stop over here at least that often."

With his arms cradling the two older siblings, he glanced toward the recliner and back at her. "Does Tripp go on my lap or my chest?"

"I can hold him. He seems satisfied that you're in the room." She forced her legs to carry her to the only other truly comfortable place to sit—her bed. "Besides, you might be able to get some rest if you're not trying to holding him too."

"I might close my eyes, but there's no way I'll let myself fall asleep and risk dropping Glynnis and Reid." He stalked toward her, the gears in his brain working on an alternate solution, if his expression was anything to go by. "What if we put them between us in your bed? You on this side to keep them from rolling out and I'll trap them in on the other side."

*Sleep in the same bed with him?*

The suggestion seemed like a slippery slope she should avoid, but temptation and a shortage of sleep proved too strong for her to refuse his proposition. "Fine. Let's get everybody settled and I'll turn off the light."

The relief in his faint smile set off alarm bells in her head, but he didn't say a word. Instead, he rounded the end of her bed, carefully placed Glyn and Reid in the middle of the mattress, and climbed in beside them.

After she settled Tripp between his brother and sister, she switched off the lamp and snuggled under the covers. Surprisingly, the tension left her body, giving way to rightness and familiarity—a carryover from missing the man she'd loved and planned to grow old with.

Truth be told, her feelings hadn't changed, in spite of her efforts to purge them.

The gentle brush of his fingertips on her cheek set fire to her long-dormant libido and then his whisper wormed its way into her soul. "Sweet dreams."

❧

FIGHTING HIS INTERNAL ALARM CLOCK, GARRETT EXHALED, FOCUSED on the dream playing out in his head, and slipped into the edge of unconsciousness. Henley fit against him as he curved around her from behind, rocking his hips slowly back and forth as he savored the smooth rhythm and being inside her. Her breathy moans encouraged him to guide her leg over his hip and send his fingers in search of the magical spot that would send her over the edge into bliss.

A gasp accompanied the descent of his hand past her belly button and through the tight curls marking his destination. Her inner thigh trembled when he eased his middle finger into her slick folds. The first pass yielded her swollen clit, and he skated circles over it with her wetness, reveling in the new sounds she made.

In the next breath, she cried out and arched against him, surrendering to the most beautiful orgasm he'd ever witnessed. His balls tightened a second later, and heat rushed up his length as he joined her in the exquisite pleasure of being connected—both physically and emotionally.

The lazy return to his body was cut short by the woman in his cocoon suddenly sitting straight up in bed and whacking him in the cheekbone with a flying elbow. He rolled away, holding his arm over his eye to prevent another mishap.

"Oh my god! We were having sex! I thought I was dreaming and…" She dropped her face to her hands and groaned—not the sexy kind, either. "I shouldn't have put the babies back in the crib, but they were sound asleep. And so were you. I can't believe we… This was such a mistake. Oh my god, were you—"

"No, it wasn't. Being with you has never been and will never be a mistake." He ran his fingertips along his cheek to check for bleeding and winced at the stab of pain from the light pressure. At least he hadn't discovered a cut. A black eye was still a possibility, though. "And it wasn't sex for the sake of getting off. It was making love, just like it always was. I love you, Henley. I will *always* love you."

She whipped her head toward him, her eyes narrowed and locked on his. His proclamation had obviously gained her full attention. "Then why did you choose to stay in Seattle? You let me leave without asking me to stay, and the only reason you're here now is because you found out you're a father."

"I—"

"I really need you to go." Tears welled in her eyes, breaking his heart into more pieces than her words. "Have your lawyer contact me about custody and visitation. I promise not to keep you from seeing our children."

Shock, frustration, and disbelief whirled in his stomach as he dug through the tangled sheets and blankets for his sweatpants. He found them at the foot of the bed and stood to pull them on over his wilting but still wet dick. How the hell had he taken off his pants without being aware of the fact?

She lowered her forehead to her drawn-up knees as he faced her, shutting herself off from him, not willing to talk to him or let him explain what he'd been feeling the day she'd decided to move out without telling him. He could cut her some slack for her reaction to their wake-up call, but kicking him out for saying he loved her and throwing all the blame on him for their split was harsh.

Beyond her, movement in the crib caught his eye. A trio of bright smiles greeted him, but the joy of being with his children got lost in the grief of Henley ordering him out of her life. His wish for a second chance with her had been a fantasy, having no real shot at happening.

Unable to simply go, he padded to the crib and picked up his daughter. "Good morning, Glynnis. It's your turn to nurse, isn't it? How about a diaper change first?"

He kept his gaze focused on Glyn, even though the weight of her mother's stare tempted him to glance at her. The baby kicked her legs and blew slobber bubbles as he unfastened her pajamas and went through the motions of his task. Her little hands patted his beard when he lifted her into his arms again.

After a quick kiss on her forehead, he carried her to the bed he'd shared with his lost love and laid her beside Henley. Without a word, he moved on to taking care of his sons and then going to the kitchen to prepare their breakfast while they waited in their swing.

Soft murmurs came from the bedroom, and he tried his best to block out her voice as he tightened the second ring. With no idea when she might let him spend time with her and their kids again, he opted to hold both of his boys while they ate, like he had yesterday with Glynnis and Reid.

The logistics of lifting them both from their swings and handing them their bottles took a bit of thought, but he finally sat at the table with a baby in each arm. His face ached, and stiffness told him the area around his cheekbone was swollen, although nothing hurt as badly as his shattered heart. "Your mommy packs a mean elbow jab, even if was probably an accident. I need to google how to reduce the bruising and inflammation from a black eye. Not sure if the steak thing actually works. Geez, Carson's going to have a field day when we meet for lunch on Monday."

Reid grinned around his mouthful for several seconds before going back to drinking his liquid nourishment.

"What am I supposed to do, guys? I fell in love with her the day I met her, and nothing's changed. She's right, though. I didn't ask her to stay. I'm ashamed to say it, but my ego took a big hit when she said she was offered her dream position without so much as an interview. She got a call out of the blue for a job in her hometown and I'd been waiting more than four years for that promotion. I don't know. Maybe I didn't go after her because of that. Like I didn't feel good enough for her." The admission triggered another surge of regret. "She's smart, you know. A lot smarter than I am. I didn't have a clue my boss was doctoring the books and making me the scapegoat. Seems like fair payback for the way I treated her."

The prospect of sharing custody instead of his life with her sobered him into silence while Tripp and Reid finished their breakfast. No solutions popped into his head, leaving him at a loss once again.

When he returned to the bedroom for a quick goodbye, she stood at the front window with Glynnis. He kissed both boys on the cheek and sat them side by side in the crib. As much as he longed to hold his daughter before he left, he didn't move any closer. "I'll be back to help at lunchtime."

A curt nod was all the acknowledgment he got, sending him through the kitchen and out the back door.

# CHAPTER NINE

THE CURSOR BLINKED AT HENLEY FOR ROUGHLY THE THOUSANDTH time, while her mind repeated the same part of the one-sided conversation she'd overheard this morning. Not once in the last fifteen months had she considered that Garrett's pride could've been a casualty of her job offer or that he'd been jealous of her success.

Neither jobs nor money had ever been a point of contention between them. They'd shared household expenses in the three-bedroom ranch his grandmother had left him in her will, never arguing about who paid for what or who had the bigger paycheck. Communication and openness had ruled their relationship until she'd gotten the email and then the phone call from her future employer. Sleeping on the offer without telling him right away and discussing it had contributed to their demise. Guilt still lived in her conscience for excluding him, even temporarily.

She jumped at the sudden email notification that flashed in the corner of the monitor screen. Beryl Drechsler's name appeared in the box, giving her an excuse to avoid thinking about the far more unsettling event from this morning.

*Unsettling. What an understatement. Orgasmic. Satisfying. Yeah, that's more like it.*

The message was short—"Call me ASAP."—and included a phone number.

Afternoon naptime would last at least another fifteen minutes, so an interruption was unlikely and her ruminations needed to end. Thinking about waking up with Garrett buried deep inside her was pointless and sexually frustrating, especially when he'd maintained a physical and emotional distance from her since her freak-out.

She tapped in the number as she crossed her makeshift office in the smaller downstairs bedroom to close the door.

Beryl picked up on the first ring. "Hello."

"Hi, it's Henley. Is everything okay? Your email sounded urgent." Pacing to the window, Henley caught sight of her tenant mowing the yard. She stepped to the side when he looked toward the house.

Despite her request that he leave, he'd shown up showered and wearing clean clothes at eleven thirty to change diapers and handle the lunch bottle brigade, bruised cheekbone and all. He'd also taken it upon himself to cross several small maintenance tasks off her to-do list on the fridge, the stubborn man. He used to hate making waves and detouring from the path they set together, but that had obviously changed.

"I haven't heard from you since you told me the babies were sick. Just checking in to see how they're feeling. And you. How are you doing?" The hesitant tone of her question sent up a warning flag. Had Garrett mentioned his possible link to Glyn, Reid, and Tripp during Thursday evening's cookout?

*My brain is too tired for this.*

She returned to her desk and sank into the chair. "They're feeling much better. Thanks. I'm wishing the weekend had an extra day or two so I could catch up on my rest, but the world doesn't stop moving. You have to know what a rare commodity sleep is."

"You aren't kidding, although I imagine having a parenting partner makes a big difference. Archer definitely pulls his weight. Anyway, do you have plans for this afternoon?"

An outing meant the chance to escape for an hour or two before the expected drop-in at the next mealtime. "I'm hoping to take a walk when naptime is over. We could all use a change of scenery."

"Good. You live close to campus, don't you? I've seen you walking through the neighborhood on the north side with your stroller wagon, which is really cool by the way. I need to get one of those for Mia and Marshall."

Henley's gaze strayed to the window again, but she swiveled her chair toward the closed door to put a lid on her ridiculous hormones. "I'm about two and a half blocks from the Fine Arts building. Transporting triplets is a challenge, so the wagon is more convenient than driving most days."

"I bet. I'm about four blocks or so east of you. Want to come to my house for a playdate? My friend Zinnia and her daughter will be here about one thirty, but feel free to come later if you need to. We'll be here all afternoon. Just moms and kids. Our husbands are going to help Zin's dad assemble a playhouse in the backyard for when he babysits Daisy."

*Zinnia. Daisy. Why do I recognize those names?*

*Ah, Dr. Needleman's daughter and granddaughter.*

The opportunity to get out of the house and away from the temptation to throw caution to the wind made the decision simple. "I'd like that. Can you text me your address?"

"Awesome. Sending you a message now. It's the lavender Victorian."

"Thanks. And thanks for the invitation. See you soon." A smile snuck up on her as she ended the call and closed her laptop.

After an uninterrupted shower, diaper and diaper bag checks, and an all-clear peek outside, she rolled the loaded wagon toward the sidewalk and crossed her fingers the directions on her phone didn't lead her astray. "This is going too smoothly. I hope it isn't a bad sign."

Tripp looked up at her from his backward-facing seat and stuffed his fingers in his mouth.

"I wish finding comfort was that easy as an adult." She followed the sidewalk, trying to enjoy the early fall sunshine and the rustle of the leaves. Unfortunately, the soft sighs from the trees reminded her too much of lying in Garrett's arms. She'd always loved their lazy Saturday and Sunday mornings.

After several blocks, she took a right onto Beryl's street. The lavender Victorian stood out among the more traditional blue, gray, and tan houses, its purple and white trim making it look like it belonged in a storybook.

The front door opened as she guided the stroller along the walkway to the wide porch. Beryl hurried down the steps, a blonde woman with glasses right behind her. "I'm so glad you were able to come. Henley, this is Zinnia Trimble-Hines. Carson Hines the geneticist is her husband, and Dr. Needleman is her mom. Zin, Henley Langston from the Physics Department."

"Nice to meet you, Henley." Zinnia smiled and then glanced toward the triplets. "Do you want us to help with the munchkins?"

Henley pressed her hand to her belly, hoping the butterflies settled down soon. Her playdate companions didn't act like they knew about her connection to Garrett, but the truth had to be common knowledge since Zinnia's husband was a friend of her children's father. "Good to meet you too. If you two can carry Glynnis and Reid, I can hold Tripp and collapse the stroller. It'll be easier to move it to the porch that way."

"Leave the stroller. Archer or Carson can take care of it as they're leaving." Without a second's hesitation, Beryl unbelted Glyn and wiggled her fingers at her, earning her a wide grin. "Look at you! You're going to keep your mommy on her toes when you start walking, but you're so darn cute she won't be able to stay mad when you get into trouble. Come to Bee-bee. That's what Daisy calls me."

Glyn reached for Beryl and kicked her feet, showing off her usual outgoing personality.

Not to be outdone by his sister, Reid raised his arms beside her.

Zinnia rescued him from the other side. "Hi there. Are you Reid? That hair is so adorable."

No sooner did Henley lift Tripp out of his seat than the football player-sized visiting scholar, Carson Hines, stepped onto the porch. His gaze locked on hers as he descended the stairs, staying longer than was comfortable. He was obviously judging her for keeping secrets from his old friend, not that she could blame him.

*Life is about choices. Garrett may have moved here when he found out I had the embryos implanted, but I would've told him eventually.*

She had to look away when Carson stopped a few feet from her. "Thanks for helping with the wagon."

His eyebrows dipped lower and he frowned. "Garrett told me what happened between you in Seattle. When Beryl mentioned your name and the fact that your kids were sick the other night, I had to talk him down from confronting you right then. He had no idea about the triplets. Is he their dad? If he is, have you told him?"

*He didn't know?*

Her equilibrium pitched and swayed from that revelation. She pulled in a shuddering breath to ward off a sudden bout of lightheadedness. "I… Yes, he is. I told him."

Carson's expression didn't budge.

The scenario that had run through her mind during Beryl's first invitation had come true. The questions and judgment were exactly as she'd imagined, kicking her flight response into overdrive. "I just remembered something I have to do. Sorry to bail again, Beryl, but I need to go."

"Carson, stop it. Look at Glynnis and tell me she isn't the spitting image of Garrett." Beryl inserted herself between them. "Henley, ignore him. He's being overprotective. Zin and I want you to stay."

Still frowning, he seemed to study her daughter's face. "Common traits. The only way to know for sure is a DNA analysis. Garrett was too worked up to consider a paternity test when he found out about them the other night, but I'm recommending it when I talk to him later."

Disbelief surged through Henley's veins at the man's audacity. She turned her back to him and buckled Tripp back into the wagon. "Don't bother. We'll stop by your lab Monday morning so you can collect your samples and process them. Then you can apologize for being a jerk when the test shows Garrett's their father. Beryl, Zinnia, would you mind putting Reid and Glyn in their seats? I'm not in the mood to socialize anymore."

ॐ

A DOOR CLUNKED SHUT SOMEWHERE BELOW GARRETT, BUT HE frowned at his phone instead of checking to see if Henley had returned from her walk with the kids. The message he'd missed from Carson while he'd been staring at the framed photo on his dresser caught him completely off-guard.

*"You should have a paternity test done. I'll do it free of charge. Not admissible in court, but it's a starting point. Come to my lab by 8 Monday morning. Blood or saliva sample works. I have lancets and swabs. Results in about 10 hours."*

He barely reined in the urge to blow up his friend's phone with a chorus of WTFs. Instead, he tried for the rational approach. *"What reason would she have to lie to me? Especially when she isn't the one who told me about our children. Back the hell off."*

His finger hovered over the Send button for several seconds, even though shooting the messenger wasn't his style. He deleted all but the first sentence.

The question popped into a bubble in the conversation and bouncing dots immediately appeared in a new one. They disappeared, reappeared, and disappeared again.

Then his phone vibrated in his hand. The screen lit up with Carson's name. He waffled between answering with the part of the text he'd deleted and letting the call go to voicemail.

A second name flashed above the first one, and he tapped the icon to answer it. "Henley, is everything okay?"

Her defeated sigh tore at his insides. "I'm taking the babies to Dr. Hines' lab Monday morning for a paternity test since everybody seems to think I lied about who their father is. I've also contacted my lawyer about drawing up a custody agreement. You're already on their birth certificates, so that should save some time. Their next feeding is at four, if you'd like to help. As I said before, I won't stop you from spending time with them."

"Did Carson call you? Damn him. I believed you. I still do. You're a terrible liar and you would never do that to me. God, how did we even get here? I'm coming downstairs right now so we can talk. Okay?" He hoped like hell she agreed, because they couldn't go on like this.

Her silence stretched on too long. "Okay."

"Thank you. I'll be there in less than a minute." He forced a slow breath as he ended the call and ignored the voicemail alert on the screen. Outside advice had no place in this discussion.

He stuffed his phone in his jeans pocket and slipped on his jogging shoes. When he reached for his keys, the envelope containing her engagement ring caught his partially blackened eye. Rather than second-guessing his gut, he grabbed that too. It might persuade her to trust that she had been his sole reason for moving to Cradle Gorge.

As promised, he stood outside her kitchen roughly half a minute later. The contraption she'd used for a walk with their kids was parked in the freshly cut grass, confirming they hadn't been home for long.

Her cautious expression when she opened the door and gestured for him to enter made his chest hurt. "Hi. The babies are playing in the crib."

He stepped into the space where he'd met Glynnis, Reid, and Tripp. Moving the closest chair toward the one a quarter of the way around the table, he waited for her to close the door. "I'm here to see you, not them. Let's sit and talk. Just the two of us."

She gave a curt nod and sat with her hands tightly clasped in her lap. "It's okay if you want proof."

Shaking his head, he sank into the seat opposite her. "I trust you. You said I'm their father, so it's the truth. If we need a paternity test for legal reasons, fine, but I'm really hoping it doesn't come to that. *You're* the reason I'm here. The kids are a bonus. If I hadn't put two and two together when Beryl said you were supposed to be at the cookout but your kids were sick, I know you would've—"

"Carson said you didn't know about them. I should've told you."

Her forehead scrunched up like it did when she was deep into a physics conundrum.

"No, I didn't, but I also get why you chose not to tell me. My stupid ego got in the way when you wanted me to move here with you. That's something I'll always regret." He covered her hands with his and gently squeezed. "To be clear, I applied for this job because I wanted a chance to fix my mistake. I accepted it because this is your hometown and I knew you were somewhere close. Whether or not we would ever have children never crossed my mind during that drive from Seattle. It was you I wanted. I still do. And I meant every word I said this morning. I love you, Henley. I will *always* love you."

Her chin trembled and wetness pooled in her eyes. "I love you too."

Relief rushed through him, giving him more hope than he'd felt since the moment she'd said yes to his proposal almost two years ago. "Hearing you say those words again makes me incredibly happy. Can we finally talk about the future? Our future."

The hurt, the sadness, the hesitation faded from her expression as she nodded.

He dug the envelope out of his front pocket, untangled her hands, and dumped the contents into her palm. Then he slid the ring onto her finger. "This belongs to you. Will you marry me? As soon as humanly possible? No waiting this time."

"You kept it." Tears spilled past her lashes as she wrapped her arms around his neck and crawled onto his lap. "Yes, I'll marry you. I've missed you so much."

Holding her close, he did his best to convey the joy pumping through his veins in a kiss that felt like coming home and falling in love with her all over again. Each slow glide of her tongue against his wiped away the pain and regrets he'd lived with for fifteen months, relegating them to the past where they belonged. Passion and devotion filled the empty spaces they'd left in his heart and soul. He was whole again.

She eased back, her breathing as ragged as his. "Stay tonight. I want to wake up next to you. And I promise not to elbow you again."

An easy smile slid across his face, triggering a twinge in his bruised cheekbone. "Every night for the next fifty or sixty years. You're never getting rid of me."

She brushed her lips over the sore spot. "I'm never letting you go."

Faint voices carried from the bedroom, with giggles and a happy squeal mixed in.

"Good." He threaded his fingers into her hair as he nibbled a path to her ear, loving the freedom to touch her. "Sounds like they're having a party. We have a lot to celebrate. Maybe we should join them."

"In a few minutes." She guided his mouth back to hers for another breath-stealing kiss, the kind that promised forever.

# CHAPTER TEN

A FLOOD OF RELIEF, JOY, AND LOVE COURSED THROUGH HENLEY'S veins as Garrett tightened his hold on her and deepened their kiss. The last fifteen months of heartache faded away with his arms around her, and the connection she'd thought long gone flared to new life. It was every bit as strong as it had been before he'd chosen to stay in Seattle for his promotion and her new job had taken her across the country. The rash decision to have the last of their embryos implanted on her way out of town had deepened their bond instead of ending it.

He eased back a fraction of an inch, his rough breathing matching her own. "Finally."

"Finally." Not bothering to fight a smile, she kissed him again. "Do you—"

Knocking sounded at the back door and a trio of louder babbles and squeals came from the other direction.

Garrett sighed as he touched his forehead against hers. "I need to get used to lots of interruptions."

"Mm-hm." She touched her lips to his beard, testing the feel of it on her skin. The thought of it brushing her inner thighs sparked anticipatory ripples in her lower belly. "We're definitely continuing this later. I'll see who's at the door if you go check on the babies."

"We also need to talk about squeezing in a trip to the courthouse for a license and a wedding between classes, meetings, and feedings on Monday." He helped her off his lap, but his hand lingered at her waist when he stood. "Our journey has been hard, but I don't think I'd change any of it if I could. I'm right where I want to be now."

Her emotions welled up in her heart, preventing her from responding. A nod and another quick kiss were all she could manage before they headed in opposite directions.

The stern expression on the man standing on her doorstep tried to chase away the good feelings, but she refused to give Carson Hines that power. What more could he have to say after telling Garrett he should insist on a paternity test?

She locked an equally steady stare on him and waited for the geneticist to speak.

Following a full ten seconds of silence, he cleared his throat. "I owe you an apology. You have absolutely no reason to lie about Garrett being your triplets' father, and I should've given you the benefit of the doubt. I thought I was protecting a friend when I offered to run a DNA analysis on him and the kids. Being an expert witness a few dozen times has jaded me, but it's still no excuse. He trusts you. That's good enough for me. I was a jerk, like you said, and I'm sorry."

Stunned by her visitor's admission of guilt, she blinked at him. "You believe me then?"

"Yes." Not a trace of dishonesty showed on his face, and his voice sounded sincere.

"Okay. I accept your apology." Giggles carried to her from the bedroom, but she kept most of her attention on Carson.

"Thank you." He glanced over her shoulder, evidently hearing Reid's and Tripp's contagious laughter. When Glynnis joined her brothers' fun with a happy garble of chatter, Carson cracked a smile. "Is Garrett here so I can apologize to him too?"

She gestured for him to enter. "Come on in. He's checking on the babies."

Garrett toted Tripp on one arm and Glyn on the other into the kitchen as their guest stepped inside. Without slowing, he headed toward the line of high chairs. "What are you doing here, Carson?"

"I was out of line. I came to apologize. To both of you. I'm sorry." Carson's gaze swung toward her and then toward Garrett, his eyebrows dipping at the latter. "Wow, Zinnia and Beryl were right. The resemblance is more than just a few common traits. Eye shape and color. Ears. Browbone. That slightly crooked smile. They have Henley's cheekbones and jaw structure, but everything else is you. Where's Reid? I didn't notice earlier. Does he share the same facial characteristics as his brother and sister? You have no idea how much I'm nerding out right now over knowing somebody with triplets."

Garrett snorted as he lowered Glyn into the seat. "I spent two years living down the hall from you. You're practically drooling over the possibility of analyzing their DNA so you can see which markers they share. We might decide at some point to let you play with their saliva in your lab, but it's not happening until after we're married—and the sources of the samples have to remain anonymous to everybody but you."

"Not a problem. Wait. You're getting married? When is this happening?" Those shifting eyebrows rose this time.

"Hopefully, Monday afternoon. Make yourself useful and plan a small reception at your house for about six o'clock. I'll text you details tonight." Juggling a wiggly Tripp, Garrett somehow managed to fasten the harness on their daughter. "Right now, we have kids who are going to start telling us they need to be fed and we'd kind of like to celebrate our re-engagement before the wedding."

"Gotcha." Their visitor's grin was accompanied by a quick wave as he turned the doorknob. "Thanks for not making me grovel, and don't worry about a thing. Zinnia, Beryl, and Archer will help me with the food, the cake, and whatever else needs to be done. Oh, and congratulations. It's great to see you happy."

The back door clunked shut, easing the weird tension in the room.

Garrett blew out a noisy breath and secured Tripp in the middle high chair. "Are you okay with Carson handling the party after the wedding? I couldn't think of any other way to distract him from the genetics stuff."

"Honestly, I hadn't even thought about having a reception." A tiny twinge of guilt tried to take root, but Henley pushed it aside to prep bottles and bowls while he went back for Reid. "If it keeps him too busy to ask about the whole DNA testing thing, it's fine with me."

Footsteps grew closer after a few rustling sounds. "Good. We have enough to do with work and the babies. I think we should all take a nap after they eat."

She caught his grin as he buckled in their middle child. "A nap, huh? Why do I get the impression you have something else in mind?"

"I didn't say we should sleep the whole time." Wrapping an arm around her waist from behind, he picked up the bottles with his free hand and nuzzled her neck. "Have to burn off some excess energy first, and let's not forget about celebrating our re-engagement. I missed you so much."

A shiver rippled over her skin from the contact, but their firstborn child smacked a palm on the tray before Henley could steal even a quick kiss. "What excess energy? I have a feeling it's going to be a while before we make up for all the lost time."

"We're together again. That's all that matters." He brushed his lips against hers and smiled. "I'll feed Glynnis."

"Feeling brave, huh?" As she reached for two of the bowls, their daughter let out a shrill squeal. "Too late to back out now."

His snort drew the attention of all three babies, and he kissed her again before carrying the bottles to the table. The way he smiled at the oldest of their kids made her heart swoon. "No chance of that. Right, Glyn? Even if I need a shower when we're done."

Almost an hour later, she laid Reid next to his brother in the crib and waited for Garrett's reaction to the trio cuddling together. Their daughter clutched the front of Tripp's shirt in her fist, her soft coo sounding like a sweet lullaby as his eyes drifted closed.

Garrett wrapped his arms around Henley from behind while Glyn and Reid slowly nodded off. She leaned into the love of her life, holding him place with her forearms over his and her head against his shoulder.

His relaxed exhale caressed her cheek. "We made them. Three amazing babies. I think it's still sinking in, but life is better than I ever imagined it could be. You, me, and the family we wanted. I almost lost hope."

"I'm glad you didn't give up on us." A wonderful shiver raced through her when he pressed a kiss to her ear. She tightened her hold on his arms and walked toward the bed, still enveloped in his embrace.

"Me too." His deep exhale perfectly embodied the exhaustion from their journey back to each other.

She turned in his embrace and rested her ear over his heart. "So, naptime?"

"I'm not quite ready to go to sleep yet." He nuzzled her hair. "Are you interested in that celebration?"

"Mm-hm. You should take this off first." Looking up at him, she tugged the hem of his shirt free of his jeans. Then she unfastened the waistband button. "These too, while I slip into something more comfortable."

His lopsided grin said he remembered exactly what more comfortable had meant during the early days of their relationship in Seattle. "I'll meet you in bed in less than two minutes."

They met under the covers in roughly half the time, skin to skin with their arms wrapped around each other and their legs tangled. She nudged him onto his back, pressing her fingers to his lips to remind him not to wake up their babies when he let out an approving hum.

His seductive dark-eyed stare made an appearance, but he nodded and lifted her to straddle him. "I promise to be good."

She couldn't help but raise her eyebrows and shake her head. "That was never in question. We have to be quiet."

"I can be quiet. Can you?" He glided a finger through her folds as he whispered the question, finding her clit and then going back to dip inside her.

She bit her tongue to keep a groan from escaping. A separate master bedroom and nursery moved to the top of her to-do list. "Maybe."

Sitting up, he kissed her again, effectively cutting off her ability to make too much noise while he teased her. "Ready for me to be inside you?"

"More than ready." She lifted her hips and guided him to her entrance. Anticipation urged her to hurry, but she lowered herself an inch at a time to savor their reunion. By the time she'd welcomed him as deep as he could go, every nerve ending in her body was on fire.

"Mm." He rocked upward and licked a circular path around her nipple. A flick of his tongue across the puckered tip accompanied the forward motion of her pelvis, nearly sending her straight over the edge. "You feel so good."

A desperate whimper snuck out as tremors rippled through her muscles. "Yes."

His hand slipped between them, his thumb massaging her above where they were joined. Lightheadedness and the sensation of flying apart struck when she grasped his head to hold him at her breast and moved against him. Every muscle trembled, carrying her into sweet oblivion and sweeping her along a seemingly endless river of bliss.

He pulsed inside her and grunted into her flesh while a burst of heat added to the momentum already prolonging her pleasure. His hold on her tightened, keeping her safe in his arms while they caught their breath and floated back to the real world. "I love you so damn much."

"I love you too." She let him guide down to the bed, still connected in every way, and savored the weight of him grounding her. "Forever."

# EPILOGUE

Giving up on trying to concentrate, Garrett logged out of his email and shut down his computer. As Mondays went, it definitely wasn't his worst. The moment he'd been looking forward to since the first time he'd proposed to Henley was finally about to happen.

He pushed away from the desk and stood to retrieve his suitcoat from the back of the chair, grateful he'd been given a second chance with the love of his life.

"Knock-knock." Dr. Needleman stepped through the open doorway, her ready smile in place. "Do you have a minute?"

"About five, if you need them." He shrugged on his jacket as she entered his office.

"I only need the one. I understand you and Henley Langston are getting married today, and I wanted to stop in to wish you all the best while I had a free moment." She held out an envelope with neat lettering on the front. "Congratulations to you both."

"We are. Thanks." Sliding the card into his pocket, he rounded the desk. "We're having a small ceremony at the park after work. I know it seems quick, but we were together for two and a half years in Seattle."

She frowned and waved away his explanation. "Velocity is less important than depth in relation to love, although I do love a good ternary plot. My daughter and son-in-law—Zinnia and Carson—filled me in on a few of the highlights. He mentioned you know each other from grad school and that you applied for the job and moved to Cradle Gorge to reconnect with Henley. As long as you're both happy, that's all that matters."

"I'm happier than I've been in a long time." A surreptitious glance at the clock on the wall told him he could leave now if he moseyed instead of walked to the daycare center.

"You look like you're anxious to go, so I'll head back to my office." She grinned and set off out the door at her usual hurried pace. "Have a wonderful rest of your day!"

"Thanks. You too." He trailed after her, pausing to lock up and then saying a quick goodbye to his secretary. Sunshine greeted him when he exited the building, but his attention landed on the woman waiting for him at the bottom of the steps.

She smiled up at him, sending his heart into the same pitter-patter rhythm as the first time he'd laid eyes on her. "Hi. I have it on good authority that we have an appointment with a justice of the peace in about an hour. Want to get married today?"

"Today and every day." Feeling lighter than he had in what seemed like forever, he shuffled down the stairs and gathered her in his arms.

Her warm breath tickled his ear as he closed his eyes to savor the moment. "Sounds like a perfect plan."

The hope he'd carried for fifteen months and twenty-five hundred miles swelled inside him. "I love you."

"I love you too. Let's get the kids and go have a wedding." She slipped her fingers through his and walked with him toward their future.

MARRIAGE LICENSE TUCKED IN THE INNER POCKET OF HIS SUITCOAT, Garrett pushed the stroller out of the county probate office behind Henley and pulled his phone from his pocket to reread the confirmation email from the officiant.

*"I'll meet you by the gazebo at 5:00pm."*

"We have fourteen minutes to walk to the park." His pulse picked up when the love of his life aimed a breathtaking smile at him.

She pressed the call button for the elevator and then reached for his hand, her engagement ring sparkling under the florescent lights. "About thirty minutes until we're married."

Lacing his fingers through hers, he nodded. "Second best day of my life. The day I met you is still first in line."

The doors swooshed open as she brushed her lips over his. "Ditto. What about the day Glyn, Reid, and Tripp were born? Where do they rank?"

He maneuvered their contraption into the elevator ahead of her, making room beside him in the tight space. His half-hearted battle against a chuckle lost. "Third, of course. Three for three. Their mommy will always be most important to me."

Glyn patted his leg and giggled. "Ma-ma-ma-ma-ma."

Her brothers joined her chant, surprising the heck out of him since he'd only started teaching them to say it yesterday.

Henley's shock morphed into a delighted grin and watery eyes. "Oh my gosh! Did you coach them?"

He shrugged and gave her hand a squeeze. "It kept them occupied while I was changing diapers. They're quick learners."

A chime announced their arrival at the ground floor and the doors slid open again, but she stopped him with a one-armed hug. "That's the sweetest wedding gift you could've given me today. Thank you."

"You're welcome. Making you happy is my top priority." He shoved his foot in the way when the doors moved inward.

The early October day greeted them with more sunshine at the courthouse exit and made for a pleasant walk two blocks to Cradle Gorge's park. As they rounded the curve in the sidewalk leading toward the creek, a gathering of people came into view. Flowers decorated the gazebo, a violinist stood at the ready, and a photographer snapped pictures in their direction.

Carson stood out among the ten or so gathered near the steps, with

Daisy perched on his shoulders. He waved, like he hadn't gone over-board—well beyond a modest reception at his house.

Garrett shook his head. "Somebody got a little carried away with his assignment."

Henley's snort triggered contagious laughter from the trio enjoying the ride. "Of course, he did."

"He's trying to make up for behaving like an idiot."

"It's fine. I only care that we're getting married." She lengthened her stride and nodded toward a gray-haired woman talking to Zinnia and Henley's parents. "There's Judge Lawson, standing by the gazebo."

Keeping pace with her, he pushed the stroller through the parting group of their friends and family—Dean Needleman and her husband, Beryl and Archer with their twins, Mr. and Mrs. Langston, in addition to Carson, Zinnia, and Daisy. A chorus of excited hellos and perfect-day-for-an-outdoor-wedding greetings surrounded them as he walked with her to their destination.

The officiant stepped forward as they approached. "Henley. Garrett. I'm Katherine Lawson. It's so nice to meet you—and your children. Look at those happy little faces!"

Henley offered her free hand. "It's a pleasure to meet you too, Your Honor. Thank you for performing the ceremony on such short notice."

"You're very welcome. I love helping couples achieve their happily-ever-afters. Let's get started." The judge gestured toward the violist, and music quieted the conversation around them. Then she climbed the two stairs into the shelter.

Leaving the babies in the care of their grandparents, Garrett followed her with the woman he loved more every day still holding his hand. The steady pressure of her fingers laced with his told him she wanted this as much as he did. Calm settled over him when he turned to face her.

The soft sounds of the violin continued in the background as Judge Lawson opened the book in her grasp. "Family and dear friends, we are gathered here today to celebrate the marriage of Garrett Wells and Henley

Langston. They've asked for a simple ceremony that focuses on their commitment to each other. Their journey has been a difficult one, but their love is stronger for it and shows it can withstand the test of time. Garrett and Henley, do you take each other as husband and wife, to cherish and support your partner through life's ups and downs, for as long as you live?"

He raised their joined hands to his heart and they spoke the words together. "We do."

"Because taking care of each other and triplets makes for a very busy day, Henley and Garrett have chosen to purchase and exchange rings in a private moment when time permits." Judge Lawson closed the book and smiled. "And so, by the authority granted me by the state of Ohio, I pronounce you husband and wife. May your life together be long and filled with joy."

Not waiting for permission, he gathered Henley in his arms for a slow and thorough kiss. "I love you. Forever."

She hugged him tighter and nuzzled his ear. "Forever."

Thanks for reading! If you enjoyed this story, please consider leaving a review on the retailer's website, BookBub, and/or Goodreads to help other readers find their next book! Find your next read on my website, join my Facebook reader group for fun discussions, and subscribe to my newsletter to receive the latest news about releases, sales, book signings, and more.

# ABOUT THE AUTHOR

**Mellanie Szereto** is the *USA Today* Bestselling Author of over sixty romcoms and contemporary romances, most with characters who have plenty of life experience like herself. Whether you call them older, seasoned, mature, experienced, or later-in-life protagonists, they deserve love too! Her stories are often set in small towns with quirky main characters, fun secondary casts, and lots of humor. She enjoys gardening, cooking, and baking—as well as hiking to work off the fruits of her labor—and incorporates food into all of her stories. She lives in an old farmhouse in rural Indiana with her husband of thirty-nine years.

Visit her website for more information about her books!